Bamford Luck

ARTHUR C. EASTLY

BAMFORD LUCK

iUniverse books may be ordered through booksellers or by contacting:

iUniverse
1663 Liberty Drive
Bloomington, IN 47403
www.iuniverse.com
1-800-Authors (1-800-288-4677)

Because of the dynamic nature of the Internet, any web addresses or links contained in this book may have changed since publication and may no longer be valid. The views expressed in this work are solely those of the author and do not necessarily reflect the views of the publisher, and the publisher hereby disclaims any responsibility for them.

Any people depicted in stock imagery provided by Thinkstock are models, and such images are being used for illustrative purposes only. Certain stock imagery © Thinkstock.

ISBN: 978-1-4917-6139-7 (sc)
ISBN: 978-1-4917-6141-0 (hc)
ISBN: 978-1-4917-6140-3 (e)

Print information available on the last page.

iUniverse rev. date: 02/27/2015

Contents

Chapter 1

Another great day for haying had arrived on the Bamford Ranch, with the sun shining from a nearly cloudless sky. The sun had come up two hours before and would be drying the grass. Clay Bamford sat at the kitchen table nursing a mug of coffee, with Alorenzo Gonzales doing the same across from him. They were waiting for Clay's parents to come for breakfast. Most days, both men would be long gone by this time, but today the senior Bamfords were leaving to travel to the West Coast. In total miles it wasn't so far from the ranch in eastern Idaho to Seattle, but still Clay wasn't sure it was a wise move with his mother fighting a weak heart and taking several medications. Well, she was excited about going to visit her sister.

Clay looked out a window. "After Dad drives away, I'll go back to moving bales into storage."

"What I figured you'd want to do." Alorenzo waved one hand. "Reckon I'll saddle my horse and take a ride through the bred heifers."

"You do that, Lorenz. Probably take you all day to see them."

"Expect so. If I don't get to all of them today, just have to ride out again tomorrow." The sound of feet walking across the sitting-room floor reached their ears.

"What's this about not seeing them all today?" Will Bamford smiled at the good shot he had gotten in at Alorenzo.

Alorenzo's white-haired head turned, and his face grinned. "Clay told me to slow down 'cause I been showing you up."

Will smiled as he slapped Alorenzo on the shoulder and then went to pour a cup of coffee. With a full cup, he leaned back against the counter and watched his son.

Clay saw the slight smile and wondered what his dad could be thinking before he asked. "Should I bring the motor home to the house so we can pack it for your trip?"

"Thank you, Clay. While you're getting the motor home, Lorenz and I will start cooking breakfast."

Clay walked to the mudroom, pulled on a pair of boots, put on his everyday working Stetson, and went out the door. While crossing the ranch yard to the machine shed, he mentally reviewed everything they had done to get the motor home prepared. The three men had vacuumed, washed windows both inside and out, checked the supplies, and wiped down the interior and appliances. While his mom put fresh sheets on the bed, Clay had checked the engine oil, air pressure in the tires, and the lights. Will and Alorenzo brought lawn chairs to add to the storage bins. To the best of his reckoning, the motor home was ready to go once his parents put their luggage on board.

The engine fired up immediately. Leaving it running to warm up, Clay walked through the vehicle doing a last-minute check. The closets were full of clothes, the kitchen cabinets seemed to have everything useful for cooking, and the fridge and freezer had so much food in them there was hardly any space not being used.

Sitting down in the driver's seat, Clay looked at the fuel gauges. The tanks were full of diesel, and the water tank with water. Shifting the automatic transmission into low drive, Clay pulled out of the machine shed and drove to the house. Everything was ready.

Mary was sitting at the table when Clay returned to the kitchen and said, "Good morning, Mom. How are you?"

"Doing just fine, Clay. How's my son this great morning?"

"We have another good day for haying. If you'd get your husband loaded up and hit the road, I could go to work."

"We'll be going in a few minutes. Be good for you to sit still for a while. Received a letter yesterday from your aunt Sadie over in Seattle. Did Dad tell you?"

Clay pulled out a chair and sat down at the table. "Not a word. He's getting cussed mean about sharing the news."

Mary turned her head to look at Will and laughed at him. "He probably didn't think it was important enough to go around talking. Sadie's letter boils down to telling me they'll be happy to see us and have us stay a few days."

Will came with a box of cornflakes and a bowl for Mary. He went to the fridge and pulled out a box of milk to bring to the table. "Sadie's letter didn't have much in it, Clay—just women's talk."

Mary swatted Will on the hip with her hand. "You men don't think anything's important unless it's about your cows." Mary poured cornflakes into her bowl and reached for the milk.

Alorenzo brought a platter full of bacon strips and a pile of whole wheat toast. Will brought a platter of scrambled eggs. The two men pulled out chairs to sit in. "You want to try some to this bacon, Mary?"

"Best not do that, Lorenz. Have to stick close to the doctor's diet. You men go ahead and eat up." It saddened Alorenzo to see Mary eating so little and hardly any of the good food. She was thin and had no color in her cheeks. Damn heart taking in after her and for all the years she was always so lively and full of fun. Now she was struggling to stay alive.

Alorenzo looked at Will. "What road you taking to Seattle?"

"Plan to go out here to the highway and follow 93 up to Missoula, then take Interstate 90 up through Coeur d'Alene and over to Spokane. Mary has some cousins up there we haven't visited with for many years. When Mary's ready to move on, we'll stick with Interstate 90 all the way to Seattle."

The men settled down to eating, and conversation faded away. When they were done, Clay brought the coffeepot and refilled cups. Mary was drinking milk with her cereal.

"You're going to finish stacking the bales, Clay?" Will said.

"Hopefully the weather stays good. Probably take a couple of weeks or more to finish up. You want bales here in the yard or loose hay?"

"When the weather turns nasty, it's always nice to have hay in the loft. For the rest of the winter, bales are fine. You do whatever you think is right. Time's getting near to separate the bulls from the herd. When you have a slow day, gather up the bulls and move them into the bull pasture."

"Sounds good, Dad. Hope you two enjoy your trip. Is your suitcase packed, Mom?"

"It's lying open on the bed with everything I want to take packed. Please close the case for me and bring it out to the motor home."

Clay stood up. "Don't forget to take your pills, Mom." He walked away and a few minutes later came back with the case. Will and Alorenzo had the table cleared, and Mary was standing at the sink washing down pills.

Will and Clay carried the luggage out to the motor home, and Alorenzo came from the house with Mary holding on to his arm. Will watched. Alorenzo doted on Mary, who had nursed and looked after him for many years after his rodeo accident. In fact Clay's grandmother delivered Alorenzo at his birthing. He had lived here on the ranch all his years. In his younger days Alorenzo became a known bull rider, until an accident happened. A bull tossed him and stomped on him real bad. He came out of it badly broken up and has suffered from a touched-up head ever since.

The men got Mary settled in the large, well-padded boss's chair and Clay buckled her in. Will did up his seat belt. Clay and Alorenzo went down the steps and stood off to one side as the motor home started moving and waved good-bye. The men stayed right there and watched the vehicle until it was out of sight.

Clay said, "Hope they have a good trip and it isn't going to be too much for Mom." Alorenzo shrugged his shoulders. Clay looked at his watch. "I've lost a couple of hours; going to drive out to the hay field. See you later, Lorenz."

* * *

The motor home rolled along the county gravel road throwing up a dense cloud of dust and came to a halt at the stop sign at Highway 93. A car was coming toward them from the south, so Will shifted the transmission into park. "Mighty dry out there, Mary; we put up a dense cloud of dust coming along the road."

"Like Clay said, it's good haying weather."

"Right you are. Close to three weeks since the last rain. Weather stays like this, the bales should be gathered up by the time we get home."

"Don't you be worrying, Will. Clay and the men will get the work done. You haven't been on a holiday in a coon's age and darn well better relax and enjoy yourself. Besides, I plan to kick your butt playing crib."

Will watched the car go past and drove onto the highway, turning north for Missoula, Montana. He looked in the large mirror at Mary, who was peering at the road map, and smiled. "How many years since we were in Missoula?"

Mary shook her head thoughtfully. "Four - five years or more. Sure is more comfortable riding in this motor home than the old pickup you had."

"Reckon you're right. We aren't so young anymore, and both of us are getting soft. More and more, we want things to be comfortable and convenient—don't want to put up with roughing it."

"You may be right, Will. Our son is sure not soft. You grab his arm or watch him, and it's obvious he's solid muscle. He moves real fast when he needs to."

"You're a very observant mother. Clay's never said much about his years in the army and mostly only about training camps and such. The training he got and whatever he did hardened him up. I can tell you one thing. Watching him since he came back to the ranch, he's not a man you want to get into a fight with. He'd be very rough."

Will focused his attention on the road while his mind thought about their son. *'Clay stands well over six feet, has wide shoulders, a narrow waist, and gray eyes. He's normally so quiet he could go all day hardly saying a word. With Robert dead he is our only son, in fact our only child.'* Will smiled. *'He isn't exactly a child; he is twenty-eight years old, made of solid muscle and bone, and tougher than an old Angus bull. Still his mother thinks of him as her child. Some little boy! Inside he has the hard steel core of the old Bamfords. Always polite, especially to women, he will fight at the drop of a hat and once started he becomes a whirling dervish with a cold, hard intensity few people can stand up to. No one can push him, a normal Bamford trait that has served the family well for several generations.'*

Looking in the mirror he saw Mary was sleeping in her chair.

* * *

Luong An Chie'n eyed two teenagers smoking outside the entrance to the building housing the Seattle Asian Youth Club. A local businessman, Luong owned a popular Vietnamese restaurant located three blocks away on the edge of this old historical part of Seattle. Many of the buildings were built way back in the 1800s, and the years of storms and weathering had given them a well-used appearance. Many sat unused and uncared for, which caused outsiders to categorize the area as a run-down slum neighborhood. Luong was a sponsor of the Asian Club and provided most of its funding. Both teenagers moved aside, making room for him to go past, and Luong noted this, briefly wondering if the slim, young girl was putting out for her older companion.

Inside, Luong glanced around the large main room at the Ping-Pong and pool tables and empty chairs, before climbing the long wooden stairs to the second floor. Each step going up caused the old, worn wooden steps to creak. No one could approach the second floor without his arrival being loudly announced.

Voices coming from the upstairs meeting room that Luong used as an office alerted him to the presence of two of his lieutenants. Conversation stopped when he pulled the door open. "Good morning, my friends," Luong greeted the two men inside. "Are there any messages?" He watched Quang, his senior lieutenant at the club, for an answer.

"No messages, Uncle."

Quang delivered messages, carried money from the drug operation to the clubhouse, and in turn delivered cash to pay for shipments coming in through their supply network. As a family member, Quang, son of Luong's second sister, rated consideration as being more trustworthy than other young people who were not relatives. Quang used the generous cash income he received from Luong to support his mother, brothers, and sisters.

Luong smiled to himself, thinking what a wise decision this building had been. When he decided to purchase this old, long-unused, brick bank building with its large vault on the main floor, many thought he had lost his mind. Luong used the vault to store large stacks of money generated from his distribution operations. The vault proved to be invaluable. Long hidden from view in a workroom behind a heavy oak door, the vault was a special feature of the building. Few people in the area remembered the existence of the vault from when a bank operated in this building during the early years of the city. Even better had been Luong's follow-up decision to sponsor a youth club located in the building, a community service that provided a cover for the real use of the building. During afternoons and evenings, the club became crowded with laughing, joking teens. Two of the top table tennis players in the Pacific Northwest played from and represented the club.

Pleased with himself, Luong's thoughts turned to the Fish Market, a business selling a large volume of seafood, which another relative operated for him on the waterfront. The business was located in a long, wooden building with its front door on a paved street and the back door exiting onto its own saltwater dock. The original owner operated as a ship chandler, selling supplies and providing minor repairs to ship owners, seagoing sailboats, and fishermen. Now, well over a hundred years in age, it was widely known as an excellent source of seafood.

"Quang, have you been to the fish market recently?"

Quang thought for a moment. "It has been two months except for the Friday night when I delivered money for the boat."

"It would please me if you went one day this week to look over the operation. Find out if it's running smoothly. Are the people on the staff happy? Are the fish being kept fresh? Are the customers happy? Those types of things. Bring me a report."

"Certainly, Uncle. I will go this coming week on a day when the store is in full operation."

Luong thought for a minute. "It will be best if you go in the afternoon and check on the building." The building enjoyed a long history at the current location on Salmon Bay, a short distance around a knob of land from Fisherman's Terminal. Old and badly weathered, the building had existed for many years. Luong's extended family operated the very popular fish marketing business, generating substantial profits. More importantly, the fish business provided a cover for the importation and distribution of drugs.

"While you're there, talk to the men in the back. Find out what they have to say about the charter business. Often, much is learned from the idle talk of employees."

Luong mused. Large numbers of shoppers came to the market to purchase seafood. His workers had been told to make sure the various types of seafood were always fresh and sold at very competitive or lower prices than available elsewhere. Particularly on Fridays and Saturdays, customers crowded the market, buying large quantities of fresh seafood. On those busy days, cars and people crowded the immediate area, overflowing the parking lot and searching the street for empty parking spaces. The noise created by crowds of jostling, hurried people and the pervading smell of seafood provided a perfect cover for Luong's primary operation, which was the importation and distribution of a totally different product. Right under the noses of happy shoppers laughing and talking in a variety of languages, the hidden product was being processed for distribution. When ready, it was shipped in what seemed to be normal vehicles leaving the area—always with a smelly fish or two wrapped in brown paper lying on the floor.

Luong smiled. He provided the brains, planning, and management, keeping himself remote from the product, relying instead on his henchmen. This arrangement required strict discipline and harsh punishment of anyone who broke the rules, stole from him, or dared to use the product they sold.

Luong's oldest brother, along with a cousin of the same generation, handled the punishment of employees who broke the rules. They also punished any customer who failed to pay promptly. The rules became an established and accepted system that worked well, based on ten years' experience building the business. Luong wasn't popular with the people he employed because of his stern, demanding manner and the severe punishment meted out to those who strayed.

Luong was of medium height and had a slim build and dark brown eyes that stared unblinking, particularly when he was angry. He always combed his black hair straight back and had it regularly trimmed. He wore baggy, wrinkled suits and shoes that rarely received polish. Luong never wasted money and didn't want to attract the attention of anyone by appearing successful. Setting aside his review, Luong walked to the desk to sit down before asking, "Do you have everything ready to make collections on Monday?"

"Yes, Uncle. The list of how much each dealer owes is ready, and they know not to miss an appointment."

"Good. As usual, keep careful records. My business plans will take me away until Sunday. Keep an eye on the club. Now, you two, leave. I need time to think."

Luong watched the door close behind the teenaged boys and unlocked a file drawer in the battered desk purchased cheaply from a dealer in used furniture. He removed a Washington State highway map and a street map of Portland, Oregon. From a brown folder, he got a computer printout of an e-mail with the name, phone number, and address of his contact in Portland.

The meeting would occur this evening. Allowing three hours for the drive, plenty of time still remained. Luong never drove fast, always staying under the speed limit. It was never wise to attract the attention of policemen. On this trip, Luong planned to propose to his contact an expansion in the Portland distribution business, which, if agreed upon, would provide growth in Luong's imports, eventually resulting in a large increase in profits for him. The Portland contact didn't know Luong had been promised a lower per unit price for increasing the total volume of his imports, and he felt no need to share these savings with his customers. Luong knew there was no hurry to commence the drive south.

Sitting quietly, he used the time to mentally review operations. Luong fathered and continued to build a business dynasty that would make his sons and their sons' rich beyond belief, and he, Luong An Chie'n, would be remembered by future generations of the family as the founder of a vast business empire.

* * *

After spending four days in the Spokane area, Will Bamford drove the large motor home west on Interstate 90, arriving in Seattle after the sun set. Over twenty years had slipped by since he last drove the streets of this city and it had grown and changed. Or maybe his memory wasn't so good anymore. Bamford resided in the country, wasn't young anymore, and never liked city driving, especially at night when it was dark. He glanced in the mirror at his wife, Mary, lounging in the leather captain's chair, before telling her, "I'm going to get off the highway and find a place to stop for the night. In the daylight, we can follow the street map easier."

"You do that, Will. I'll make sandwiches and give you a crib lesson."

Will was pleased to hear Mary so perky. In the mirror, he grinned at her and said, "You never saw the day." Bamford took the off ramp and drove slowly along the dark streets, thinking, *'This is an old neighborhood.'* A service station, closed for the night, appeared as he approached the next street corner. He stopped on the street and for several minutes considered the service station. He could see nothing that disturbed him, so he drove in, turned the motor home around, and backed up to park for the night. After lowering the hydraulic jacks to level and stabilize the vehicle, he went out with a flashlight to look around.

When he came back, Mary asked, "Everything look okay to you?"

"Seems to be fine. From what I can see, this is an old area of the city. Can't see much of it; in the morning, we'll get a better look at things."

Mary took sliced ham, mustard, and dill pickles from the fridge and began making Will a sandwich. With a wet cloth, Will wiped the tabletop off before filling two glasses with water. He kept an eye on Mary; she wasn't eating near as much as he thought she should. Mary brought his sandwich and put it on the table before going back and cutting a slice of bread in half and topping it with a small slice of ham.

Sitting at the table, Mary bit off a bite of bread and chewed. She had a thoughtful look on her face, and Will recognized something was coming. "Wonder how Clay is making out on the ranch."

Will grinned. "Probably working twelve to fourteen hours a day stacking those big, round bales. Don't you go worrying about our son."

"He's always so darned quiet."

"Clay's always been quiet." Will put his sandwich back on his plate. "Actually more quiet since he came home from the army."

"I always get the feeling there's something bothering him. Maybe it's bad memories of something that happened in the army."

"Don't know about that, Mary. You remember the general who came out to the ranch to visit Clay?" Mary nodded. "He said Clay had seen some tough action and spent time overseas visiting other countries. Told me we should be proud of our son. Clay's never mentioned anything about what he did or where he went."

"Well, he hasn't been back for two years yet." Mary sighed. "Maybe more time will take care of things."

Will went back to eating, and Mary nibbled. When they were done, he gathered the dishes, washed them, and stored them away.

Mary held the deck of cards and put a pad of paper to keep score on out on the table.

* * *

Quang, accompanied by three younger Vietnamese boys, swaggered along the sidewalk in the evening darkness, two blocks from their destination at the clubhouse. Their youth group controlled several square city blocks, and those with inflated egos considered this as their area of the city. A trusted lieutenant in the organization, Quang carried responsibilities, while the other three were minor functionaries—errand runners and trainees. The secret Hong Society they were members of ruled this city area first settled back in the mid-1800s and filled with well-aged buildings. During the dark of night, they were in undisputed control. The Seattle City Police rarely ventured into the area during the night, and when they did, it was with backup and force. During daylight, patrol cars regularly passed through the area, the officers seldom stopping for one of their coffee and donut breaks.

At the corner ahead, they would cross the paved yard of the closed service station, shortcutting the left turn into the last block to the clubhouse. There they would join other club members for the evening. With luck, there might be orders that would earn some of them extra cash. Not yet trusted enough to know the inner secrets and workings of the Hong, they were simply aware of large amounts of cash being generated, not knowing their estimate of large fell far short of reality.

Dim window lights shining from a motor home parked near the service station building were so out of place in this section of the city they could only stand in stunned silence for several seconds. No one in this part of the city owned a motor home. Nor could they remember one ever stopping in the area. Obviously the motor home didn't belong here. Silent in their Reebok-clad feet, they approached the vehicle and listened near the curtained windows. Through a roof vent, a man's voice came clearly. "Fifteen two, fifteen four, and two pair is eight."

Gathered near the rear of the vehicle, the teens conferred in muted whispers on a course of action to teach these interlopers a lesson. These strangers needed to receive the message to stay away from this part of the city in the future. Their usual solution to a strange vehicle involved slashing tires. This large motor home had duals on the rear axles, so the one carrying a knife sturdier than the switchblades of the others moved forward to the front right wheel. Kneeling on his right knee, he held the knife point to the tire with his left hand and pushed hard with his right. The hiss of escaping air seemed loud in the darkness, and the vehicle's settling weight wrinkled the tire, entrapping the knife in a solid grip of tire rubber. Still holding on to the knife, his head swiveled to look over his shoulder as a man wearing jeans, boots, and a red and black checkered shirt banged open the motor home door and stepped down to the pavement. The older, gray-haired man stared at the young Asian. "What the hell are you doing, fellow?" a deep, raspy voice demanded.

Too frightened to move for an instant, the boy loosened his grip on the knife and started to stand up as the large man stepped forward and reached to grab him. "Damn boy, you got some answering to do." A large right hand clamped down on the teen's shoulder, and he felt the power in the fingers as his friends ran toward the man's back. Quang, the largest of the three, carried a four-foot-long steel pipe in his hand.

A women's voice asked, "What's going on out there, Will?" She appeared in the doorway at the top of the steps just as the pipe swung in an arc and crashed into the back of Will Bamford's neck. As Will's firm grip loosened, the small Asian shoved him away, and Will collapsed on the pavement with his head and left arm in the light from the doorway. The woman rushed down the steps, one hand going to her mouth. "Oh God, Will! What's happened!" Her slipper-clad feet touched the pavement, and suddenly she gasped, both hands clutched at her chest, and she fell sideways.

Four pairs of hooded eyes stared for a long moment. The pipe swinger tossed his weapon aside, and it bounced and clattered across the pavement toward the back of the yard as he announced, "Guess we showed them."

Neither the man nor the woman moved. Slowly the teens began to realize what had happened. "Do you think they're dead?" one boy whispered in a soft, scared voice.

A third stated, "Looks like it. We should get away from here before someone sees us." Knife forgotten, three of the boys started away while Quang bent to lift the man's left arm and look at the wristwatch. A Rolex! After removing and pocketing the watch, he followed his friends, leaving two bodies lying there, the twelve-volt light from the open doorway shining on them.

Chapter 2

At six o'clock, the early morning silence was broken by the sound of a siren as a police cruiser rushed to the scene, answering a 911 call from an excited service station attendant who spoke very poor English. A female officer drove the car with her new partner, a beginning officer, in the passenger seat. The cruiser turned into the service station and swung until the headlights lit up the motor home and two bodies lying on the pavement. After staring for a moment with both hands gripping the steering wheel, the female officer muttered, "Shit. It looks like we have another mess on our hands." Sighing softly, she added, "Ted, you look at everything carefully and tell me what you see."

Officer Ted Hanson looked carefully at everything visible in the headlights. "Two people are down, looks like a male and a female." He paused and added, "A motor home, which seems fairly new, maybe a year or two old, with the door standing open and the inside lights on. The yard is a mess of old car parts, and there are piles of junk lying around."

Angie Hoffman's head turned. "See anything else, Ted?"

"Not right now, except for the one male inside the service station."

"Look at the license plate." Hoffman frowned; Hanson still didn't pay enough attention to details. "It's from Idaho. What does that tell you?"

"Oh, I see. I bet these people are on holidays."

"Good guess." Hoffman remained silent for a moment. "Probably arrived in Seattle last night, after dark, and stumbled into the wrong part of the city." Hoffman started to open the car door and stopped. "We better take our shotguns with us. This is a tough neighborhood, and backup might be awhile getting here." They exited the car, both with shotguns. Standing beside the cruiser, Hoffman looked across the car roof and instructed, "You stay here and watch everything. Make sure the man in the gas station stays in there. I'm going to check those two and see if it's worth rushing them to a hospital"

"Okay, Angie. You be careful until help gets here." This was the first potential murder Ted had encountered in the few short months of his duties on the police force.

Angie Hoffman, a seven-year veteran of the force, walked slowly toward the bodies, watching everything around her carefully. She took note of the knife sticking in the front tire and sighed, thinking, *'Not again.'* Kneeling beside the man, Hoffman put her fingers on his wrist to feel for a pulse. Nothing. The arm was cold and clammy. Hoffman thought, *'Probably been dead for several hours.'* She checked the woman, with the same result. Looking at the open door of the motor home, she had an impulse to check the interior to see if there was anyone else. No, it was unlikely, and Hoffman didn't want to disturb the scene and ruin it for the experts who would be coming. This looked like robbery and homicide. This would quickly be way over her head; it was a situation for the homicide detectives.

Walking back to the car, Angie looked at her partner. "Both are dead. Keep a sharp eye on things while I call this in." Reaching through the open car window for the mike, she pulled it out and used her thumb to push the button, turning her back to the car. "Dispatch, this is Hoffman, car 801. Do you read me?"

"Loud and clear, Ange. What do you have for us?"

"We found two bodies—white, male and female, cold, more than middle aged, probably sixty or more. The motor home is sitting with the door hanging open and inside lights on. Looks to me like homicide and robbery. Nobody around except one male in the service station, and Hanson is keeping him inside. Need help ASAP."

"Gotcha, Ange. The duty sergeant left a few minutes ago. We'll send help. Do you need an ambulance?"

"Not right away, both bodies are cold." Hoffman grimaced, not liking this situation one little bit. "Looks like both people have been dead for several hours."

"Okay." The dispatcher's voice came back over the radio.

"Hoffman, this is Roberts here, five minutes away." The gruff voice of her sergeant came as a welcome sound.

Angie pushed the button. "Thanks, Sarg."

Hoffman replaced the mike and dug out her notebook. "Ted, you get the crime scene tape out of the trunk and seal this place off while I write up what we have here. It's going to get hectic in a few minutes when all the experts arrive."

Angie watched Roberts drive up to the curb as Officer Hanson was finishing a double row of police tape across the two street sides of the service station. Roberts sat watching for a moment from the car, nodding his head in appreciation. Both officers were carrying shotguns, and this district warranted that type of caution. With the area taped off, it would keep the media out. Soon enough there would be reporters swarming, asking their dumb questions before the police even got a chance to start investigating. Roberts made a mental note to commend both officers for their efficiency. Angie saw Roberts exit the car and duck under the tape. As he straightened up she started walking toward him, her notebook in hand. He listened closely as Hoffman reviewed her notes for him, before he asked, "You didn't disturb anything?"

"No, sir. I watched where I put my feet and only checked the bodies for a pulse."

"Any other details you noted?"

"Yes, sir. There's a knife stuck in the front tire of the vehicle. Looks like another tire slashing. Also, it appears the man's wristwatch is missing. His arm is well tanned, and the white band left from wearing a watch is very evident."

Roberts watched her closely. "Did you enter the vehicle?"

"No, sir, I didn't want to disturb anything." Hoffman pointed at the motor home. "The man's watch may be inside."

"Well done, Hoffman." Roberts smiled. "Where is the vehicle from?"

"Idaho, sir. I have the license number written down. Likely they came to Seattle as tourists on holiday."

Roberts frowned at the new information and thought for a minute, "I agree with you. The media will be here soon. Hanson, you cover the license plates so the reporters can't get pictures. It'll buy us a little extra time." Roberts squared his shoulders and stretched his back. "Hoffman, you call in and request a check on the license number. Find out who the owner is and where this motor home is registered. This could be a stolen vehicle."

Over the next hour, the street filled with police vehicles, TV crews, newspaper reporters, and a handful of gawkers. Roberts, Hoffman, and Hanson were doing crowd control, making sure no one crossed the police tape. Two TV crews were shooting pictures. A reporter from the *Seattle Times* kept yelling at Roberts, wanting information. Inside the tape, homicide Detectives Justin Brand and Barry Heftner systematically checked outside the vehicle, while the department's pathologist waited patiently for the police photographer to finish recording the site. Pictures were being shot from every angle. Roberts watched the department people examine the crime scene and deliberately ignored the reporters, his back to the crowd. Hoffman commented, "Sir, there's something odd about this crowd of onlookers."

Roberts turned to look at her. "What makes you think so?"

Hoffman looked him straight in the eye. "If you eliminate our people and all the media people milling around, there are very few residents from the area in this crowd." Hoffman shrugged. "Seems odd to me that more locals aren't taking an interest. Usually a crime scene attracts plenty of attention."

Roberts swung around to scrutinize the street for several minutes. He put his hand up to hide his mouth from the cameras when he replied, "Good eye, Ange. It does seem odd. This is your area. You got any ideas?"

"The local Asian gang operates from a clubhouse one block up the side street. If they're involved in this, the locals will stay as far away as possible. People may watch from windows, but they aren't going to display any interest. Besides, they get more protection from the gang than from our police department, and most of them don't trust us anyway."

"Why do you suppose that is?"

"Sir, there are a large number of Asian immigrants living in this area, and they brought their mistrust of authority with them from their homelands. Probably we haven't done much to help change their attitude."

Roberts stared at her for a moment. "Hoffman, go to your cruiser and write this conversation in your notebook, along with your observations. When we meet with the detectives, tell them what you think."

"Yes, sir." Angie turned and started away, Roberts call to her, "Good job, Hoffman."

Detective Brand supervised removal of the knife, hoping the technicians would be able to recover fingerprints from the handle. A hydraulic jack positioned under the frame was lifting the vehicle to remove weight from the tire. A techie stood ready with a plastic evidence bag to hold the knife.

Detective Heftner slowly inspected the motor home entrance for signs of forced entry and found nothing. Next he worked his way up the steps until he stood where he could survey the interior.

On the table, he noted a crib board and scattered playing cards. A pair of small western boots stood against the cupboards. *Must be the women's*, he thought. They were small, and the woman was wearing slippers. His head slowly swiveled as his eyes inspected everything in sight, until he found himself looking at the driver's seat. On the seat lay a Seattle city road map with a handwritten note pinned to one corner by a safety pin. Safety pins were mostly out of use especially for binding paper pages together, after all paper clips were easier to use. Bending forward, Heftner reached for the map and straightened to read the note written by a woman's hand. His face paled, and he stood staring at it for several seconds before backing down the steps to the pavement. Turning toward the front of the vehicle, he called, "Brand, you better come and take a look at this."

They looked at the note together before Brand asked, "Do you think this is the judge?"

"Hell yes, Justin. How many Edgar Winehousers can there be in this city? If he's connected to these people, we better be damned careful how we handle the investigation."

Brand ran a hand over his chin. "He's a tough, old bastard all right, and not one for fooling around. Barry, you better get on to the superintendent or the chief and ask for advice. Have the address in this note checked to see if it fits with the judge."

They looked at the note again without touching it. "I'm going to drive to the station. Reporters may be listening in on the radio network."

"Smart move, Heft. I'll carry on here."

"Okay. Go slow and easy and make sure everything is done right." Heftner took a step and stopped. "Be back to help you, just as soon as possible."

Brand looked across the lot at Sergeant Roberts, and after catching his eye, he waved him over. Brand walked away from the motor home and waited for Roberts. "Sarg, get more uniforms down here to make this place secure. We're going to have the top brass looking over our shoulders in short order."

"How many do you want, Justin?" Roberts wondered what could be so important.

"Up to you, Sarg, you've been doing this a lot longer than me. Heft just found a note that appears to link these people to federal court Judge Winehouser. He's on his way to the station to talk to the chief."

"Winehouser is a good man and no friend to criminals, Justin." Roberts smiled. "He's a stickler for detail and accuracy. Still, it's easy to see why you're concerned. Give me an hour, and this place will be sealed up tight."

"Thanks, Sarg." Brand watched Roberts walk to his car and stop to talk to Hoffman. Both Brand and Heftner had started their careers as young rookies under Roberts, who encouraged and helped them both move up the ladder to become detectives.

* * *

Detective Justin Brand neared the end of his report on the Bamford crime scene for Chief Otto Kruger, Deputy Superintendent Stanley Reeser, and other department people crowded into a meeting room. "In the vehicle, we found a man's wallet and a woman's purse. From the contents, we have identified the two people as Robert William Bamford, aged sixty-two, and Mary Elizabeth Bamford, fifty-seven, residents of Challis in Custer County, Idaho. The vehicle is registered in the name of Bamford Ranch Company." Brand paused to turn a page. "First on the scene were officers Hoffman and Hanson, soon followed by Sergeant Roberts."

Kruger's eyes shifted to look at each individual as they were named. "Sir, Officer Hoffman's initial inspection of the scene and her astute observations, combined with her tentative identification of the suspected murder weapon, are important in this investigation. After checking the bodies for vital signs, she recorded the knife lodged in the front tire of the vehicle and observed the wristwatch was missing from the man's left arm, which we believe was stolen. Amongst the junk and refuse lying around, Hoffman found what appears to be the murder weapon. Both the weapon and the knife are currently in the lab for examination. Nothing appears to be missing from the interior of the vehicle, and we believe the assailants probably didn't enter."

"Do you have any clues on who's responsible?"

"Not yet, sir. We hope the lab results will give us a lead. Officer Hoffman proposed a theory on who maybe respons—"

Reeser, known for his sarcastic treatment of all subordinates, interrupted, and Brand fell silent. "What does a junior office like Hoffman know about motives?"

Angie Hoffman blushed and remained silent while the superintendent stared at her with hard eyes. Brand straightened in his seat, the look on his face hardening. "Officer Hoffman regularly patrols this area of the city. Her experience with problems in the area in total is greater than all the rest of us combined, including you, Superintendent."

"That's enough, Reeser," the chief growled. His voice softened slightly as he said, "Hoffman, you were first on scene. Give us a rundown."

Reeser's attack had unsettled Hoffman besides she didn't come to the meeting expecting to give a report; Kruger's request surprised her. She opened her notebook and slowly thumbed through to the proper page. Without looking at Kruger, she started, not realizing the chief's intent was to give her a chance to gain experience and show her stuff. "Sir, at 5:50 this morning, dispatch directed us to answer a 911 call from a service station. Officer Hanson and I arrived at the scene at 6:12 and began our investigation."

While Hoffman gave her report, the chief listened closely. Once his eyes glanced at his old friend, Sergeant Ian Roberts, and he nodded his head. Roberts smiled. When Hoffman finished, Kruger suggested, "Brand said you have a theory."

"Yes, sir, I do." Hoffman's face flushed again. "Sir, the right front tire on the motor home had been slashed. Tire slashing occurs in this area more often than is reported to us. It always happens to a vehicle that doesn't belong in this area of Seattle. It's the Asian gang's way of warning strangers to stay away. I believe in this case they slashed the tire, the man who was inside came out to see what happened, and they hit him with a blunt instrument."

Kruger glanced at Hoffman and almost smiled. "Are you privy to the medical examiner's report when these detectives are still waiting for it?"

"No, sir." This time Hoffman looked back at him, straight in the eye. "During my inspection, I found a length of two-inch pipe, which is possibly the blunt instrument. There were hairs on it similar in color to the victim's. Also, sir, while checking the victim for a pulse, I noticed his head was at a peculiar angle, leading me to believe his neck had been broken."

Kruger let the silence hang while the suspense built. His voice softened. "Well done, Hoffman. You're a credit to your father." His head swung back to Brand, and he growled, "Go on with your report, Brand."

Brand waved his hand for Heftner to take over. "Chief, while Brand was supervising recovery of the knife from the front tire, I entered the vehicle and found a road map on the driver's seat with a handwritten note attached." Heftner produced a plastic bag with the map inside, folded so the note was visible. "Sir, the note contains the name and home address of federal court Judge Edgar Winehouser. It's possible the Bamfords may be acquaintances of the judge."

"Is that why you requested my office set up a meeting with the judge?"

"Yes, sir. The judge volunteered to stop by the station around five thirty or so, on his way home."

Kruger glanced at the wall clock. "Twenty minutes." He looked back at Heffner. "How much does the judge know about this investigation?"

Heftner shrugged. "We asked for a meeting to discuss a case we're working on. At the time, we didn't have the names or address for the victims. The judge agreed to meet with us as a favor."

"Okay, let's get ready for the meeting." Kruger said, "Brand, Heftner, and Hoffman, you three will attend the meeting with me. Roberts, you get on the phone and track down the local police in that area of Idaho. Get whatever information you can on the Bamfords without giving out details of this investigation." He held up a cautionary hand. "We still don't know what happened here in Seattle, so just see what you can find out."

* * *

County Sheriff Tom Odleson was busy putting away files and cleaning off his office desk in preparation for going home for a late dinner when the phone rang. He sighed, thinking, *'Already late for dinner, and now the damn phone has to ring.'* Leaning back in his office chair, he picked up the phone. "Sheriff Odleson. How may I help you?"

"Sheriff, this is Sergeant Roberts with the Seattle City Police Department. If you have a few minutes, there are some questions I need to ask you."

Odleson suddenly found himself sitting up straight with his elbows on the desk, his weariness after a long day forgotten. "Seattle is a lot of miles away from southern Idaho, Sergeant. What do you need?"

"The department needs a little information, Sheriff. What can you tell me about a man named Robert William Bamford?"

"Will Bamford? Hell, I've known Will since I was a kid." Odleson laughed. "Reckon I can tell you anything you want to know, except maybe how much money is in his bank account."

"Do you recall when you last talked to him?"

"Talked to Will a week ago Saturday at the store. Haying at the ranch was over, and he was taking Mary up to Spokane in their motor home to visit some distant kin folks of hers." Odleson paused. "From what he said, I believe they intended to go out west to take another look at the ocean."

"What does Mr. Bamford do to earn a living?"

Odleson laughed again. "Don't tell me Will is asking for credit somewhere?"

"Not at all, Sheriff. I'm just trying to put together background information."

Suddenly Odleson became disturbed. Something about these questions didn't sound right. His voice firmed, and his humor disappeared. "Sergeant, you better level with me. What's going on? Has Will been in an accident? Give me the facts or you get no more information from this office."

"Yes of course, Sheriff Odleson. My orders are to not give out any information until we gather all the facts. What I'm going to tell you is in the strictest confidence, between you and me. As soon as possible, I promise to phone you back with the details. Robert and Mary Bamford were killed earlier today, and we're trying to figure out what happened." The silence lasted so long Roberts thought the phone line had gone dead. "Are you still there, Sheriff?"

"Yeah, I'm here," muttered Odleson. "This is one hell of a shock. The Bamfords are two of the best people I know. As a teenager, my very first job was working summers on the Bamford Ranch for Will. He always treated me fair."

"Sorry to be the one to inform you, Sheriff. He sounds like a solid man."

"Damn right he is—as solid as those mountains he lives in." Odleson's eyes glared at the phone. "Sergeant, I don't feel like talking right now. You call back in the morning."

"Just one more minute, please, Sheriff. Is there anything you can tell me about Mary Bamford?"

Roberts could hear the sadness in the deep voice that replied. "Mary's a mighty fine woman. She's been ailing the last two or three years with heart problems. Takes a bunch of pills every day. Can't tell you what they are. The doc would know. Will bought a motor home so Mary could rest while he drove her around. Will didn't want Mary to become house bound."

"Thank you, Sheriff, for taking the time to talk to me. I'll call you tomorrow."

"You do that." The phone went dead in Roberts's hand. He glanced at the receiver before hanging up, thinking, *'Country people haven't changed since I was a kid growing up on the farm. They care about each other.'* Picking up his handwritten notes, he walked out of his office to the meeting room.

Kruger glanced up. "Were you able to get any information on the Bamfords, Ian?"

Roberts related his conversation with Odleson, and Kruger nodded. "Winehouser is late, probably held up in rush hour traffic. Phone the lab, Ian, and tell them about the bad heart. Check to see if the pictures of the Bamfords are ready—and get them if you can. They might help jog the judge's memory. If you have time, come back and sit in on the meeting."

* * *

The duty officer from the front desk escorted Judge Winehouser to the meeting room and held the door open for him. Winehouser smiled when everyone stood up. "Sit down, folks. This isn't a court room." He held out his hand to shake. "Hope you're having a decent day, Chief." He went around the table. "Roberts, haven't seen you in some time. You're looking fit for all the years you have on you." Roberts smiled. "Who is this young lady you have here, Sergeant?"

Roberts stood up and turned so he could see both of them. "Judge Winehouser, this is Officer Angie Hoffman, a seven-year veteran with the department."

The judge shook her hand and held on to it. "Hoffman, are you related to Detective Albert Hoffman?"

"Yes, sir, he's my father."

"How's he doing, Officer?" Angie could detect the caring concern in the judge's voice.

"He has good and bad days, sir. His asthma acts up real bad from time to time."

"Say hello to him for me. One of the most efficient detectives I ever worked with. Isn't that right, Kruger?"

Kruger nodded in agreement. "Yes, sir, one of the best."

Winehouser moved on to the end of the table. "Heffner and Brand, are you two still running together?" Both men nodded and shook the judge's hand.

Winehouser rounded the table and looked at the chief. "Where do you want me to sit, Kruger?"

"Please come along the table and sit opposite Ian."

Winehouser pulled out the indicated chair, sat down, and looked back at Kruger. "Chief, whatever it is you want to talk about today, tell me right now, does it have anything to do with any of the cases before my court or likely to come before it?"

Kruger looked at the stern face and sharp, piercing eyes. Winehouser had just demonstrated to everyone that his memory remained excellent by speaking to all those in attendance using their names. "No, sir, we're asking for your help as a citizen, on a new case that started this morning." Kruger waved a hand at Hoffman. "Hoffman and Roberts were the first on scene at an accident, and they called Heftner and Brand in."

Winehouser nodded his gray-haired head. "Proceed."

Kruger looked at Heftner, who opened a file lying on the table in front of him, before he asked, "Judge, are you acquainted with a man named Robert William Bamford?"

The surprised look on Winehouser's face changed from its normally stern demeanor. "Of course I know him. Will Bamford is a good friend and my brother-in-law. He's married to my wife's sister. They're on their way here to visit us." His voice sharpened. "Why are you asking?"

Heftner shuffled his papers into a neat pile and closed the file. "Sorry to be the one to tell you, Judge. The Bamfords are deceased. We found them this morning outside their motor home."

Winehouser's face turned gray, and he looked down at his hands for a long moment. When he spoke, his usually firm voice sounded hesitant. "What happened, Detective?"

"We're not sure at this point, Judge. Officer Hoffman arrived at the scene first and has a very plausible theory." Heftner suggested, "Perhaps you would like to hear her report?"

Winehouser listened to the report without comment, then accompanied the detectives to the morgue to identify the bodies, thanked them, asked to be kept informed, and went home to explain the sad news to his wife.

* * *

Noon hour was well over when Sheriff Odleson hung up the phone after being brought up to date by Sergeant Roberts. He swore bitterly, folded the sheets of paper his notes were written on, put them in a shirt pocket, and left his office. On the way out, he told the office receptionist, "Got a message to take out to the Bamford ranch. See you in the morning."

Leaving the police cruiser with the engine idling outside Johansson's General Store, which sold just about everything a person needed, Odleson entered and walked to the counter. Lars

Johansson came to serve him. "Afternoon, Sheriff. What can I do for you?"

"Give me a bottle of Jack Daniels like Will Bamford buys and some plastic glasses."

Tom Odleson had long been known as a man who rarely drank, and the request surprised Lars. While he went for the items, he wondered what could be going on. "Anything else you need, Tom?"

"Nothing else, Lars. Put these items on my bill." Odleson walked away from the counter, and Lars watched him go.

Thirty miles later, Odleson drove into a ranch yard that was empty except for one of the collie cattle dogs and three barn cats. Not unusual; on this ranch they worked from seven to seven and often later. This was haying season, so he continued to drive through the yard and along the ranch road past the close in pastures, heading out to the hay fields where he had worked as a teenager. Tractors were busy moving large, round hay bales and stacking them in fenced enclosures. Odleson parked beside Clay Bamford's GMC half ton and got out with the bottle of Jack in one hand and two glasses in the other. Standing there waiting beside his patrol car, he found himself feeling as low as a man could. He waited for Clayton William Bamford, now twenty-eight years old, the same age as Odleson's oldest son. The two boys were in the same grade all the way through school. Now with his parents gone, Clay would be all alone with this big ranch to run. Too bad Clay's only brother got killed in Iraq during Desert Storm. It would be much easier if Robert Bamford were still around to help run the ranch. To the best of Odleson's recall, Bamfords had fought and died in every war the United States ran up against. Every war since old Bob Bamford gave up being a mountain man and rode in here during the gold rush days of the 1850s. Old Bob came back to a string of valleys he remembered from years of trapping beaver. He brought with him a money stake in gold coins from selling beaver pelts and two men, one Spanish and the other

Shoshone Indian. Descendants of Old Bob and both his men still lived and worked on the ranch. Old Bob figured there would be more money to make selling supplies to miners than digging for gold. He laid claim to all this ranch land by settling smack in the middle of the narrow entrance to a series of valleys that covered several thousand acres and were completely surrounded by mountains. No one could drive a vehicle in or out of the ranch without passing through the ranch yard, although there were long, unused horse trails through the mountains. Buying cattle from eastern settlers headed for Oregon and rounding up strays along the Oregon Trail, Old Bob and his men herded the animals here and started raising beef, which they then sold to miners.

Occasionally over the years, Will Bamford related bits and pieces of this long history to Odleson. As a young boy, Clay always listened and rarely commented. He grew up a quiet boy. He was friendly enough—he liked people and was well liked in the community—and he was smart. At seventeen, Clay went off to university to study computer engineering, and the US Army grabbed him right after graduation. Odleson mused, must have worked on something secret because there never was a hint of what Clay did while in the army. He served two hitches before refusing to reenlist after his mother developed heart problems. Clay had come home a year and a half ago so his dad could spend more time with Mary. Suddenly Odleson remembered Mary commenting on an army general flying into the ranch by helicopter to talk to her son, not long after he came home from the military.

Odleson watched two John Deere tractors come across the hay field and place large, round bales on a stack. Bamford backed his J.D. out of the way and turned off the engine. He climbed down from the tractor cab and walked toward Odleson carrying his Stetson in his hand. He was a tall, wide-shouldered man with the Bamford light brown hair that was almost blond. He had the narrow waist and muscles, hard as rock from all the horse riding and working on the ranch. He grinned and waved his hat at the

Sheriff deciding to poke a little fun at him. "Hi, Tom, you get yourself lost?"

"Came out to see you, Clay." Odleson held out a glass and poured it half full of Jack before doing the same for himself. He motioned toward the trees near the creek. "Let's sit in the shade." Clay sat on the grass with his legs crossed, Indian style, while Tom leaned his back against a tree, pulled up one knee, and stood the bottle upright on the grass between them. "Where's Lorenz?"

Bamford's face showed he was puzzled. "He rode off to check on the heifers. Should be coming along anytime now." Tom sipped his whiskey, and Clay did the same, looking over the glass at the sheriff. Clay kept silent and waited. A noisy tractor came in with another bale, the engine growling loudly. They sipped Jack and watched the bale go on the pile. Suddenly Clay's left arm went up, and he pointed. Tom turned his head and saw Alorenzo Gonzales riding toward them, sitting up proud and straight in his saddle. Tom stood up and walked to the cruiser for another glass.

Gonzales ground hitched his horse and accepted a glass of Jack. Tom bent to add to Clay's glass, replaced the bottle, and picked up his own glass. "Here's to you, Lorenz." Both men nodded and sipped their drinks. They sat in silence for a while, enjoying the whiskey. Odleson looked at the two men. "Damn it!" He shook his head, "Reckon I'm bringing tough news." Neither man responded to the statement. They sat there watching him and waited. "Clay, I got a phone call. The hard fact is Will and Mary got into an accident." Tom watched Clay's eyes harden. His face didn't change, and he just waited. "I'm sorry, Clay. They were both killed." Odleson hurried on, wanting to get this over with. "The sergeant who called said the police talked to your uncle Winehouser, and he confirmed their identity." Tom removed his flat-brimmed police hat and wiped a hand over his forehead.

Clay finally spoke. "What happened?"

Odleson shrugged. "An accident of some kind happened out in Seattle. All I know right now. The police sergeant said they were still trying to figure it out, and he would call me as soon as they know." Odleson put his hat back on. "I'm sorry, Clay. Will and Mary were the best." His eyes glanced at Alorenzo. Both of the old man's cheeks were wet. Alorenzo had aged, way up in his seventies now; no one seemed to know for sure. His Spanish ancestor arrived with old Bob Bamford. Tom felt himself choking up and cleared his throat. "Sure am sorry, Lorenz. Didn't want to bring bad news."

Clay interrupted. "Don't be sorry, Tom. You're our friend, and its best you came instead of someone else."

Lorenz held up his glass. "To Will and Mary." They drank, and Tom reached for the bottle.

* * *

News spreads fast out in the country. In the morning with only a few hours' sleep, Odleson went to inform the preacher and followed up by stopping at Johansson's store. Lars and Hilda Johansson were close friends of the Bamfords, and Clay wanted them to know. By evening, all the neighbors for miles around knew.

Chapter 3

Hoffman and Hanson knocked on doors of houses along streets surrounding the service station, searching for people who might have seen or heard anything, even the smallest detail to give them a lead. They were on foot, backed up by two police cruisers following along in the street. Two full days of knocking on doors, and it was always the same—no one home or elderly grandparents babysitting who rarely knew more than a few words of English. Most were Asian, with an assortment of whites, blacks, and others of undetermined lineage. The few who spoke English denied any knowledge, claiming they were sleeping or watching TV. Both officers recognized how small the chance of learning anything could be. These people were scared of both the police and gang members, having long ago learned their own safety depended on remaining blind and deaf.

Brand and Heftner visited with the coroner to be led, line by line, through the reports. Doctor Keith Herman, a small, careful, precise man, knew his reports often ended up in a courtroom where lawyers tried to discredit his findings. Over the years, everyone learned that no one could rush Doctor Herman in doing his autopsies or in presenting his facts and conclusions. The detectives listened politely, often not fully understanding the technical medical terminology that the good doctor, of his own accord, took time to explain without being asked. Mary Bamford died from a massive myocardial infarction most likely caused by sudden surprise, excitement, and the exertion from moving too quickly. In layman's terms, she died from heart failure.

It took less time to listen to the report on Robert Bamford, who was found to be in remarkably good physical condition for a man of sixty-two years. In the doctor's opinion, Bamford died instantly from a fractured spinal column due to a blow from a blunt instrument, which also shattered two vertebras at the base of his skull.

Brand cautiously inquired, "Doctor Herman, could the blow have been from a two-inch-diameter steel pipe?"

This question resulted in a dissertation on the nature of the fractures and all the doctor's observations. In the end, he agreed the pipe was possibly the blunt instrument used.

* * *

Clay Bamford spent a restless night after Sheriff Tom Odleson left. At first light, he saddled a horse and rode away alone, wanting time to think about the situation, to remember, and to consider the future.

Alorenzo watched Clay preparing to leave, hoping he would be asked to ride along. He used a corner of the kerchief tied around his neck to dab at his eyes. Long ago, he had taught Clay to ride, just as he did the older brother, Robert Bamford, and their dad himself all those years ago. Alorenzo rubbed his forehead; his head hurt just like it did most days. Clay disappeared around a turn into the valley and might be gone all day. The ranch work must continue; the animals required caring for, so he would fill in for the boy and organize the men. Yesterday everything came to a halt when they informed the men of the accident, and that was okay. Now a new day was beginning, and if Will Bamford were here, he would expect the ranch work to get done while this good weather lasted.

Alorenzo looked at the GMC, momentarily tempted; he hadn't driven for many years and once again decided against doing it. If one of his spells occurred with him driving, it would result in an accident. Even dead drunk, he could stay on a horse and often had. In any case, his horse would bring him home if his head went blank.

The sound of tractors stacking bales, dimmed by distance, accompanied Alorenzo as he finished herding three hundred head of Angus cows into a fresh pasture. He closed and firmly latched the gate before removing his Stetson to wipe the sweatband and replace it on his head. Swinging into the saddle, he turned his horse, figuring it was time to start home. Taking a last look around, his eyes spotted Clay coming, still half a mile away. From the angle of the sun, he figured it must be all of six o'clock. The sun would disappear behind the mountain before long. He waited until Bamford arrived, and both horses moved out, side by side, holding to a steady walk. After the horses took a few steps, Alorenzo queried. "You doin' all right, boy?"

"Reckon I'm fair to middling, Lorenz." Clay placed both hands on the saddle horn and leaned forward to ease his seat in the saddle. "Expect it's time for me to phone Uncle Edgar this evening. Have to drive into town tomorrow and talk to the preacher, get arrangements started."

"Do what you have to, boy. We'll look after the ranch."

"Thanks, Lorenz." Clay waved a hand around. "Won't feel like the same ranch now with Mom and Dad no longer here."

The silence lasted as the horses stepped along. "Tough times, Clay." Alorenzo sighed. "We've seen our share of tough times. Your two uncles killed in Nam, and Will wounded. Robert while he was over there in Iraq. Will, he always said you got to look ahead, not back; a man must keep moving forward. Your mom and dad would want you to keep going."

Clay sighed and removed his Stetson. "Reckon I know that, Lorenz."

"All those years you were in the army, Will kept building and planning so this ranch would be here for you. You eat anything today, boy?"

Clay smiled, waving a hand. "Not so you'd notice."

"Reckon we best be getting home." Alorenzo touched a spur to his horse, and they loped toward the ranch yard, still a mile and a half away.

Clay phoned Seattle, fully expecting his uncle would describe a traffic accident of some sort. "Winehouser residence, hello."

"Hello, Edgar, this is Clay calling."

"Clay, I'm so glad you called. Your aunt Sadie's been calling for two days and getting no answer."

"Tell Aunt Sadie I apologize for that. We've been out on the range. The sheriff drove out from town to bring news of the accident."

"What did he tell you?"

"Not much. All he knew for sure seemed to be that an accident happened, and Mom and Dad were killed."

"It's much more serious than that, Clay." Clay listened silently as Edgar related details of his meeting with the police. When their conversation ended, Clay talked to his aunt and promised to call again the next evening. Clay set the phone down, his face screwed up with sadness, and tears started coming from his eyes and running down his cheeks. With both hands clenched into tight fists he wiped his eyes but the tears kept coming. He paced the house in his stocking clad feet, hardly able to see through the tears. Every few minutes he waved his fists in frustration. Finally he slumped into a leather clad arm chair before the unlit fireplace and just sat there.

In Seattle, the Winehousers drank their evening tea, sitting in Edgar's study. Sadie told him, "It's worrisome to think about

Clay being all alone. He hardly said a word to me. Do you think I should fly to Idaho to spend some time with him?"

Edgar considered the idea. "No airline lands anywhere near the ranch. Clay would have to drive a long way to pick you up."

"That's true." Sadie sipped from her cup.

Edgar watched her. Finally he suggested, "I have an existing back log of holidays from past years I never got around to taking. When we go to Idaho for the funeral, we could stay at the ranch for a couple of weeks."

"Oh, Edgar, that's such a wonderful idea." Sadie rewarded him with a wide smile, the first one he had seen in days. "When Clay phones tomorrow, ask him if he'll mind having his old relatives under foot for so long." Her face sobered. "Are you sure you'll be able to arrange so much time away?"

"Don't worry, Sadie. I received a letter not long ago threatening to cancel those days if I didn't use them soon."

Three days later, Clay made his usual evening phone call, and Edgar brought him up to date. "The medical examiner and the police lab have finished their work. Will and Mary will be released in the morning, so I can send them home as we discussed."

"Thanks for looking after everything."

"We're all family, Clay. Do you want the motor home put into storage until you can come for it?"

"No, I don't want it back. It would be a constant bad memory. Why don't you and Sadie keep it?"

"A very kind suggestion you are making Clay. We would never use it. Your aunt's idea of camping is a five-star hotel." Clay laughed, pleasing Edgar with the effect his little joke had.

"Edgar, would you mind looking after selling the motor home for me?"

"Of course I will. What do you want done with the clothes in it?"

"Don't want them back. Give them to someone—your church or maybe the Sally Ann?"

"Certainly, Clay. We'll bring Will's wallet and Mary's purse when we come and take care of disposing of the rest. Sadie and I plan on driving to the ranch as soon as everything is arranged at this end. Do you want to talk to Sadie?"

"You say hello for me. Talk to you tomorrow night."

"Good-bye, Clay."

* * *

After two weeks, Detectives Brand and Heftner reviewed their files. All the lab reports were in, and they could find no solid clue as to who had been responsible for the murders. There was a missing Rolex watch, which Judge Winehouser described as a gift to Will Bamford from his son. The lab had positively identified the weapon, and there was nothing else to go on except for Officer Hoffman's theory regarding the Asian gang. Without a solid lead, they had small chance of getting a search warrant to enter the gang's clubhouse, and even if they did, they didn't know what to search for. Sure they might get lucky and stumble on drugs, which they suspected the gang might be distributing. Language problems made investigating even harder. Every time the police stopped one of the gang members, they immediately lapsed into Vietnamese, pretending to understand very little English. Brand closed the last file and suggested, "We may as well set this case aside for a while and hope for a break of some kind. We have nothing to go on."

"A damn shame." Heftner shrugged. "They killed a good pair of people who had been married a long time and unless we get lucky, they may get away with it."

"Heff, you always say there are no perfect crimes. Sooner or later, something will turn up." Brand stretched his arms over his head and mused, "We need to find a way to put pressure on the gang."

"Very hard to do without stepping across the line."
Brand pushed the file away, "I know, Heff. I know."

* * *

Three weeks after the funeral, things were taking on normalcy for Clay. Having the Winehousers visit proved enjoyable even though a sad occasion prompted it. All the immediate demands of the ranch were satisfied, and there would be a lull until the steers needed to be brought down from the high country to winter in sheltered valleys at lower elevations. Clay sat on his horse in the middle of a pasture watching cow/calf pairs grazing. To anyone watching, he would appear to be studying the animals. Actually, his mind wandered far away; he was considering a plan to even the score. He possessed knowledge of powerful weapons that were at his disposal, and he knew how to use them. Such thought caused a slight smile. His mind flipped back to the summer he turned nineteen—the summer he discovered two things, women and computer hacking. Actually, the woman discovered him, and it became an exciting few weeks as a woman twice his age gave him a stimulating education. The computer hacking he discovered on his own.

He never tried to steal anything; it was the thrill of knowing he could do it. Over a period of months, he became efficient at computer hacking, using his expertise in computer engineering to access computer networks and reach out ever further from the university. His proficiency in Spanish led him to look south into Mexico where he stumbled on messages travelling between drug dealers in Mexico, Columbia, and Europe. At first he considered the curious messages to be only interesting, until he realized what they really were about.

Early in the new year, half-frightened at doing it, Bamford walked into the local FBI office with a manila file thick with computer printouts and asked to speak to an agent. After waiting, he was handed over to a junior officer with only a few months' experience. The officer casually leafed through the file. He couldn't read Spanish, which was to be expected in the northern tier states. The agent asked a few questions, obviously seeming to doubt the answers, asked for Bamford's name and phone number, and thanked him for coming in.

Clay went back to his studies and his hacking. He found it to be exciting even if the FBI showed no interest. A week later, his life changed. Walking home from classes to his off-campus, rented apartment, Clay watched a plain gray car parked on the street behind his GMC half ton. As soon as he turned up the walk to the apartment building, the car doors opened. He heard the doors closing and turned to look. Three men wearing suits were coming toward him. Shifting the briefcase to his left hand, Bamford turned to wait. Two of the men who appeared to be in their thirties stopped some five feet away while an older man watched from the public sidewalk. The burlier of the two men asked in a tought voice, "Are you Clayton Bamford?"

Clay didn't like the man's manner or his rough tone of voice. His slate-gray eyes hardened as he watched the man for a moment. "Who the hell wants to know?"

The sharp retort set the men back, and they took another look at the tall, broad-shouldered, young man dressed in jeans, western boots, and a wide-brimmed Stetson hat. Before the first man could speak again, the older man interrupted. "Excuse me, Waite. May I speak to Mr. Bamford?"

Both men stepped aside onto the grass, and the well-dressed, gray-haired man approached on the sidewalk. "My apology, Mr. Bamford. We had no intention of being aggressive. May I introduce myself? I am General Thompson Thorsen of the US Army, and these two gentlemen are FBI agents. If you don't mind, I would like to discuss a file you left at the local agency office several days ago."

Clay's gray eyes softened and he stuck out his hand. "Pleased to meet you, Mr. Thorsen." There was a slight smile on the well-tanned face. "As you already know, I'm Clayton Bamford."

Thorsen smiled. "Without your hat, you look exactly like your yearbook picture." Thorsen almost winced from the firm handshake. He was already familiar with Bamford's background from a hurried FBI report, and now he was learning something more important. Bamford possessed what the military referred to as a strategic mind, the ability to look beyond the obvious facts and discern a larger picture. His thoughts were interrupted.

"Would you care to join me in my apartment, Mr. Thorsen? It will be more comfortable than standing here."

"Thank you, that's very thoughtful." Thorsen inclined his head. "And my companions?"

Clay smiled. "Your choice." He turned and walked to the building with three men following him. On the second floor, Clay unlocked a door and held it open for the men to enter. All three heads swiveled to appraise the rooms. There were two bedrooms with a bathroom between, a small kitchen, a large dining/living room, and most surprising, everything was spotlessly clean. Everything, even the windows, shone. Thorsen immediately suspected a female roommate lived with Bamford.

Clay waved a hand. "Find yourselves seats while I put coffee on."

They watched Clay take his briefcase to a table obviously set up to be used as a desk. He went into the bathroom, from where they heard the sounds of him washing his hands. In the kitchen, Clay filled a pot with water and added coffee before setting it on the stove and turning on a burner. Clay came from the kitchen with cups and placed a plate of store-bought cookies on what served as a dining room table—a typical wooden kitchen table with four wooden chairs. Thorsen said, "I see you have two bedrooms. Do you have a roommate?"

"No, sir. The extra bedroom is for my parents when they come to visit." Clay stood watching them. Finally he suggested, "You said you wanted to discuss the file."

Thorsen thought, *'A clean living man, strong family ties, and not one to waste time.'* "Yes, that's correct. Would you mind telling me in what manner the information came into your possession?"

Clay looked him right in the eye. "I was computer surfing and stumbled on the first messages. They were interesting, so for the next few days I kept going back. Each time I dumped the messages to a floppy. When I finally came to fully understand what they were about, I printed copies and put them in a file. Figured someone should see them, and the FBI office seemed logical. No one there showed any interest."

"You read Spanish, Clay?"

"Yes, sir." Clay turned his head to look into the kitchen before going to get the coffeepot. He came back with the pot and a carton of milk. "Everyone want coffee?" They all agreed. Clay poured four cups and sat down at the table with his back to the kitchen. Thorsen pulled out the chair on Clay's left and turned it so he was facing Clay.

"The Agency apologizes for seeming indifferent regarding the file. No one in the local office reads Spanish, so they didn't appreciate what the messages contained. Do you speak Spanish also?" Clay nodded. "English and Spanish. Any other languages, Clay?"

Grinning, Clay rattled out an answer he knew none of them would understand—just having fun with them. Thorsen smiled at the demonstration. "What language are you using now?"

Clay smiled. "Shoshone. In Shoshone, I told you, 'I speak the Shoshone Indian language, Mister White Eyes.'"

Thorsen laughed, pleased with this young man's directness, although not complete openness. He'd return to that in a minute. "Any other languages?"

"No, sir."

"Clay, my given name is Thompson. Not all that common a first name, still it's the one my parents gave me. If I'm going to address you as Clay, would you please use Thompson?"

"I can do that, Thompson."

"Good! The information in the file you provided, while not complete, is very valuable to the efforts I direct on behalf of our government. You said you were surfing when you got the information. You really mean you were computer hacking, do you not?"

Clay turned to look at the agents and then back at Thompson. "I believe computer hacking is illegal, is it not? It's considered an invasion of privacy even though the FBI and CIA do it all the time."

They stared at each other, and Thompson realized Clay was well informed and not going to be intimidated. He turned to the agents. "Would you both please wait for me in the car?"

When they were alone, Thompson moved to the chair opposite Clay. He slumped down, put both elbows on the table, steepled his fingers in a praying position, and placed his chin on his thumbs, the first fingers of each hand rubbing the sides of his nose. He was silent for several minutes. "Clay, I've been in the military for a long time, more years than you've lived. For several years now, I've been in charge of a special operation on behalf of our national government with the purpose of stopping the importation of drugs into this country. Stopping is rather an unobtainable objective; let's just say to slow the volume as much as is humanly possible. When your file arrived in my office, it seemed like a ray of sunlight. It gave us a glimpse through a door we've been trying to open for some time. I don't need to know how you got the information. What I need is your help."

Clay's face didn't change. He just waited, and Thompson thought, *'This kid would make a great poker player.'* Thompson sat up straight and reached for his cup. The coffee was cold. Clay took the cup from him, emptied it into the sink, and refilled it with hot coffee. Thompson grinned. "Thank you. You're in the third year of Computer Engineering, so you'll graduate in a year and a half with your degree."

"That's the plan."

"Would you be willing to work for me on a consulting basis until you graduate?"

"Don't know what you do." Clay frowned. "You said you're with the government. Is what you do legal?"

Thompson laughed. "To be honest, most of the time it is. There are occasions when we have to bend the rules to achieve important objectives. On those occasions, we ask for approval to go ahead from a high-level oversight committee that rarely refuses us permission." Thompson rubbed his nose. "Hundreds of people surf, as you described it. The hard fact is very few are really good at it. I've never understood what the difference is, what makes a few people highly proficient at surfing. Maybe it's a special quirk in their brain or some kind of intuition. In any case, you seem to have that special talent, and your country needs it. I don't expect to walk in here unknown to you and have you jump on board with my projects. May I suggest something?"

Clay nodded his agreement.

"The things my agency does are classified top secret. Therefore, I can't discuss our activities with you until you're assigned a security clearance. Please grant me your permission to have a security check done, and after you're approved, I'll come back to meet with you again. At that time, we'll discuss the types of things you can help us with."

"You won't find much to check on me." Clay shrugged. "All I've done so far is go to school and work on the ranch. You do what you need to—only don't go upsetting my folks with a bunch of foolish questions. I'll listen to what you have to say, but that doesn't mean I'll agree." Clay glanced at his watch.

"Thank you, Clay."

Clay wagged his head. "Almost seven, you hungry? I was planning to cook up a mess of scrambled eggs and sausage meat. You may as well eat with me."

"Sounds good, Clay. Is it all right to use your bathroom?"

Clay waved toward the bathroom door. "Go ahead and make yourself at home." Clay grinned. "There are no secrets lying around here; all those are safely cached in my head."

They sat across from each other to eat large plates of scrambled eggs with pieces of sausage meat mixed in, hash browns, medium salsa, whole-wheat toast, and fresh coffee.

* * *

Clay's head came up suddenly, and his eyes focused. A pair of calves frolicking around kicking up their heels had brought Clay's mind back to the present. He started his horse moving to walk on through the herd, thinking about his plan and how best to start making progress on it.

Chapter 4

The bedroom, where Clay slept ever since he became big enough to climb out of a crib, contained a single bed, a dresser with six drawers, a large closet, and a single window opening onto a veranda that went around three sides of the house. A countertop covered in computers, printers, spare parts, and tools went along one complete wall. Shelves above the counter held textbooks from university, computer manuals, and a large assortment of paper supplies, disc storage, and ink cartridges. This was his bedroom, but even more, it was his office.

Using his engineering training, Clay built his own open-frame computers, with the computing power and storage he wanted. He purchased the motherboards, processers, hard drives, and other computer components directly from suppliers. To unknowledgeable people, it appeared to be somewhat of a hodgepodge of unworkable pieces slapped together. This was caused by the lack of the standard metal and plastic cases used for customer appeal in computer stores. Clay didn't bother dressing up his computers. In actuality, he built mini mainframe computers much more powerful than any PC available on the market.

Settling into his office chair in front of the keyboard, Clay turned on the power switch and considered the best computer hubs to use while the computer went through its startup procedure. Locating a back door into the Seattle Police Department's computer system was his most immediate objective, and he knew it would be a tough task. All operating systems have weaknesses available to be exploited by people in possession of the required expertise. Basically, the challenge came down to finding system weaknesses without alerting and setting off protection devices, which themselves contained other weaknesses. It was a game Clay discovered and became proficient at while in university. Ever since the first meeting with General Thorsen, his skills at computer hacking were used to seek information, disrupt systems, and do such mundane things as tracking financial transactions and money transfers. Many were mundane, everyday transactions, which often proved to be very profitable. Early in his career with Thorsen's Agency, Clay suggested commandeering drug funds. They secretly did just that, providing finances for expanded operations outside their approved budget. Hundreds of millions of dollars in cash resided in offshore operating accounts.

For this operation, Clay planned to bypass the Agency's large IBM mainframe computer center in Washington. Thus would he avoid leaving any trace of his activities that the agency could pick up. Clay reached to retrieve from the overhead shelf a well-worn and thumbed operating manual for an IBM mainframe, a manual he never used now because time had outdated it. He kept the manual to serve a special purpose. Opening it to the proper page, he perused the list of codes handwritten below where the printing on the last page in chapter 8 stopped, leaving most of the page blank. The writing appeared to be notes, put there by a technician working to solve a problem. In reality, they were the codes necessary to access a number of computer hubs around the world.

After selecting the mainframe at the University of Texas as his first stop, he moved on to a large banking hub in Mexico City, and from there to San Francisco to a hub he would use to start a search in Seattle. Now, with midnight gone by, it seemed unlikely anyone would notice the unusual activity taking place. If someone did, Clay would immediately shut down the connections and disappear into cyberspace. After two hours of probing and feeling his way around the police department's system, he shut down the computer and went to bed. The next night he continued to search for a weakness.

On the third night, at eleven minutes past three, Clay gained entry to the Seattle Police computer system. He started probing and quickly identified a commercial operating system he had knowledge of from past projects. Obviously Seattle purchased the system to save money. Clay had become familiar with the system because many police departments did the same thing. In one of his notebooks, he found the previous codes used to access a similar operating system while working on a project on behalf of the Agency.

It was enough for tonight. Clay stretched before shutting down the connections and turning the computer off. He padded down the hallway to the bathroom, wearing his robe, and returned to the bedroom to roll into bed and catch a few hours' sleep before the ranch came to life for another day.

Three days later, Clay downloaded to a hard disk the contents of the police reports on the Bamford accident, including the investigation, lab and autopsy reports, and conclusions made by the officers. Included were names for everyone involved, the address of the accident, and an attached report on the Asian gang detailing what the police knew of their activities. It had taken a week to get this far, and now the difficult work lay ahead of him— trying to gather intelligence on the gang. First there was one little detail to take care of. He wrote a program code to be left buried in the police computer operating system. It would automatically transmit to an electronic mail drop in Denver any new information added to the Bamford file. Clay could now access the mail drop whenever convenient and download new data without directly accessing the Seattle Police computer system.

In early October, the ranch crew finished moving the steer herd down from high country pastures to spend the winter in sheltered valleys where the weather was better and it was easier to look after them. The men completed the move back from line camps with the two married men going about getting their wives resettled in the ranch houses supplied for them. In a few days, everything necessary had been done to shape up for the coming winter. The temporary men hired for the summer returned to their families. Hopefully, the big snows wouldn't start until after Thanksgiving. In reality, in this country you never really knew; heavy snows in October did occur.

Now the ranch yard hummed with activity. There was a huge amount of catching up to do after the long summer, and people were always around chatting. Bamford particularly enjoyed having Shoshone Mike and his wife, Peggy, back. Mike's parents named him Jason, but his grandfather, who came to the ranch with Old Bob, went by Shoshone Mike, and the name stuck to each generation. It was their way of honoring ancestors. Both spoke good English, but Bamford liked to practice his Shoshone words and refused to talk to them in English unless other people were involved.

Working days on the ranch and nights on the computer, Clay began losing weight. He felt more tired than normal on Saturday morning as he drove to town with a long list of supplies to purchase. He stopped at the bulk fuel dealer to ask him to fill up the ranch's fuel tanks, just in case winter came early, picked up pails of oil, antifreeze, and tubes of grease before driving to Johansson's with his shopping list.

Walking into the store, Clay found a seat on a high wooden stool at one end of the counter to wait his turn. He pushed his Stetson hat up and looked around. The place seemed busy with mostly ladies from around the area picking up items for the next week. Those who passed by spoke to Clay, and he replied to each with a smile. In a small town like this, there weren't many people he didn't know. Lars came along the counter and stuck out his hand. "Been awhile since seeing you, Clay."

Clay nodded. "Things have been busy at the ranch. Now we're getting ready for winter."

"You think winter's coming this early?" Lars shook his head. "Hope you're wrong."

"Just getting prepared in case the weather doesn't cooperate." Clay shrugged. "Here's a list of things we need. Can you put it together while I take care of some errands?"

"Let me have a look at it." Lars ran a finger down the list, reading the items. "You appear to be stocking up for a long winter."

"Never hurts to be prepared." Clay grinned and tipped his hat to a lady going by. "Mike and Peggy will be in next week. Put what they need on the ranch account."

"Will do, Clay. Give me a couple of hours to put this order together."

Clay nodded and stood up, accidently bumping an older lady going by in the aisle. He turned, quickly putting out a hand to steady her. Grabbing the Stetson off his head, Clay started to apologize. She cut him off before the words got out. "Clayton Bamford, you watch where you're going."

"Sorry about that, Mrs. Olsen. Are you all right?"

"Of course I am, Clayton." He heard the same stern voice during his English and history classes in high school. Mrs. Olsen stared at him. "You look tired, and your face is thin. You're not looking after yourself, Clayton." Her eyes took on a gleam of humor. "It's way past time you found a nice girl and settled down." Mrs. Olsen wagged a finger at him as she had so many times in school. "You need a wife to look after you."

Grinning at her, Clay responded, "You're probably right Mrs. Olsen. Not very likely I'll find a girl willing to put up with me."

She gave him a stern look. "That is a problem. Let me see." Mrs. Olsen smiled. "Maybe if you showed up in church more often, we could reform you so nice girls would show some interest." Her eyes shifted to look past him. "Do you agree, Hilda?"

Clay turned to look. Hilda Johansson was standing beside Lars. "Now, Elsie, don't be too tough on Clay. He has a big ranch operation to look after, and he doesn't get to town very often. Clay isn't out partying and running around like some we could name."

Mrs. Olsen put a hand on Clays arm and smiled. "Mary always told me if Clayton got out of line, I should take the strap to him. Never did get to do that. If he starts partying and carrying on, I will take the strap and drive out to the ranch, just to give him a sore hand." Everyone within hearing laughed, with Clay joining in.

Lars admonished the women. "You ladies quit picking on Clay." He lifted a hand and started away. "See you later, Clay."

After excusing himself, Clay left the store. He went to the Bumper to Bumper to buy oil and fuel filters, completed his other errands, and stopped at his accountant's office for a meeting. At half past noon, he edged his truck up to the sidewalk in front of the Ranchers Grill and Tavern to eat a meal he hadn't cooked himself, before returning to Johansson's.

Sheriff Odleson saw the GMC backed up in front of Johansson's and pulled in alongside. Getting out, he leaned one arm on the truck box as Clay came from the store with another carton to add to the load already in the truck. "You need help, Clay?"

"No need, Tom. Wouldn't want you getting your fancy uniform dirty." Clay grinned. "Have a few more things to load, and we can talk." Clay made three more trips, which filled the bed of the truck box. He got the tarp and covered the box to keep out dust and left the tailgate down. Sitting on the back of the truck, legs dangling, they caught up on the local news.

After visiting with the sheriff, Clay fired up the GMC and started for the ranch, thinking while he drove that now he could begin to put his plan into action. Hacking the Seattle Police's system had taken time. He had been careful not to cross the protection systems, and it took several days. The Asian gang proved impossible. If they used a computer connection, he hadn't found it, so as they did in the Agency, the time had arrived to put feet on the ground. The road slipped away under the truck as he mentally plotted how to get off the ranch unseen. With his appearance in town today talking to so many people and seen by many more, his whereabouts were established. None of them would think anything of his not coming back to town for the next two or three weeks, even a month.

Arriving at the ranch, Gonzales and Shoshone Mike came to help unload and store away the supplies. Clay related what news he had picked up in town and ended by relating Mrs. Olsen's threat to give him the strap. The men got a good laugh at his expense. In the evening, Clay sauntered over to Alorenzo's cabin and talked to him in Spanish. Gonzales understood when told Clay would be away for two or three weeks, and if anyone asked for Clay, to tell them he had gone out hunting. Alorenzo wouldn't be lying because Clay was going hunting, just not for elk like people would think. From long experience, he had become accustomed to Clay's coming and going and never questioned it.

At three in the morning, Clay loaded the truck with a small duffle bag of clothes, a few special items, a battered, old tool case containing tools and testing gear for working on computers, and drove away from the ranch. A wad of hundred-dollar bills taken from the hidden cache on the ranch were in Clay's pocket along with a passport and matching driver's license, made out in a Spanish name. The passport was so good it had taken him through US Customs several times. He only needed to darken his hair to match the pictures before using the passport.

Two hundred and thirty miles later, the GMC drove past Mountain Home and kept going. Mountain Home was the one place where there was a chance of running into someone who might recognize him, if they happened to be in from the air base.

At a small diner in Boise, they served him a plate full of crisp bacon, eggs, and hash browns. With the truck fueled up, Clay got back on I-84 and drove into Oregon, heading for Pendleton.

In Pendleton, he found a cheap motel, checked in, and went looking for a thrift store. After searching around the store, he found a worn pair of black jeans, several T-shirts, a light wind breaker, a slouchy, round hat like golfers wear, and a used pair of black runners with rubber soles. Putting all these things together, it cost Clay twenty-one dollars, and he left the store feeling happy.

On the road at first light, I-84 took him along the Columbia River Gorge to the Dalles, where he went north across the river into Washington State and turned west on Highway 14, being careful to stay under the speed limit and drive courteously.

After turning north onto Interstate 5, Clay ran into a rainstorm. The GMC pulled into Lacey late in the day, and he found a motel for the night, paying cash. The plan called for the GMC to stay parked in Lacey while he went into Seattle. By doing that, the truck and the license plate wouldn't get caught on a surveillance camera.

In the morning, he woke excited about the challenge ahead. Clay took time to darken his hair and cleaned up the bathroom sink. While in Seattle, he would be Manuel Sanchez in accordance with the driver's license. Waiting for his hair to dry, he dug into a bag of donuts picked up the night before and drank a Coke.

Before doing anything else, Clay gassed up the truck and bought street maps for Lacey and Seattle. Next he drove the GMC to a car rental place named Rent A Wreck to get an older, small car that would get around without attracting attention. From a parking spot on the street a block away, Clay walked to the car lot with a baseball hat pulled down to shade his eyes and wandered through the vehicles toward the small office. A teenager came out to meet him. "Looking for a car, Mister?"

"Yes, it's for a holiday." Clay's spoke using a Texas drawl. "Maybe for two weeks. You all happen to have a Honda or small Ford?"

"Where you from, Mister?" Clay smiled inside at the boy's reaction.

"Texas. Brazos County, Texas." As hoped, the teenager reacted.

"Figured you were from down south somewhere, with the drawl you have."

"Didn't know I spoke with a drawl. Of course down in Texas, everybody sounds like me."

The kid ate it up and said, "Come on and take a look at what we have. There's one Honda Civic and a couple of Fords." They walked around and checked all three, even though Clay already knew which one he wanted. He left it to the last. When they got to it, Clay walked around looking at it and asked for the keys. After sitting in it and listening to the engine, he got out and kicked the tires and opened the trunk. "How much do you charge for a car like this?"

The kid didn't hesitate; he had heard the two weeks. "Ten bucks each for days one and two, and after that, seven dollars a day plus insurance, and you pay for the gas."

Rubbing the two-day growth of beard on his chin, Clay let it all hang in the air for a moment before going to look at the car again and hitting the hood with his fist to test its firmness. "What kind of mileage does a Ford Focus get?"

"My dad gave this one a tune up last month; it should get thirty miles or more."

Pretending to be calculating the cost using his fingers, Clay finally asked, "What will the insurance run me?"

The boy smiled, figuring he had Clay hooked. "Come in the office, and we can work out the cost." Walking ahead, he held the door open for Clay, and they went in to make a deal. Since Clay was using cash, the boy insisted on being paid for the full two weeks in advance. "Are you here on holidays, Mister Sanchez?

"Yes, sir. I figure to catch myself a salmon and look around a mite."

"Well, you enjoy yourself and drive safely."

"Figure to do just that. See you in two weeks." Driving out of the Rent A Wreck in the dark blue Focus, what he needed now was a place to leave the GMC. Parking the Focus behind the truck, Clay transferred all his gear to the trunk of the car and locked the doors. Three blocks away, in a residential area, he spotted an old timer out raking his front lawn, and it was a large yard. Pulling up at the curb, Clay got out and asked the man if he had room to store the truck for two weeks. The old timer wanted to know why, and when he heard Clay planned to go fishing, he agreed to keep it for thirty dollars, half down and half when Clay got back. Seemed like a lucky day to Clay. After hiking back to the Focus, Clay drove around looking for a different motel for the night. By tomorrow, the beard would be three days old, and the dark brown hair curled around his ears. A coin laundry served to wash and dry the used clothing.

Chapter 5

Greater Seattle is a city spread out on a north-south axis, divided by ocean inlets, lakes, islands, mountains, and forests of large trees. Such geography presents a difficult city for a stranger. Anyone unfamiliar with the streets and trying to find his way around has a problem. Clay might have been ten or eleven years old when they came to see the Winehousers on summer vacation. Navigating the streets wasn't something he remembered. With a city map on the passenger seat, it still took him hours to find the part of the city where the Asian gang's hangout was located. It was an area of old, well-used buildings, now mostly uncared for and left vacant. After finding it, he got out of the area and went looking for a motel, hoping to get one within walking distance.

Clay found a Super 8 some ten or twelve blocks away, parked the car, and went into the office. A nice young lady with bright red fingernails smiled at him. "Do you have a room for one?"

She tapped on a keyboard and a moment later looked up. "Do you prefer the ground or second floor?"

"The second floor would be nice if you have a room."

"Certainly, sir. We have a single with a double bed and a color television. Would you like that one?"

"It'll be fine. I'll take it for two nights and may want to stay over for another day."

"No problem, sir." She placed a form on the counter. "Please fill this registration form in for us."

She looked at the form after he pushed it toward her. "You're driving a Ford Focus, dark blue. Do you know the license number?"

"Sorry, miss." It was a lie. "Never been able to remember it. You want me to go out and look at it?"

She smiled again. "It won't be necessary, Mr. Sanchez. How will you be paying, credit card or cash?"

Reaching into a jean pocket, Clay pulled out several bills, folded in half, and paid her. "If I decide to stay another night what time, do you need to know?"

"Checkout time is noon, so before that." She gave Clay directions, and after washing up, he walked three blocks to enjoy dinner at a seafood restaurant and start familiarizing himself with the area. He followed a different route back.

After two days of walking and driving an ever larger area of the city, avoiding several blocks around the gang's hangout, the area became familiar ground to him. Midafternoon on the second day, the Ford Focus cruised sedately past the service station where Will and Mary were found. Three blocks past, Clay made two left turns and came back to go past the gang's hangout. It was an old, two-story, dark red brick building. At the front, two young Asian men were leaning against the wall smoking. They didn't bother to look at the Focus as the car went past them and kept going. The next morning, Clay drove past going the other way, and right across the street from the hangout was a corner grocery store. His eye caught a sign advertising a room for rent. The second floor of the building seemed to be living quarters above the store. Clay's heart jumped. The store was right across the street from the gang's clubhouse, and renting a room there would give him an excuse for being in the area.

Back at the Super 8, Clay paid cash for one more night, went to the room, and lay on the bed to think it all through carefully. If the rental room happened to be still available, there was no reason not to just stay right there and begin watching. To fit with his cover, he would be wearing the well-used clothes, speaking English with a Spanish accent, and being one more man fallen on hard times. It would be important to not take anything along that would be out of character.

The Focus, parked at the side of the building near an exit, was out of sight from the motel office. In the morning after retrieving his old backpack from the trunk, Clay packed the tool kit that held special items he hoped to use, an extra T-shirt, a pair of boxer shorts, a small shaving kit, and the khaki jacket. Back in the motel room, he changed his clothes, returned to his car wearing the used clothing, and locked the suitcase in the trunk. His plan was to park the car, take the backpack, and leave the seats bare so there was nothing to attract attention.

Exiting the motel parking lot onto a side street, the Focus turned right and drove to a quiet residential street near a park entrance. Parking the car at the curb under a large tree, he retrieved the backpack and placed it on the car hood. Clay locked the car and put the ignition keys in a metal container with a magnetic bottom. Leaning against the front fender giving the appearance of resting, while looking casually around to make sure no one was watching, his right hand slid under the fender and left the car keys hidden.

Donning the backpack and striding away like a hiker out for the day, Clay followed a trail into the park, turned at the first opportunity, and walked the mile or so to the corner grocery store. Before entering the area, he stopped to lean against a building, fished out a Zippo lighter, and lit up a cigarillo. After donning a pair of glasses with thick glass lens and heavy, dark brown frames, he pulled the Houston Astros baseball cap down to shade his face. At a slower pace and affecting a slight stoop, Clay wandered slowly along the sidewalk, finally coming to the corner grocery. Stopping on the corner to look around, he slowly turned until the For Rent sign was right there in front of him. A little Asian lady watched through a front window as Clay rubbed his chin and looked at the sign for a minute before walking toward the door and entering.

She was middle aged with black hair and not much over five feet tall. "What you need, mister?"

"Senora, over there is a sign, room for rent."

She stared at Clay. "You talk funny. Where you from, mister?" She had quickly picked up on Clay's drawl and mixed language.

"From Texas, Senora. My name is Sanchez."

"You want see room, mister?" Clay nodded yes, and she led the way out a side door and up a flight of enclosed stairs. The room was small, with a single bed his six-foot-two-inch frame would fill, a small table in front of a window, one chair, and a standup cupboard with four clothes hangers. Looking around and peeking out the window, it couldn't have been better. The room was clean and, most important, located at the front of the building with a perfect view across the street. An old style, wooden framed window faced the Asian clubhouse, and when he lifted, the lower half slid up easily. The Asian lady showed him the bathroom down the hallway before telling Clay, "Ten dolla for one week. You no cook, no girl, no party." Nodding his head in agreement, Clay smiled and dug out two fives. The lady pocketed the money and walked away, going back to look after her store business.

There were no clothes to hang up. Clay's gear included a laser microphone, a small tape recorder, and earphones to plug into his ears. Setting up the laser and cracking the window he scanned the laser over the windows of the gang's hangout. A very old brick building with single-pane windows through which the laser picked up sounds very well. Voices, music, or noise of any kind caused the single pane of glass to vibrate in sympathy with the sound, just like a diaphragm type microphone. The laser picked up the glass vibrations and translated them back into sound. He could either listen with the earphones or record sounds on tape and listen later.

The sounds coming from a ground-floor room took a while to understand. It seemed like three or four men were playing pool. In one second-floor room at the front of the building, someone was asleep and snoring loudly. The other rooms were quiet. It was four thirty in the afternoon, so with the tape recorder turned on, Clay decided to go find something to eat, figuring activity in the clubhouse would pick up in the evening.

At the foot of the outside stairs he paused to light a cigarillo while his eyes scanned the area for anyone showing interest in him. There was no one in sight, so he walked along the side of the store to the street, crossed toward the clubhouse, and walked slowly past, displaying no interest in the building. Two blocks further along the street, in a Chinese restaurant, Bamford chose a window table and ordered food. There was a shelf with used pocket books. After looking through them, he bought two.

On Saturday, after three days with very little to show for all the listening, he went downstairs to the store to pick up some Hershey bars, potato chips, and a Coke. As he walked to the counter to pay for them, a young lad came from a back room to talk to the Asian lady. They argued about a computer that wasn't working, and she told him it was too expensive to get it fixed. Bamford stood at the counter for a minute listening, before she turned to him. "Grandson get computer, now it no work." She waved her arms. "What does poor woman do with grandson?" She started adding up the cost of his items. Looking at the boy, Clay asked him what went wrong with the computer. He explained, and Clay offered to take a look at it for him, after mentioning having worked with computers in one of his jobs. The boy led the way to a room at the back of the building and turned on the computer. There wasn't much wrong, nothing serious. Clay fooled around with it for a few minutes, updated the operating system, cleaned up the hard drive, and it began running smoothly again. The boy said he was ten years old, in grade five, and used his PC and inkjet printer to write reports for school. He showed a poor-quality printout and asked if the printer could be fixed. Going upstairs, Clay returned with his tool kit, which was six inches thick and looked to everyone like a beat-up briefcase. After opening up the printer, it didn't take much to clean the print head and wipe off the feed rollers and platen. While Clay worked and talked with the little boy, his older brother walked in and stood watching them. He didn't seem overly happy seeing Clay there. Clay told the boy to write something and print a copy, which he did, and it came out clear and sharp. It excited the boy to have his computer working again, and he ran to tell his grandmother. Clay followed along to pay for his purchases. The Asian lady wanted to give the items to him. He refused, telling her it had been fun to help the boy. Leaving, he noticed the older boy standing at the back of the store watching.

Saturday night provided the first real good information. Clay located what appeared to be an office on the second floor of the Asian clubhouse where the lights were on. The people inside were discussing a shipment coming in. They were waiting for confirmation of its arrival. Gradually it became clear to him; they were talking about drugs coming in on a fishing boat they secretly owned. The captain who operated the boat worked for them, pretending to be the owner. Tonight the boat couldn't get to its usual dock and would dock at some place named Port Gamble on Puget Sound. From there, it would take several hours for couriers to drive the shipment to what they were referring to as the market, since it was after hours to catch a ferry. From that information, Clay figured Port Gamble must be located on the west side of the Sound.

Clay listened and wrote down names and places for future reference, using what light came through the window. His watch read 2:47 when the phone in the office rang. After the phone was hung up, they discussed the call, their voices sounding happy the shipment had arrived at the market. After a moment, a sharp voice barked orders to four men to immediately go and start dividing the shipment into smaller packets, ready to move by Monday to their network of distributors. Clay wrote down the four names. From his bedroom window, he watched four men come out of the clubhouse and noted their faces as they stopped under a streetlight to unlock a light blue Chevy car. After they drove away, he turned on the tape machine to catch any further conversations and went to sleep.

There was no sound from the clubhouse when Clay woke up, so he put the equipment in his tool kit and locked it before going out for breakfast at a small restaurant. After eating ham, eggs, fried potatoes, and toast, with good strong coffee, he sat there thinking about the information from the night before. If that female police officer's theory proved to be correct, he had a score to settle with these people. Now it was time for him to figure out how best to use the information to hurt them. Still the fact remained, while the information gave him a clue as to what they were doing, it wasn't yet sufficient to formulate a plan.

Keeping the handwritten notes wasn't wise in case someone happened to see them. They should be in the rental car and away from both him and the rented room. A walk to the car would do him good, and in a couple of hours he would be back.

Monday evening, at a Vietnamese restaurant three blocks from Clay's room, the waitress placed an order of hot, spicy soup on the table. A group of young Asians entered and commandeered a table. Keeping his head down and concentrating on eating, he watched them from the corner of his eyes. One among them was the older brother from the corner grocery. They kept glancing at Clay, and he felt sure they were talking about him. Big brother was explaining something. Mentally reviewing the past few days, there seemed to have been nothing to attract attention to him, so what was going on? Obviously, they would have seen him along the street, mostly coming and going for meals and occasionally just walking around. Finishing the soup and leaning back in his chair, Clay stared up at the ceiling for a moment, finished drinking the glass of water, and looked at the bill. Fishing out money, he put enough bills to cover the cost plus ten percent on the table. He left without looking at the boys.

Standing on the sidewalk outside the cafe, he lit a cigarillo and puffed before walking slowly away along the street. The damn cigarillos stung his throat. Using the cigarillos was part of his cover as a down and out workingman. Hopefully these people would accept him. In case the police talked to someone who remembered seeing the Texan, what the police received as a description would be very different from the real person. Twice during the past week, police cars had passed by him as they drove along the street.

Next morning, after eating breakfast, Clay picked up a copy of the *Seattle Times*. Sitting on a bench, on the sunny side of the corner grocery, he read the paper to catch up on the news. After going through most of the paper, dropping the sections on the bench beside him, he started looking through the help wanted ads as the big brother came out of the store. He walked closer and asked, "How you learn to fix computers?"

Clay's head turned and looked up. "Mostly I just picked it up." Clay's left shoulder shrugged, causing his head to tilt left. "I worked a couple of years for a company whose business was selling computers to the drilling rigs in Texas and Oklahoma. They put me in a car and sent me out to fix problems."

Big brother came closer and sat on the other end of the bench, with the scattered newspaper sections between them. "What are drilling rigs?" He truly looked puzzled.

"A drilling rig is equipment oil companies use to drill oil wells."

The light came on in his eyes. "Ah, oil wells." Big brother pulled a pack of cigarettes out of his shirt pocket, tapped the pack to shake a cigarette out, and offered it to Clay.

Clay shook his head no. "Thank you, senor. I like my little cigars." Unrolling the left sleeve of his T-shirt, Clay removed a cigarillo from the box, and big brother held out his lighter. While big brother lit his cigarette, Clay wondered, *'Why the sudden interest in me? For a week, not one word, and now he's suddenly acting friendly.'*

"Why you leave Texas?"

Clay's laugh caused the boy to watch closely. "My boss, he has this wife, ooh la la." With his hands, Clay made the shape of an hourglass in the air and pretended to lift a pair of large breasts on his chest. Big brother laughed. Clay continued, "The boss, he's a jealous husband. He promise he'll shoot me, so I go." Big brother laughed again and slapped his leg, liking the answer.

After a moment, big brother asked, "You are Mexican?"

"I am American. My grandfather came from Mexico."

Big brother puffed his cigarette and blew smoke out his nose. "Why you come here?"

"On my way to Alaska, and my money ran low, so I stopped here. I have an uncle in Alaska who owns a commercial fishing boat. He writes he'll hire me to work on his boat." Looking down at the cigarillo, Clay tapped it against one shoe runner to knock off the ash and told big brother, "My money isn't enough to get a ticket." Waving the want ad section at him, Clay continued, "I've been looking for a job to pay for a ticket. Don't see anything in the paper."

Big brother smiled slightly, seeming pleased with the story. Without another word, he got up and walked away. Going back to looking at the want ads, Clay pretended to be reading while his mind tried to figure out what big brother was up to. Very curious behavior and it seemed unlikely he did it just to be friendly.

In the evening, Clay went back for more hot spicy soup, and while placing his order, big brother came in with two of the Asians Clay had seen under the streetlight, along with an older Asian man. Clay figured the older man might be thirty-five, although Asians were hard for him to judge—he might be forty or fifty. The way the boys and the restaurant staff treated him, the older man must be somebody. Opening a pocket book to read,

Clay showed no interest in the activities around him, except each time he turned a page, he checked them out from the corner of his eye. With the baseball cap pulled down low, and wearing the thick, fake glasses, no one could see what his eyes were doing while his head was tilted down. The soup came, and he smiled at the pretty young girl. He knew the men were watching him.

After breakfast the next morning, Clay went for a stroll, poked around in a secondhand store, picked up a newspaper, and wandered back to the corner grocery. He claimed his usual spot on the bench to start reading the paper while enjoying the morning sun. Finished with the paper, he gathered up the sections and put them back together for disposal. It was ten fifteen in the morning, and so far today he hadn't accomplished a thing. Big brother came along the street and stopped near Clay. "You want job fixing computer."

Putting a surprised look on his face, Clay stood up. "Has your little brother's computer quit again?"

"No, not brother's computer. Computer at the office in clubhouse is not working. Boss say to hire you to fix."

Again Clay looked surprised. "Sure, I can take a look at it. If it's something I can fix for you, I'll do it."

"You get your tools. We go now."

"Yeah, sure, be right back." Leaving him there, Clay went around the building and up the stairs to his room. Removing the laser mike and the recorder from the tool case, Clay taped them to the bottom of the tabletop before leaving with the tool case.

It turned out to be the same upstairs room the mike picked up conversations from. Nothing fancy about it. A desk, a few tables, two sofas, and a mixture of armchairs. On a small table in one corner sat a PC, sixteen-inch monitor, keyboard, and a laser printer. It was fairly good equipment although there was nothing special about it. A modem connected to a telephone line sat there beside the PC, so they were probably using e-mail. Clay's heart thumped in his chest when it hit him; this could be the big break needed to give him an opportunity to gain access to the gang's computer, without them knowing it. The hard drive might contain everything needed to pin them down, although gaining access to the computer would be a problem. All four men from the streetlight were there, and big brother didn't offer to introduce them. The older man wasn't around. Sitting down in a chair in front of the computer, Clay turned on the power. The monitor was black, so its power was off. One hand felt under the front for the switch and turned it on. Quickly accessing the document file and the computer in quick succession, Clay kept moving too fast for the men watching to follow what he was doing as they kept an eye on him from several feet away. Humming quietly to himself, Clay scanned through the computer settings and list of devices as they crossed the screen one after the other. When something like ten minutes had gone by, Clay murmured "ah" and stood up. Turning the PC around, to get at the side, he reached for the tool case and opened it to select the right screwdriver to remove the screws securing the case. With the PC open for inspection, Clay went about checking the various components. A few minutes later, after fishing out a small flashlight and using a mechanics stethoscope, he listened at various points to the components. Finally he zeroed in on the hard drive, listened to it, and put one finger on it to feel for vibrations. Muttering, "Hmm, running rough," Clay turned off the power. Looking at the men, he asked, "Do you have another computer I can use to test this hard drive?" His fervent hope was they didn't. Clay waited anxiously.

They looked at each other. The one who gave the impression of having more authority than the others asked, "Why you want another computer?"

Sitting down, Clay explained. "If you have another computer, I can go to a computer store and buy an enclosure and cable to use to test the hard drive. If you don't have another computer, it will be necessary to take the hard drive to a computer store to get it tested."

The young man looked at the computer. "You show me."

Using a screwdriver, Clay pointed at the hard drive. The young Asian reached across in front of Clay to touch it, as he had seen Clay do, and his shirtsleeve pulled up his arm. Clay saw the Rolex, and his throat tightened until he almost choked. The man was wearing Will's Rolex, the very one Clay gave him. There could be no mistake, because Clay paid a jeweler to add a small diamond on the side of the watch, and it was shining right there in front of him. It took all of Clay's self-control not to react violently. The Asian man stepped back, and Clay looked up at him, wanting to remember his face, his build and size. Finally the Asian shrugged. "This is only computer. You take to store."

Turning back to the computer, Clay took a moment to regain his composure before asking, "Can someone drive me to a computer store? I don't know where to go."

The man said, "Ching, you take him." Clay removed two screws that were holding the hard drive in place, unplugged it, and, being elaborately careful, removed it. Sliding the drive into a dark-gray plastic bag, Clay folded the top of the bag over and placed it gently in the tool case, where he covered it with foam rubber. Turning back to the computer, he took time to replace the small screws so they wouldn't get lost and replaced the side on the computer before commenting, "Don't want dust getting in."

Closing the tool case, Clay stood up with it hanging from his hand before requesting. "Can you give me money to pay for parts?"

The Asian stuck a hand in his right pants pocket and pulled out a roll of bills. "How much you need?"

Using his fingers, Clay ticked off the possibilities. "An enclosure and cable around thirty bucks, computer rental maybe fifty, if we need a new drive probably another eighty or ninety. What's that come to?" Clay started adding, and the man held out three hundred-dollar bills.

"You bring receipt and change." After nodding, Clay shoved the money into a jean pocket and followed Ching to the door. Not a word was spoken as they descended the noisy wooden stairs, exited the building, and went to a car parked on the street.

Chapter 6

Ching looked young enough to still be in high school, and his driving gave the impression this might be his first time behind a wheel. They made it to the computer store without having an accident or the police pulling the car over. Clay was tempted to volunteer to walk back, but he decided against doing that.

Ching followed Clay along the aisles until he located hard-drive enclosures, looked at them all, and selected a good one. With the enclosure in his hand, Clay walked to the service-and-repair counter, where three men waited on customers. Choosing the oldest man, who looked to be somewhere in his thirties, Clay stood in the line as the man helped a customer. He might be more adaptable to the request Clay planned to make. When his turn came, he smiled at the service man. "How are you today?"

The service man returned the smile and took the enclosure. Clay added, "Want to make sure this is the right enclosure." Ching stood a few steps away, listening.

The man glanced up. "What hard drive is it for?

"Have it right here." Opening the tool case, Clay's hand gently removed the hard drive and showed it to him. The man didn't hesitate. "This enclosure will work, although we do have cheaper ones." He looked at the open case with all the tools. "You work on computers?"

"Had a job servicing specialized computers on drilling rigs while living down south in Texas."

"Are you looking for a job? We're short of technicians right now, and work is piling up." It was an opening that might help get Clay into the back room, which was necessary to carry out his plan.

It didn't make Clay happy to mislead the service man, but after hesitating, necessity overruled his feelings. "Only been in Seattle for a few days. Right now I'm working on a little job. Will it be okay to come back and talk to you in a couple of days?"

"You do that." The service man opened a drawer and brought out a business card. "Take this with you, and give me a call."

A sign on the door behind him warned, Employees Only beyond This Door. "Will you rent me one of your test stations to use to check out this drive?"

"Can't let anyone—oh hell, if you're going to work here, you might as well have a look around. Your friend will have to wait here."

Ching shrugged his shoulders at Clay's glance. "It may take a few minutes." Ching nodded, and Clay added, "Be as fast as possible." Closing the tool case and carrying it and the enclosure, he followed the service man to the back room. There were four guys working, and only one bothered to look up before turning his attention back to what he was doing. Computers, printers, parts, and boxes filled shelves on functional metal storage racks like those seen in factories and warehouses. The manager stopped at an empty workstation and pointed. "You can use this one. If there's time, I'll come back to see how you are doing."

Clay moved quickly to open the cardboard box and extract the enclosure. It took a few minutes to have the hard drive inside the enclosure and plugged into the computer. Firing up the work computer, he soon had the contents of the drive displayed on the monitor. A quick run down the list of files found e-mails, favorites, and document files. They were all there. From a stack on a shelf, Clay selected a writeable disc, inserted it in the computer, and started copying files. Bringing up system files while the disc ran and going through the motions of checking them kept Clay occupied, both using up time and for the benefit of anyone who looked to see what was going on.

It took about fifteen minutes to download the files stored on the hard drive. Ejecting the disc and putting it into a paper sleeve for protection, it slid easily under the egg carton foam lining of the tool case. After the computer shut down, Clay figured it would be wise to leave the hard drive in the enclosure for protection. With it and his tools back in the tool case, Clay snapped the lid down and went back to the service counter. The service man saw him coming and waved. Leaning on the counter, Clay asked, "How much do I owe you?"

The service man took the box the enclosure came in and scanned it. He looked at his computer and announced, "Thirty-three dollars and forty-nine cents."

Smiling and pointing at the door to the back room, Clay asked, "What about the use of your workstation?"

The service man waved it away. "You were only back there half an hour or so. Not worth worrying about. Is your hard drive okay?"

"It is now." When Clay handed over a hundred-dollar bill, he received a puzzled look, thankfully with no comment. The service man held out a copy of the invoice and counted out change into a pile on the counter. "Give me a call when you finish your job."

Stuffing the change into his pocket, Clay nodded. "Will do, thanks for your help. You have a good day." Waving with one hand, Clay headed for the door and held it open for Ching.

Back at the clubhouse, the first thing Clay did was hand over the invoice and leftover money to the guy who had given it to him, although he would have felt better breaking his neck. While Clay got busy recovering the hard drive from the enclosure, the Asians stood across the room talking. Ching gave them a report on the trip to the computer store.

Holding the hard drive in his left hand, Clay carefully replaced the adapter plug on the hard-drive contacts so it would mate with the computer plug. That done, the hard drive slid into place in the frame. It took only a few minutes to plug the drive in and replace the hold-down screws before reassembling the enclosure so the parts wouldn't go astray.

Now for the real problem, which happened to be in the operating system; it needed to be cleaned and the latest updates downloaded. After pushing the power button and leaning back to wait, it took a minute for the computer to warm up. As soon as it did, Bamford brought up the CPU and started making changes. On a sheet of paper, he noted, *PSU may be a little weak.*

Switching to the Windows Vista OS, which was out of date, Bamford started downloading updates to the system from Microsoft. This would take some time. While keeping an eye on the screen, he started cleaning up. First the side cover went back in place on the computer, and he tightened the screws on the case. From the toolbox, he got a cloth and a small spray bottle of alcohol to clean the enclosure, wiping down the computer, monitor, and keyboard. This wasn't for the benefit of his Asian friends; it was to make sure none of his fingerprints were left behind.

By his watch, it took forty minutes to update the OS, finishing at three thirty in the afternoon. Shutting the system down and turning off the power, Clay told the senior man, the one wearing Will's watch, "You should find the computer is working well now." Pointing at the enclosure with one hand, he added, "Keep this enclosure in case the drive acts up again, and this note is to alert you—the PSU seems a little weak and may need to be replaced in the future. Try the computer out; if it doesn't run properly, you can get me to come back."

The blank look on his face made it plain he didn't understand. So what? That was his problem. Picking up the tool case, Clay started for the door. The Asian hurriedly asked, "How much I owe you for fixing computer?"

Glancing at his watch, Clay told him, "Almost six hours. Whatever you think it's worth will be fine with me."

The Asian seemed surprised and discussed it with his pals. His hand dug out the roll of bills, and he peeled off three big ones. Clay thanked him for the money before big brother escorted him down the squeaky stairs to the front door. While he was inside working, the sky had clouded over, and rain was now falling, which meant the laser mike wouldn't be effective. Their discussions this evening might well be interesting. No matter; with the disc, even better information was already stored in Clay's tool case.

Having been very careful with his money since arriving, it seemed likely they would expect something different from him now with $300 in his pocket. At the usual time, Clay entered the Vietnamese restaurant and ordered a more expensive dinner. Half his meal was eaten when the four men arrived and found a table. Looking up and seeing them, he raised a hand and nodded. They waved back and sat laughing and talking together.

Now, with nothing left to keep him in Seattle, Clay's brain hatched a new plan of action. With four days left on the second ten-dollar rent payment, this would be a good time to disappear. Before first light in the morning, he walked softly down the outside stairs wearing the backpack over his jacket and, in the rain, headed for the Ford Focus.

When the car rental agency in Lacy opened, Clay was there to return the car and then go to recover his half ton. The GMC rolled smoothly south on Interstate 5. It gave him a great feeling to be away from the troubled area in Seattle. At the junction, the GMC turned off to go east on Highway 12 to Yakima, then southeast to the Tri Cities, where he found a motel in Kennewick. Clay stood in the shower getting clean and washing his hair to remove the coloring. The used clothing went into a bundle for disposal. Putting away Manuel Sanchez's driver's license and passport made him Clayton Bamford again. Early in the morning, at a Dumpster, the used clothes disappeared before the truck started east on Highway 124, heading for Lewiston, Idaho.

Stopping in Lewiston long enough to get a haircut and a bite to eat and gas up the truck, Clay started south on Highway 95 to finish a long day, which would get him back to the ranch sometime after dark. Once again it brought home how big the country was, and to think, his great-grandfather, Old Bob, came there riding on a horse's back. In the dark of night, Clay drove past Challis and headed for the ranch. No lights showed in any of the buildings. Parking alongside the house, he went in, fixed a sandwich to eat, and crawled into bed, happy to be home.

Alorenzo came for breakfast to discuss what needed to be done on the ranch. After he left to deal with the men, Clay cleaned up the kitchen and went to the office to spend the day catching up on mail and paying bills. It was not what he wanted to be doing with that disc sitting beside his mainframe computer. The disc would have to wait until he caught up on all the necessary tasks and made an appearance in town.

Saturday morning in town, Clay stopped at the garage, went in, and leaned on the counter in the small office. It was an old building with concrete floors and well-used walls decorated with out-of-date calendars, each displaying a partially dressed girl. Good-looking girls too. Calvin was working on a car up over his head on the hoist. He stopped working and walked to the office, wiping his greasy hands on a rag, his coveralls already spotted with oil. "Morning, Clay. You fall out of bed?"

He received a grin for that. "Lorenz was rousting around before first light, so I got up. How are you, Cal?"

"Doing okay. You want a cup of coffee?"

"Don't bother. Lorenz and I drank a pot earlier. You got time to put new tires on the truck? They've still got some miles on them, but this morning Lorenz said the air smelled like snow, so I want to have it ready."

Cal wiped his hands again. "Hope he's wrong. Sure hate to see snow this early."

"Me too, Cal. Lorenz has been predicting the weather all his life, and he gets it right as often as the weatherman on the radio does."

Cal pointed at the hoist. "Have to finish up a lube job on this car. Promised it would be ready this morning. Could do your truck next and have it ready for you after lunch."

"Sounds good, Cal." As Clay straightened up, Cal stuck a hand into his coverall pocket and tossed a set of keys on the counter. "You take my truck and use it to get around town."

"Thanks! There are a number of people to see while in town. Might take me a few hours." Cal went back to the hoist, and Clay took Cal's truck and drove to his accountant's office.

* * *

It snowed a little, just enough to serve as a warning that winter would be arriving soon. Clay spent time digging into files on the pirated computer disk and pulling out information useful to go after the gang responsible for the death of his parents. The police files didn't prove they were guilty, just suggested it. It seemed doubtful until he came across the asshole wearing the Rolex he bought in Switzerland as a gift for his dad. What knowledge he had might not stand up in a court of law, but he now felt sure about it, and they were going to pay. Not much different from things he did for General Thorsen for the past nine years, except with Thorsen they were fighting large international drug cartels with billions of elicit dollars changing hands. These guys were small potatoes by comparison, although it would take time to learn the extent of their operation, who their contacts were, and how they moved money around. Whenever possible, Clay planned to drop a tip to the police if it could be done without his involvement becoming known. He planned to go back to Seattle to use all his training and experience. If the plan worked, at the end the gang would be gone, and no one would know of his involvement. *'In like a ghost, operate like a ghost, disappear like a ghost'*, the motto of Thorsen's group; leave the local people with the results, not knowing the ghosts had even been there. Except this time it would be just one ghost.

By the Saturday before Thanksgiving, a cookie, carefully written and planted in the gang's computer, began relaying all new information entered or received by the hard drive to a mail drop on a server in San Diego. Unless the Asians came up with a reason to call in a computer expert, the cookie would operate until he sent it a code to stop. Any time Clay chose to access the mail drop and enter the proper codes, his computer downloaded all new information. By using different access routes each time, no one could trace the transmissions.

For years, Clay's mother always roasted a turkey, and everyone on the ranch came for Thanksgiving dinner, a tradition that went back at least to his grandmother. This year it was up to him. With a grocery list, he walked into Johansson's to shop. A crowd filled the store; probably most of the shoppers were there for the same reason as Clay. Finding a stool at the end of the counter, he settled down to wait his turn. Lars finished with a customer, looked around, and saw him. Lars waved and took two steps toward Clay before Hilda touched his arm. Watching them in conversation, it seemed likely Hilda needed help with something. Lars nodded and disappeared into the back of the store.

Clay tucked the list away in a shirt pocket, after looking to see if there might be something missing that should be added. He sat still waiting his turn. Only a few minutes later, a soft voice asked, "Can I help you, Clay?" Turning his head to see who it was, Clay sat there stunned. There stood Jennie Mae, all grown up, tall and slim, with beautiful, wavy blonde hair just like Hilda's. She smiled, and Clay jumped to his feet, grabbing the hat off his head. He stood there like an idiot, tongue-tied, staring at her. Jennie wore blue jeans and a white blouse that did nothing to hide her curves. Last time Clay saw her, she was a gangly teenager, four, maybe five years before when Clay was home for a visit. Where had she been all this time?

Clay managed to stammer, "Jennie Mae, you're all grown up."

Jennie laughed, her voice making a merry, tinkling kind of sound. "Been all grown up for quite some time now, Clay. How are you?"

"Me, oh I'm doing okay." His damned hat kept changing hands, and Clay's feet wouldn't stay still. His face felt hot.

Jennie held out her hand. "Can I see your list?"

Clay fumbled in his shirt pocket for the list, still staring at her. About that time, Hilda arrived; she was all business. "Here, Jennie, let me look after that list. Why don't you take Clay to the office and get him a cup of coffee? I made a fresh pot."

Clay followed Jennie to the office where she poured coffee for him. He took a sip, noticing she didn't have any herself. When Clay asked why, she pointed at the clock. "It will be lunchtime soon."

Finally getting his wits back, Clay quickly asked, "Will you have lunch with me? We could go to the Ranchers."

"It would be very nice to do that. Thank you, Clay. Do you want to go now?" Clay nodded, and Jennie put on a blue eider down ski jacket. When Clay looked for it, his Stetson was lying on the counter where it had been left. With it on, Clay escorted Jennie out the front door to the street, and they walked the block and a half to the Ranchers, starting to catch up on the years.

They were there early, and only one table was occupied. Both stopped to say hello to those people before Clay steered Jennie to a table beside a front window. The owner herself came with glasses of water and menus for them. She asked Jennie how school was going, and Clay listened carefully as Jennie brought the owner up to date. When the owner walked away, Clay asked, "What are you studying?"

"I majored in English and earned a BA. This is my first semester in the Creative Writing program, working toward a master's degree." Jennie pushed her hair back behind her ears. "Because of maintaining a three-point-nine grade point average, the graduate school allowed me to enroll last spring. My plan is to complete work on an MFA in Creative Writing by the end of next year."

It was enjoyable looking at Jennie and listening to her voice. She told Clay all about her four years at the University of Idaho. People came in, and most stopped to speak to them, but Clay hardly noticed; the interruptions seemed somewhere far away on the foggy side of his mind. A waitress asked twice if they were ready to order before they looked at menus.

Back when she was five years old, Jennie started coming to the ranch for a summer holiday. Clay taught her to swim in the hole at the creek. Alorenzo taught her to ride a horse and how to handle a rifle. A bookworm even at her young age, Jennie always brought bags of books from the library and never went anywhere without a book under her arm. She learned to operate the computer in Clay's bedroom, and he needed to chase her away in the evenings when he wanted to use it.

Now here was Jennie at twenty-one, a beautiful, graceful lady, and Clay wondered how she could have grown up without his being aware. Jennie asked about Clay's years in the army and heard about basic training, going through Ranger School, qualifying as a sharp shooter, and various bases around the country. He didn't mention that most of them were just a cover for what he really did.

Jennie ate a chicken salad, Clay got a cheeseburger with a Bud, and they talked. Suddenly it was three o'clock, and Jennie said she should get back to the store before closing time. Looking around, they realized they were the only people in the place. After paying the bill and apologizing for staying so long, they walked back. Standing at the counter, Clay asked her, "Will you come out to the ranch for Thanksgiving? I'm going to cook a turkey."

Jennie looked at Clay, smiling slightly. "It's very kind of you to invite me, Clay. A lady must be careful of her reputation. What would the neighbors say when they found out?"

The comment turned Clay beat red. "I wouldn't … didn't mean … how could anyone think otherwise?"

"It's not about you, Clay. The neighbors are something else. Often, perceptions take precedence over reality, and people love to gossip. Next Sunday, it will be time to return to school. If you're in town before then, possibly we could have lunch again. I would enjoy that very much."

* * *

Jennie left early on Sunday morning to return to Moscow and her studies. The two of them went to dinner the evening before. Hilda had become concerned by the time Jennie came home. She was relieved when Jennie told her they spent the whole evening at the Ranchers.

With an hour to waste before going to church, Hilda asked Lars, "Do you remember the summer Jennie Mae turned twelve, and we drove to the ranch to bring her home after her holiday with the Bamfords?" Lars looked at her and shrugged. "Lars, how could you forget? I've been thinking of that day all week. You were driving away from the ranch, and Jenny sat in the backseat with her books. It went something like this …" Hilda tilted her head, trying to recall exactly.

"Mom, do you think it would be proper for me to ask Clay to be my boyfriend?" Hilda gasped, and Lars quickly looked in the rearview mirror at his daughter. She was a very bright and determined little girl, usually with her nose stuck in a book. They both worried she spent far too much time reading a wide variety of subjects, some of which Hilda considered inappropriate for a child. Jennie always rebutted her mother's objections by pointing out the books came from the library, so they must be acceptable. Hilda had yet to find a good argument to use against that fact.

"You're only twelve years old, dear. You're too young to have a boyfriend," Hilda said. Lars listened, sure that would stop Jennie. "Beside, Clay is in university and is seven years older than you."

"Well, you see, when I finish school, I'm going to marry Clay and live on the ranch. I'll have my own horse to ride, like Mrs. Bamford. My name will be Jennie Mae Bamford, and I'll write famous books that all the libraries will have for their readers."

Hilda glanced at Lars as she fought to control the turmoil in her mind. *'A twelve-year-old girl talking about marriage? Ridiculous. Where did the child get such ideas? It had to be from those books.'* Hilda turned in the front seat to look at Jennie sitting in the middle of the backseat with her books and clothes piled around her. "Clay has been your friend for years, and you're too young to think about boyfriends and getting married." Hilda hesitated before asking, "What caused you to start thinking like this?"

"Well, I'm going to marry Clay. If he's my boyfriend, and everyone knows it, I won't have to worry about some older girl coming along and running off with him before I grow up."

Lars hid a smile and looked at Hilda from the corner of his eye; she was still looking into the backseat. "Did you say anything to Clay or Mrs. Bamford about this?"

"No, I didn't. I thought it best to discuss it with you first."

Hilda smiled at her daughter. "Very wise, dear. You did the right thing. Clay is a good friend to you, and I don't think you should say anything to him. You might scare him. Clay is still a young man, and you know men are often very foolish. The thought of marriage at his age might be very unsettling to him. This should be our secret for now."

"Thank you, Mom. I wouldn't want to scare Clay. Have to think about this some more and not say anything to anyone."

Lars smiled, "Now that you remind me, I do remember that. After this past week, it wouldn't surprise me if Jennie Mae's prediction comes true. It appeared Clay fell right off a cliff when he first saw Jennie Mae at the store. Clay is usually so in control and sure of himself; it surprised me. Seeing Jennie Mae, he acted like a pimply-faced, tongue-tied teenager."

"She's a very intelligent, good-looking young lady."

"Yes she is." Lars grinned at Hilda. "All of which she gets from her father."

"From you! You old reprobate. If Jennie Mae looked like you, Clay would be hiring her to herd cattle, not courting her."

They laughed together and Lars went to put a tie on.

Chapter 7

Thanksgiving was over. The dinner Clay put together went reasonably well, even if it didn't measure up to his mother's standards. With practice, he figured to improve his dinners in the future. Everyone on the ranch shared dinner, played cards, and talked up a storm.

Shoshoni Mike's wife, Peggy, entertained everyone with a humorous story of an amorous coyote who kept hanging around the line cabin, trying to get friendly with her collie cattle dog while the dog was in heat. Peggy chained the dog to the cabin and for two days tried to shoo the coyote away, afraid it would lure her dog into the trees where the pack could attack it. Finally Peggy stood her Winchester beside the door, kept watch, and each time the coyote came near, she shot at the ground to scare it away. Finally in exasperation, she shot at a large boulder and stung the coyote with rock chips. The animal disappeared and didn't come back.

In the evening, Shoshoni Mike and Alorenzo lit a fire and piled on wood. Clay took the opportunity to sit beside Jason Jr.—Mike and Peggy's son—to find out how his studies were progressing at the university in Boise, making him explain in Shoshoni. Jason worked on the ranch during the summer months and now was in his first year at Boise State, studying for a teaching degree. The cheery sound of pine pitch snapping and sparking in the big stone fireplace created a happy atmosphere. After a long, busy summer, the hands were happy to be back at the home place; being together again was the important thing.

Jennie drove back to the university in Moscow on Sunday and left Clay to wonder about her and the week just past. She was a very intelligent lady, well informed, and easy to talk to. Jennie came out of nowhere at the store to blindside Clay, and his reaction to her was ungainly, to say the least. He seemed to lose his poise and stumbled trying to find the right words to say. With Jennie back in Moscow, probably she would be telling everyone about her tongue-tied and inept friend. The telephone rang. Could it be Jennie? Clay hurried to the phone on the kitchen table. "Bamford Ranch."

"Can we meet on Wednesday?" It was General Thorsen.

"What time?"

"Noon."

"Agreed." The line went dead. Clay replaced the phone, refilled his coffee mug, and sat thinking, *'It must be something serious.'* More consulting, more challenges, and another paycheck. No doubt, it would delay his personal project in Seattle. The plan to disappear from the ranch for a while before Christmas would probably have to wait past the year's end.

Five minutes before noon on Wednesday, Clay parked the GMC outside the gates at Mountain Home Air Force Base, wearing one of the base's ball hats and dark, aviator, wire-rim sunglasses. He knew the security guards were keeping an eye on him. A minute later, the gates to the base opened, and a black car with tinted windows came through, swung around, and pulled in beside Clay's truck. The back window went down, and Thomson waved. After locking the truck, Clay opened the car door and slid in beside Thomson, who stuck out his hand. "Good to see you, Clay."

Clay nodded at him. "And you too." Thompson told the driver to move, and the car backed out, went through the gates into the base, and glided along toward the headquarters building. Stepping out of the car, Thomson and Clay were greeted by the usual sounds of jets coming and going and helicopters making *thrump, thrump* sounds as they flew around the base.

The duty officer, a staff sergeant, met them at the door. "Please come this way, General Thorsen. The base commander assigned an office for your use." They followed the sergeant up a flight of stairs and along a hallway to a corner office where the staff sergeant opened the door before stepping back. "There are sandwiches and a thermos of coffee on the table. If you need anything, call the number written on the paper pad beside the phone."

Thompson said, "Thank you, Sergeant. I'm sure everything will be satisfactory."

The door closed behind them. Thorsen rarely wore a uniform, and Clay noticed his gray hair was whiter than it used to be. As always, he walked erect. Funny thing about Thorsen, even when his face smiled at a person, his eyes rarely did. His face smiled at Clay now. "On the flight out from Washington, it occurred to me that it will soon be ten years since we first met outside your apartment."

"A lot of water has flowed under the bridge since I cooked you scrambled eggs that day." Pulling out a chair, Clay sat down, ready to hear what brought Thompson all this way.

Thompson paced over to a window to look out. Clay watched his back as Thompson replied, "As hard as we tried, we haven't stopped the bastards."

"No, sir, we haven't. We did make some big dents in their operations and have caused them a lot of misery."

Thompson came and sat down across the table. "They're like mushrooms, Clay. We pick one off the manure pile, and three more spring up."

"The real problem is right here inside our own country, sir. Close to 40 percent of the world's cocaine consumption is in the

United States. The police can't catch all the importers, distributers, and street dealers. There's so much money floating around to pay bribes, buy big-time lawyers, even judges and congressmen—whoever they need. Our government pours billions of dollars into countries to the south to bankroll their military and police. What happens? The problem grows and gets bigger. The money would be better spent at home to hire police officers, redevelop slum areas, and expand training and education programs. The government should make the damn stuff legal and sell it at a low price. Take the profit out of it, and the big cartels will disappear."

Thompson watched Clay for a moment, his face showing nothing, "You've always been far too practical. Even if the president wanted to do what you say, he would never get it through Congress. Besides, he wants to get reelected, and even proposing such a thing would get all the religious nuts and do-gooders up in arms."

"Seems to me it wouldn't be any worse than selling alcohol; we have drunks, but the majority of people don't abuse it." Grinning at him, Clay added, "What our country needs is politicians who don't care about reelection, just doing the right thing."

"You're trying to bait me." Thompson smiled. "Is this what you think about while out riding a horse around the ranch?"

"Sometimes!" Clay shrugged. "Having a conversation with a horse is all one sided. They never reply, just shake their heads and rotate their ears, pretending to listen."

Thompson laughed and slowly relaxed. "Remember those two days I spent at the ranch after you resigned?" Clay nodded. "Always thought it would be nice if I came back to the ranch some time."

"You come anytime you want, sir; be happy to have you."

Thompson drummed his fingers on the table for a moment. "What was the name of the old cowboy who always carried a rifle?"

"Alorenzo Gonzales. He was born on the ranch, third generation."

"That's him. He offered to take me riding and show me how to handle a horse." Thompson fell silent for a minute before straightening. "Clay, something big appears to be coming down the pike. We're getting hints from low-level informants of meetings taking place in Mexico, Columbia, Guatemala, and Europe. Nothing we can get our teeth into, just hints that something's in the works. We increased the number of agents in South America to stand watch and are spreading money around trying to buy information. At our request, satellite monitoring of phone calls in all those places has increased, which is yielding some details. The local police in those countries are cooperating, but as you know, they're never reliable and most likely have alerted the drug lords of our interest. Most likely, we'll start getting a flood of false information planted by them, just to lead us astray.

"You were always my best man at breaking through their security curtains to get into computers and communications systems. I need your help. It would be best if you agreed to come east and work from your old office."

"Can't do that, Thompson. The ranch won't run itself. There are over twenty-five hundred head of cows along with all the steers and heifers to care for. Also, there are the people who work on the ranch. I'm responsible for all of it now. Slipping away for a few days at a time, especially during the winter, is okay. It's not fair for me to be away for very long."

"You have your satellite dish and your computers, Clay. Will you see what you can do?"

"Of course. You know I'd never let you down; just don't expect quick results. Those people have become much more sophisticated over the years, and it's harder to break into their systems now than it was ten years ago."

"Thanks, Clay. Do you have everything you need?"

Clay thought for a moment. "All the data accumulated over the years is enciphered on discs and safely hidden away. I could use any new codes, names of new players, addresses, phone numbers, and such things your people have come up with in recent months."

Thompson lifted his briefcase off the floor and slid it across the table. "Everything we have is on discs inside. Included is a list of the latest codes, copies of reports, and such. The combination to open this case is 9731. Anything you need or want, just call me. You might update me from time to time." He smiled, giving Clay a little shot. In the old days, Clay sometimes got so involved he forgot to communicate. "Included is a package of crisp, new hundreds for any expenses you might incur along the way."

"Thanks, Thompson. They'll add to my rainy day stash, just in case a need should arise." Clay reached for the coffee thermos and poured two cups. Thompson uncovered the sandwiches and pushed a plate across the table. Thompson selected a roast beef sandwich. There was more than enough beef on the ranch, so Clay took pastrami on rye. Air force sandwiches weren't fancy, but they kept the body and soul together. Looking at Thompson thoughtfully and munching on pastrami, a thought occurred to Clay. "Sooner or later, a way for me to beat their security will show up. Under the circumstances, I would be uncomfortable sending information to you electronically, even enciphered."

"No problem, Clay. You send a message, and one of our planes will pick you up here at Mountain Home and bring you to Washington—three days at most."

Clay reached out to tap the briefcase with a finger. "I'll start getting familiar with the data and information tonight. Afterward, the hunt will begin."

"Just one thing, Clay. Don't wait to accumulate a big picture. As soon as you uncover useful leads, bring them to me. We don't know what the timing may be on whatever it is they've been planning, so regular briefings are vital."

"Will do, sir. Anytime you're ready, you can drop me off at the gate."

They each ate another sandwich, visited the washroom, and left the building. In the car, Thompson told Clay, "When you come to meet a plane, wear the same hat and sunglasses. There will be someone at the gate to pick you up."

After the 240-mile drive home, arrival at the ranch was in the dark. Sitting in the living room, Clay aligned numbers on two locks, opened the case, sorted through the items inside, and took out the written reports. Reading them would be enough for tonight.

* * *

Luong An Chie'n arrived in the upstairs room at the clubhouse, which he used as an office, and ordered everyone to leave. He sat down to think about the decision he wanted to implement. He felt confident the right time to expand the operation had arrived. After careful study, Luong made a decision to choose Portland as presenting the best opportunities for immediate growth. The simple supply chain they operated to bring in drugs seemed to go completely unnoticed, right under the noses of the Coast Guard, and moving a larger volume shouldn't attract attention.

When Luong started importing by sea, the shipments needed to be timed to avoid those days when commercial fishing quotas were open and fishing boats left port to grab their share of salmon before the quota closed. The system vastly improved after they began using the fishing boat to take charter groups of tourists and local fishermen out on day trips. This charter work took place on days when no commercial fishing occurred. On days when a scheduled drug shipment came, arrangements were made to charter the boat to a small, handpicked group of Luong's own people who spent the day with fishing rods, fishing, and occasionally catching their limit. At an agreed time, the boats met at an old fish cannery wharf, with collapsing and decaying wooden buildings, once used by a viable local fishery. In the small, sheltered cove, hidden from view, watertight bales of drugs went on board Luong's commercial fishing boat in exchange for a sailor's sea chest full of cash. In this manner, hard drugs from South America, and marijuana from British Columbia, flowed into Seattle by sea.

Now, Luong's drug supplier had offered a substantial price discount on condition he increase his orders to a larger volume. Expansion offered the way to take advantage of this great opportunity. Luong believed his carefully thought-out plan would work smoothly and turned his mind to reviewing the past eight years.

Starting out small, smuggling marijuana, the business grew until Luong was looking for a way to increase the great white powder's share of the operation. A chance meeting with a longtime acquaintance wanting to buy a commercial fishing boat and needing financing proved fortuitous. They bought the boat and a commercial fishing license, and Luong even worked a few days on the boat, to become familiar with the coastal area while he made arrangements with suppliers. When fishing quotas opened, the boat and crew fished, under orders to be friendly and polite to everyone and to meticulously follow all the rules and regulations. A full Vietnamese crew on a fishing trawler proved an oddity in the Puget Sound area and for a few months attracted attention from other fishermen, until they all became accustomed to it.

While the fishing crew became accepted, Luong kept busy planning and putting in place agreements for his supply chain. With marijuana, it proved relatively simple to change from trucks to boats for shipping into Seattle. Dealing with his Mexican supplier of cocaine involved more difficulties, but in the end, they saw the logic of sea transport. It would be easier and safer than smuggling across the land border between California on the Pacific side and Texas on the Gulf of Mexico. Now it had proved so successful, they were pushing Luong to take larger volumes and ship it south by land routes to supply California and other western states.

Luong decided he needed to meet with his Portland contact one more time to finalize arrangements. The big black man talked loudly, dressed in flashy clothes, drove bright-colored Cadillac's, and attracted far too much attention, which made Luong uncomfortable. Still, after four years of selling weed to the black brother—which he liked to be called instead of Richie—the man didn't know Luong's assumed Chinese name of Henry Wong was an alias. Only a handful of Luong's closest lieutenants in the drug trade, most of whom were relatives, knew his true name. Richie loudly referred to Luong as Wong, an insult to an Asian. Luong accepted being called Wong in such a friendly, backslapping way, keeping his annoyance hidden. After all, Richie paid promptly, which was very important, and he always willingly shared the young, big-chested girls who accompanied him. Luong liked big tits. His wife was thin and almost flat chested. Still, she produced two sons for him and was obedient, as a good wife should be. She efficiently managed their Vietnamese restaurant located three blocks from the clubhouse. Carefully run, with an outside accountant to do the books and pay the taxes, the restaurant provided Luong with an excellent cover as a legitimate businessman.

Luong looked across the room at the computer, which now worked so well after that smelly Mexican from Texas repaired it. He walked to the computer and sent an e-mail message to Richie, requesting a meeting in Woodland in two days. Richie would have a thirty-mile drive north from Portland, which would be an annoyance to him once again. Even so, Luong felt safer meeting away from Portland, where he suspected the police were totally aware of all the money Richie flashed around and were probably watching him.

Settling back in the chair, Luong considered the operation. It ran smoothly, and he kept himself away from contact with the actual product, letting his lieutenants take the risks. To ensure loyalty, they enforced rigid discipline using a tried and proven Chinese triad method—decapitation. Older brother, Luong Duc Huynh, did the enforcing. Huynh had never been the sharpest knife in the family drawer but made up for it with reliability. Tough and sadistic, Huynh actually enjoyed hurting people. Anyone who failed, or they even suspected of disloyalty, would be found with their head cut off, the head sitting on their chest. They didn't need to do it very often to get the message out. No one talked willingly to the police, knowing what awaited them if they did. Luong made sure his people always had money in their pockets, which provided the incentive part of the carrot and stick approach. Luong's head came up as his ears caught the sound of footsteps on the stairs. The door opened, and Quang came in, accompanied by one man. "Ah, Quang, how are you today?"

"Very good, Uncle Luong, and you how are you today?"

"All goes well for me. Thank you for the inspection you did at the fish market and the suggestions you made to improve the operation."

The praise pleased Quang. Before he could come up with a reply, the computer beeped, announcing the arrival of an e-mail. "Please print out the message, Quang, and bring it to me."

Luong read the message and smiled. Richie had accepted his proposed meeting. Six weeks before, Richie listened to Luong's proposal, and they discussed it in detail. Richie worried about the trouble it would cause with other dealers on the streets of Portland, when the city would be hit with a new supply of cocaine, and Richie would start stealing customers. The whole time Richie talked about the problems involved; Luong could see greed taking hold as Richie recognized the potential to deal in far larger amounts of money by expanding his operation.

Looking up, Luong commented. "In two days' time, I must travel to Portland and will be away for one or two days."

* * *

In Moscow, Idaho, Jennie Johansson and her roommate cleaned up the kitchen and put the dishes away. Jennie settled down at her desk to write a few more pages of a short story project for one of her classes. Sandra came out of her bedroom wearing a tight sweater over her ample chest. She picked up her jacket and announced. "Going to a party. See you later."

Jennie glanced up from her computer. "Enjoy yourself, Sandra." She watched the door slam shut. Once again, she shook her head in dismay. She liked Sandra, who could be good company; despite the fact Sandra enjoyed being a party girl. She very frankly and openly claimed she intended to screw her way through university (her words)—classmates, instructors, professors, any man who caught her fancy. She often came home tipsy from drinking, her clothes disheveled. Sandra explained these were the best years of her life, and she wasn't going to waste them, as she inferred Jennie was doing. Three semesters before, when Sandra moved in to share the apartment, she constantly tried to fix Jennie up with a man, exclaiming. "You're a good-looking woman, and any man on campus would love to get into your panties and show you a good time. What the hell are you waiting for? Before you know it, you'll be old and wrinkled, and the good times will have passed you by." Jennie smiled. She still occasionally got those sorts of comments from Sandra, though not as often as that first fall. It was kind of exciting having Sandra around and Jennie filled pages in her notebooks with observations on Sandra's lifestyle and behavior. She even wrote down the vivid descriptions Sandra occasionally threw out, although many caused Jennie to blush. For as long as she could remember, Jennie had strived to be a writer. At ten years of age, she began writing down descriptions of scenery, sounds, storms, accidents, parties, facial expressions, and the way people talked, walked, and behaved. In the past eleven years, her notes filled a large stack of notebooks, and she never went anywhere without one close at hand. She believed to be a great writer you needed material to flesh out your stories, to make them come alive. She remained alert to everything, like sounds, colors, smells, and texture, anything she might use in her writing sometime in the future.

Clay's reaction when Hilda sent her to wait on him in the store puzzled her, until realization hit her; Clay still thought of her as the little girl he knew before he went into the army and seemed surprised she was now a grown woman. During their first dinner at the Ranchers, he stared at her so much it became embarrassing. On her last evening at home, they went to dinner and then spent hours at the Ranchers and had great fun. Clay chatted with her and everyone who came in. She drank Coke, and he had mugs of beer. They went to the tavern side and alternated dancing there to the band, made up of local people they both knew, and sitting back at their table talking. It was Jennie's first time ever in a bar. The dancing lessons she took her second year in Moscow proved valuable. All evening, she hoped he would kiss her goodnight. He didn't. He walked her to the house, held the door for her, and said goodnight after Lars and Hilda came to greet them. Jennie stayed up late, describing her reactions in a notebook.

Jennie laughed softly to herself, remembering his comment, "You're a lady," which said a lot. In his mind, a woman was a lady or she wasn't. His attitude was probably based on how Mary, Hilda, and other wives he knew behaved. It was a very tough standard to use and in many ways an unfair way to judge women. No middle ground or gray area between the two. Country people judged men much the same, although more loosely. Jennie Johansson mused about it being a peculiarly rural standard, probably brought about by the lower population density, and the fact everyone knew each other, knew who they could trust, who they could rely on, and there were very few secrets. In the city, things were different, although much the same in small groups of acquaintances. The difference in the city was that a person could go a few blocks from home, and no one knew them, which allowed people to live a double life with different standards of behavior—both men and women.

What would Clay's reaction to Sandra be? Jennie pondered the question, deciding he would be polite and respectful. If he came to understand Sandra was—at best—rather loose, he would still be polite, just more reserved and distant. Being a single man and given the right opportunity, he might well take Sandra to bed and enjoy whatever special talents she possessed. Because she and Sandra were roommates and friends, she felt sure he would never go near Sandra. That didn't mean he had no interest in women. From experience, she knew he did, given the right circumstances. In fact, she knew for sure. What had that woman's name been? Nineteen years of age at the time, Clay came home from university for the summer, and the woman came to the ranch to paint pictures of mountain scenery. The two of them developed a relationship where every night he slipped out through his bedroom window and went to visit the woman in the ranch cabin she lived in. Twelve-year-old Jennie Johansson, from her bedroom next to his, observed the nightly ritual. At the time, she didn't really understand why he acted the way he did.

Jennie shook her head. She would look up the woman's name in her notebook from that time, just out of curiosity. This was the type of thing that made writing fiction so interesting and exciting. You could think, plan, and write stories on any subject you wanted, places you would never go, things you would never do in real life. To do it well, you needed to observe. How did you write about a drunk's behavior when you had never been drunk? Observation! That was the key.

Chapter 8

With the days moving into December, work on the ranch reached low ebb. Every morning the men rode out to check the status and health of the cattle, and when required by weather, large round hay bales were rolled out to feed the animals. Clay always found it enjoyable going out to help the hands, help they didn't really need. It gave him an excuse to get out of the house for several hours each morning, still leaving most of the day free to sit at the computer and systematically hack into a multitude of websites, terminals, and operating systems. Each day followed much the same pattern. Three or four hours spent with the men, on the computer until late afternoon when Alorenzo arrived to share dinner, and afterward on the computer until midnight.

Alorenzo's tastes were old school. He liked to eat beef, potatoes, and beans every day, spicing the food with Tabasco sauce from a little bottle he carried in a shirt pocket. This habit was an oddity in Idaho, attracting comment from people when they observed Alorenzo doctoring his food for the first time. Four little bottles came in a small box measuring two by three inches. Each bottle contained one-eighth of an ounce of Tabasco. A longtime rancher friend in Texas mailed a new supply to Alorenzo every spring when calving time arrived and the men were preparing to go out on the range.

After sharing dinner and spiffing up the kitchen, one of them always poured two shot glasses of Jack Daniels. They listened to the news and weather on the radio and discussed the day. Recently Alorenzo had begun prodding at Clay to find a good woman and get married. It had been several days since the subject came up, and tonight Alorenzo took a different approach. "Boy, you shouldn't spend so much time hanging around the house. It ain't healthy. You need to get off this here ranch, go into town, and have a look at the women who are available. Pick yourself out a good one and marry her. We need a Mrs. Bamford around here."

Clay took a sip of Jack before smiling. This was an old argument. Alorenzo worried about him, especially because there weren't any little Bamfords coming along to carry on running the ranch. "I know most of the ladies in town and haven't seen any who look like they want to be ranchers." This little white lie gave Clay a twinge of guilt. There was Jennie, who Alorenzo really liked and found fascinating, although he hadn't gotten around to considering her for marriage. Alorenzo didn't know that Jennie and Clay had been out for dinner twice.

"Shoshone Mike told me he heard a new school marm came in September to teach the kids." Alorenzo waved one hand. "You go to town and meet her."

Clay's face glared at Alorenzo. "You old buzzard, why are you always prodding me to get married?"

Alorenzo looked straight back. "We need young'uns around here while I'm still able to teach them what they need to know." He grinned. "How to ride a horse, handle cattle, and such. Hell, they won't learn from you; those years in the army, you forgot everything worthwhile you knew."

Clay laughed, knowing Alorenzo was only half joking, and conceded, "Next time in town, I'll ask Lars if there are any likely women around." Of course Clay didn't mean it. While Alorenzo kept talking, Clay started thinking of Jennie in a different way. He liked her.

After Alorenzo left for the night, it was time to get back on the computer. Slowly building a list of names and mailbox addresses for people in the drug cartels in Mexico and South America had become tedious and time consuming. This evening he decided to take time to go back through the existing list and check for any messages or activity of interest. Near midnight when he was thinking of shutting down the computer, a message turned up, going from Mexico City to Bogota, Columbia, discussing a meeting to be held in Rome between Christmas and New Year's. The message described why meeting in Rome at a time when thousands of Christians would flood into the city to celebrate the special season provided a perfect cover for them. The message seemed interesting. What really caught his attention was the message being copied to people with addresses in Panama, Honduras, and Venezuela in South America and Italy, France, and England in Europe, along with Iran and Pakistan in Asia.

Instantly wide awake and energized, the message laid out a puzzle for Clay to consider. Why were the Asian addresses included? Leaning back in his swivel chair, he thought about the oddity of it. To his knowledge, Asia wasn't a producer of cocaine; instead, it was the major source of opium. He didn't know much about opium, he admitted to himself. He just knew they made opium from the seedpods of poppy plants. He quickly wrote a note, as a reminder, to research poppies and opium. It would take time to search out information on all these individuals, and today was the tenth of December. If General Thorsen wanted to act on this information and send people to observe the meeting and see who attended, he needed to know real fast. A quick trip to Washington suddenly seemed necessary, to brief the general and get help in profiling the individuals. In fact, there might already be files set up on some of them.

Burning two discs, one to take to Washington and the second to keep as backup, Clay packed a briefcase with everything he needed to take. Washington was two hours ahead, so Thompson would be in his office at five in the morning, Idaho time. With his alarm set, Clay fell asleep minutes after crawling into bed.

At 4:50 a.m. the clock started clanging. A large left hand reached out to turn off the alarm. Slowly stretching his muscles, Clay sat up before padding to the bathroom. At the sink, he used hands full of cold water to wash the sleep out of his face and come fully awake. Looking back at the image in the mirror, it was obviously past time for a hair trimming. Washed and brushed, he donned a robe and walked to the office.

Sitting on the corner of the desk, Clay picked up the phone and punched in one and the two-zero-two area code for Washington, followed by the numbers for General Thorsen's direct line. On the third ring, a familiar voice said, "Good morning."

Clay's request was short. "This cowboy could use a ride."

"Excellent." Clay sensed the smile on Thompson's face. "Will call you back in a few minutes." The line went dead.

Dressed for the morning and busy frying bacon, the phone rang. "Bamford Ranch."

"Thirteen hundred at the gates work for you?"

"Very good." Clay hung up and went to the stove to turn the bacon. He put two plates and coffee mugs on the table and had begun taking eggs out of the refrigerator when Alorenzo came through the door wearing a sheepskin jacket and gloves. "Cold this morning, Clay. Smells like snow coming."

"Winter time. You think we'll have a white Christmas?"

"Could be. Want me to fry potatoes?"

"You do that. Scrambled eggs okay?"

Alorenzo nodded agreement, and a few minutes later they were seated across the table from each other, eating. When they finished their breakfast, Clay took the plates to the sink and came back with the coffeepot to refill the mugs. Reseated, Clay leaned back in his chair sipping coffee. "Going to be away for a couple of days."

Alorenzo looked up, a question in his eyes. Clay shrugged. "Got to go east and help out for two or three days."

After staring at Clay for a moment, Alorenzo inquired, "That general fella again?"

Clay nodded. "He told me he might come to the ranch for a few days and take you up on the offer to teach him how to ride a horse."

Chuckling, Alorenzo advised, "You best tell him to wait till spring; winter is no time for a green horn to start learning to ride."

Laughing, Clay agreed. "I'll pass on your advice. He's a busy man. More than likely he'll never get around to it."

"When you leaving?"

"This morning."

"What you want me to tell folks who come looking for you?"

"No reason for anyone to come around this time of year. You can say I went down to Boise on business."

"Okay, boy, take care of yourself. Don't let those fast-talking city folks take advantage of you."

Clay laughed, thinking, *'Alorenzo has always been like a second father, only he worries more than Dad ever did.'* Clay corrected himself. *'At least he shows it more than Dad did.'* He started clearing the table while Alorenzo finished his coffee.

* * *

Chief Kruger opened the morning briefing, holding a sheaf of papers in his left hand. "First thing on today's list. Brand, the judge wants to know what progress you and Heftner are making in solving the Bamford homicide."

"Nothing new, Chief. We pulled all the files and reviewed them ten days ago. It's a dead end until something new turns up."

"Keep trying, Brand. What are you working on right now?"

"We have seven files on the go, including a new one yesterday. Another body turned up with his head sitting on his chest. That's four in the last three years. This one is Caucasian, which is different from the first three, who were Asian. If the lab reports confirm our identification of the body, this one worked the street as a drug pusher. Heft suggested maybe all four were into the drug trade, although we have never found anything to tie Asians to selling drugs."

Kruger's head swiveled. "Cantrell, have you narcotics boys got any ideas on this?"

"Brand talked to us last night about this new beheading. When the ID is confirmed, we'll put a man on it with Brand and Heftner. It's been obvious for two years that whoever's supplying the pushers runs a smooth operation. It has to be a tight-knit group. We've pressured our sources, and they don't know anything or are too damn scared to talk."

Kruger put his papers down on the podium. "You may be onto something, Cantrell. If you knew you would be handed your head for talking, it would silence everyone. Put a man on this and find out if there's a history somewhere of groups like the Mafia using beheading to enforce discipline. Maybe back in Italy or some other parts of Europe. The news media made a fuss over the previous beheadings. With this new one being a Caucasian, they may get more rabid and demand action. It this thing gets played up by the media, the mayor's going to be unhappy, and we'll hear about it. Make it a priority."

Kruger looked at his papers. "Getting back to the judge for a moment, Officer Hoffman, how are things in your district?"

"Quiet, sir. Ever since the Bamford incident, the whole area seems to have gone to sleep. It could be because of all the police activity at the time. It's a long established and poor area of the city, and they don't like attention from outsiders. It could be someone put the word out."

"Thanks, Hoffman. Keep your eyes open, and if anything at all comes up, pass it on to Brand.

"Now for traffic. We're receiving more than the normal number of calls about cars speeding through school zones. The traffic boys are planning to lay on a push to slow the drivers down. Probably happen in a week or so, and many of you will be asked to help out in order to put enough manpower on the project to make it effective. I'll keep you posted."

Kruger selected a page and waved it. "Nine of you guys are late getting annual medicals. You know who you are; get with it. Next week the list goes up on the board for everyone to see. This is your last chance before I come down on you like a ton of ..."

* * *

Quang was in the passenger seat of a three-year-old, white Chevrolet Sedan following a small orange U-Haul truck across the Columbia River Bridge on Highway 5 into Portland, Oregon, where they took Exit 307 and followed it south east to Columbia Boulevard. Turning right, the U-Haul traveled west toward Smith Lake Park. Quang felt proud for having proved himself, now promoted to handle more responsibility in this new operation started by Luong. This first shipment was priced with a value of $160,000. All future shipments would have a value of half a million. An untalkative, former UPS driver fired for stealing and drunkenness drove the U-Haul. Unable to find a job, Quang hired him. He would be well paid upon their return to Seattle and could stay drunk for a month if he chose to. Quang didn't care, as long as the man followed orders exactly, and so far he had. Two cars were between the U-Haul and the Chevy as they made their way west. Everything looked familiar and normal after two trial trips in the past ten days to check the route, the time involved, and the meeting place. Drugs would be transferred to a local vehicle in under five minutes, and while it happened, Quang would collect full payment. No one wanted to spend more time than was necessary, to minimize chances of being seen.

Quang watched the U-Haul turn into the tree-lined parking lot and proceed across to where a dark green SUV sat with the engine idling. Both cars ahead of him continued west. His driver signaled properly before entering the parking lot and stopping near a large, four-door Cadillac. Quang got out of the car and removed a red duffle bag full of smelly gym clothes from the backseat. A black man carrying a package wrapped in plain brown paper came to meet him. Standing together in the fading light of dusk, they watched the transfer take place across the parking lot. When the SUV started moving, the black man held out the package to Quang before walking back to his Cadillac.

Unzipping the duffle bag, Quang placed the package in the bottom before covering it with clothes and gym shoes, wrinkling his nose at the distasteful smell of stale sweat. His driver opened the car trunk and watched Quang throw the duffle bag in before slamming the lid down.

The U-Haul drove away as Quang got into the car, and they trailed behind, leaving a gap of several hundred yards. Suddenly, the Cadillac sped past them, and Quang leaned over to check their speed. Ten mph under the speed limit, just as mandated by Luong. He glanced at the driver. "Our black friend will attract attention of any police around and make our trip safer; they won't notice our car with him speeding."

* * *

Like a feather, the Cessna Citation gently settled onto runway 33R, the shortest runway at BWI Marshal` south of Baltimore, Maryland. It was a runway reserved for the use of small aircraft and corporate jets. Clay watched through the window as the Cessna slowed and turned onto the ramp to taxi to a stop at a private hanger. As always, it struck him how slow the taxi speed seemed as compared to the speed the plane landed at. General Thorsen's private car sat near the hanger doors, his driver standing beside the car. Clay momentarily wondered if Thomson had come to meet him. He walked forward to speak to the pilot, an old friend, before coming down the steps carrying his briefcase. He stood waiting for the copilot to open the storage hatch and retrieve his travel bag. Glancing at the car again, Clay saw the driver walking toward him. Clay stuck out his hand. "Good to see you again, Thomas."

"Likewise, sir. You haven't come to Washington to see us for a long time."

Clay smiled. "It's been awhile; in fact, it's almost two years since my last visit to Washington. How are your kids doing?"

"Very well, thank you for asking. They're both teenagers now and starting to date boys. It's scary to see your daughters going out with horny teenaged boys. I told their mother to talk tough to them."

"Thomas, you're just afraid those boys will behave the way you did at that age."

Thomas looked grave. "Probably some truth in that, Major." Thomas shook his head. "In my day, the regular girls would only let you go so far—have a little fun, never all the way. Now they have the pill, there are drugs, and things are different; kids all have money, cars, and access to booze, porn, and all sorts of other things. It's damn scary being a father of good-looking daughters. I love them—still many a day I wish they were boys."

Clay slapped Thomas on the shoulder. "Stop worrying, man; just make sure their mother gives them all the facts. Kids these days are smart and, with information from the Internet, very well informed." When the copilot arrived with Clay's bag, he turned to look at him. "Thanks for the ride."

"You're welcome, sir. Have a good stay in Washington."

Clay nodded before picking up his bag. Thomas immediately reached for it. "Here, sir, let me take that for you."

Clay gave up the bag, knowing Thomas would argue if he didn't. On the way to the car, he mentioned, "I'm a civilian now, Thomas. Just an ordinary Joe."

"Yes, sir, except we all remember the things you did. You'll never be ordinary to us. When I got my leg wounded, you carried me out of the jungle in Columbia and put me on a plane home. When I couldn't pass the army medical anymore, you got me this job driving for the general. A man doesn't forget things like that."

When Clay sat in the passenger seat, Thomas didn't consider it proper. This was an officer who never acted like an officer, in the normal course of things. Always quick to act when necessary, his men learned to respect him, although most of them were older than Bamford. Thomas didn't argue. He placed Clay's bag on the backseat and kept his peace.

The copilot watched their passenger walk away wearing a Mountain Home cap and amber-colored sunglasses. He was a tall, solidly built man who gave the appearance of being in excellent shape. His manner of walking and moving possessed a flowing, rippling, feline quality that reminded the young pilot of a cat stalking a mouse. Maybe more like a tiger, he thought. After reentering the Cessna, he asked the pilot, "Who is that guy?"

The pilot looked at him. "He's been around for a few years and did things you wouldn't believe. Never mind who he is and take some advice; forget you ever saw him."

Chapter 9

Thomas Manning eased the car away, leaving the hanger behind to drive around the Cessna and along the airport road to Aviation Boulevard, where he turned west to the access ramp for Highway 195. A mile and a half later, he negotiated the cloverleaf to join the Baltimore/Washington Parkway, and Clay settled back for the thirty-mile drive into Washington.

Clay remained silent as he tried to analyze his sense of happiness and contentment at being back in Washington. He had lived here from time to time and visited Washington on numerous occasions during his military service. As the car cruised along Pennsylvania Avenue, it came to him. Washington was one of the best-planned and most beautiful cities in the world, at least as compared to other cities his travels had taken him to. A city that exuded a sense of power along with its rich history. A trace of a smile crossed his face at the thought; two hundred odd years seemed relatively young when compared to London, England. In London, history went back ten times as far, and everywhere it confronted and reminded you of Normans, Romans, Vikings, and many others.

Thomas turned onto a side street that led to the parking ramp for just another nondescript government building. Clay watched for the surveillance cameras he knew would be there. Upstairs, the security guys would see the car arriving. Thomas parked in the parking garage, and Bamford donned his cap and dark glasses, knowing as soon as he stepped from the car his image would be recorded. Just to have a little fun with the security geeks, he kept his head tilted down. He waited as Thomas retrieved the luggage bag from the backseat, and together they walked to the elevator.

Coming off the elevator on the seventh floor, only a single door greeted them, bare except for the number 701 on its grayish white surface. Thomas inserted a plastic card and faced a camera peering out from the wall. A faint clicking sound signaled a bolt sliding back, and the door opened. Thomas led the way to the security desk being manned by two guards, the older of which came to his feet. "Welcome back, Major."

"Thank you, Frank. It's nice to be back and see familiar faces."

Frank grinned. "Are you playing games with our security, sir?"

"Just checking on you, Frank."

"Won't do you any good, sir. I'd recognize your walk every time." Frank smiled. "Besides, we have some new tricks. Ron, bring up number eight on the big screen." Clay glanced up and watched a video of him and Thomas walking toward the elevator, taken from a camera obviously mounted low and pointing up to record their faces.

"Well done, Frank. It's a comfort to a man, knowing you're keeping up to date."

A woman's voice interrupted. "Don't show him all our secrets."

Clay turned, his face grinning. There in the door leading to the offices and workrooms stood Mrs. Maxine Cherrett, office manager, executive assistant to General Thorsen and a woman who mothered everyone on staff. Clay didn't know her carefully guarded age, which was probably sixty or more, as he eyed the good-looking, well-dressed woman with the figure of a thirty-year-old. Her hair seemed grayer than he remembered. She smiled. "Are you going to stare all day or come and give me a hug?"

She got her hug before Clay stepped back. "Clayton, did you find a girl and get married like I told you?"

"No, I haven't." Clay smiled. "Still waiting for you."

"Now, Clayton, don't you try to soft soap me. I'm not looking for another husband." Maxine shook a finger at him. "Twice I married two-legged critters of the opposite gender. The maintenance cost on men is too high. Neither was worth the trouble. Now I have a four-legged critter who meets me at the door bouncing with joy and wagging his tail. He's so happy to see me come home and is hardly any bother to look after." Clay laughed at her description of men. "Come along, Clayton. The general is waiting. Thomas, you bring his bag."

"Mrs. Cherrett, the major hasn't signed in." Everyone stopped, and Maxine turned to look at Frank as Clay walked back to the security counter.

While Clay signed the book, Maxine informed Frank, "You must improve your efficiency. You let this man wander around before properly checking in. Next thing I know, you'll be letting hobos wander in off the street."

Frank grinned. "We'll make sure that doesn't happen, Mrs. Cherrett."

"See that you do." Maxine smiled. "Hurry now, Clayton. There's work to be done."

The steel door closed behind them with a solid sound, and Clay heard the safety bolts slide into place to secure it from forced entry. Mrs. Cherrett led the way along the hall with its yellow tiled floor and plain gray walls. When they turned the corner, General Thorsen stood in the doorway to his office. He held out his right hand. "Welcome, Clay. It's good to have you back." Clay shook his hand and took his bag from Thomas before following the general through the door. "Maxine, do you think we could have coffee and a few sandwiches?"

"Of course, General. The kitchen will take care of it immediately." The door closed softly as Mrs. Cherrett left. Thorsen motioned to his conference table.

"Your flight was satisfactory?" Clay nodded agreement. "How are things on the ranch?"

"It's winter now, and so far the cattle are doing fine. A few mornings we've fed them hay—more just to have something to do rather than from necessity. One of these days we'll get a real snow dump, and the hard work will start."

"So, Clay, have you found something for me on what our friends are planning?"

"Hopefully, sir. A meeting is set to take place in Rome in two weeks that will bring together people from a number of countries, including Iran and Pakistan. The timing is very tight, so I came to inform you rather than waste time searching for more information."

"Well done, Clay." Thorsen rubbed the side of his nose with his left thumb as he eyed Clay. "Do you know the subject of the meeting?"

"Not even a hint. All the messages have been about arrangements for the meeting, with no discussion of agenda. Presumably they all know what the meeting is for and are only trying to agree on the actually timing. The Christmas season is considered an ideal time because Rome will be filled with tourists, and it's unlikely that anyone will notice a few more foreigners. What I found particularly peculiar ..."

A knock on the door interrupted Clay. Thorsen turned his head toward the door and called, "Come in."

Mrs. Cherrett opened the door for a kitchen staffer pushing a serving cart with sandwiches, which they wheeled to the table. Clay smiled at the steward as Thorsen commented, "Thank you. We'll help ourselves. See you in the morning, Mrs. Cherrett. Have a good evening." They watched until the door closed, leaving them alone again. "You were going to tell me about something peculiar, Clay."

"There may be a perfectly logical explanation, even though it seems odd to me for drug suppliers from South America and Europe to meet with people from Middle East countries."

Leaning back with a thoughtful sigh, Thorsen mused, "I don't recall coming across a connection between the groups in the past. You didn't find anything to indicate a reason for the gathering?"

"No, sir. In the intercepted messages, there's no mention of agenda items. Keep in mind, I brought a list of people who are sending and receiving these e-mails and didn't take time to access everyone's computer. The meeting is only a few days away, and I wanted to alert you, to allow time for planning on how to deal with the meeting. While you're organizing that, we can put people on each of these targets to start drilling into their files, which should result in some clues as to the subject of the meeting."

Thorsen didn't hesitate; he stood up and started for the door. "Come on, we'll find Pat, and you can brief her." Thorsen led the way with Clay following, carrying his briefcase. They were looking for Patricia Gowdy, a career government employee and Thompson's longtime manager in charge of the Communication Section, a purposely vague department name intended to go unnoticed by the public, media snoops, and the huge Washington bureaucracy. Gowdy's office was empty, with the door standing open. Thorsen continued along the hall until they heard her voice coming from a small meeting room. Thorsen knocked before opening the door, interrupting Gowdy, who was explaining the operations manual to two new recruits who had recently joined the team. Conversation stopped, and three heads turned to look. Gowdy placed both her hands on the table and came to her feet. "Good afternoon, General."

Thorsen stepped into the room and moved aside, a slight smile on his face. He watched Gowdy's eyes widen in surprise as Clay entered. "Major Bamford, I heard you were helping us. It's so good to see you again."

Clay advanced on her and put his free arm around her shoulders, giving her a squeeze. Clay noted that Pat had grown even larger than two years before. He estimated she must weigh over two hundred pounds now. An almost round face, Clay noted her green eyes were still sharp. Patricia Gowdy's policeman husband had the misfortune of being gunned down while participating in a raid on a drug house nine years before, and she took the loss hard. When the funeral was over, Pat threw herself into her work, putting in long hours at the office, often grabbing a few hours of sleep on the office floor at night, devoting her energy to the fight against drugs. Each victory won by Thorsen's team became a personal victory for her, a small revenge against drug pushers. Clay released Pat's shoulders and set his briefcase on the table. "How are you, Pat?"

"Eating too much and grossly overweight." Pat's eyes twinkled. "Even so, I can still pound a computer with the best of them. Are you bringing something for us, Major?"

Thorsen said, "Clay brought a few leads for us, Pat. Why don't you take him to your office and review the data with him. Afterward, get people on it. This one has a short fuse."

"We'll get right on it, General. Major, come and meet the two newest members of our team." Clay followed Gowdy around the table, watching the two new hires stand up. Clay found himself eye to eye with Graham Eiler as Pat introduced them. "Graham graduated from Southern Cal last spring with a programming degree, and we convinced him to bring his talents to our war on drugs." The two men shook hands.

"Pleased to meet you, Graham. Welcome aboard."

"Thank you, Major. I've heard about you and wondered when we might meet."

"Call me Clay, Graham. I'm not in the army now." Clay put a hand up to pat Eiler's shoulder as he moved past.

"Major, this is Margot Lass who has a master's degree in Computer Science. We managed to steal her away from Intel. She can explain anything you want to know about computer chips."

Gowdy stopped beside Lass and turned to face Clay. "You can see why we nicknamed her Ugly Duckling."

Clay estimated Lass was five foot ten. She had flaming red hair and a figure no man could miss seeing and appreciating. Her face still showed traces of the freckles she hadn't outgrown, and her brown eyes sparkled as she smiled at him. Clay stuck out his hand, and they shook. "I'm very pleased to meet you, Margot. With a name like Lass and red hair, would I be correct to assume you're Scottish?"

"Aye, Major, you would. It's nice to meet you. As Graham said, we've listened to stories about you."

Clay laughed. "Don't believe a word of what they tell you, especially from Pat. I was always able to fool her. Where did you go to university, Margot?"

"The University of Edinburgh, Major."

Gowdy interrupted. "You two go back to your projects. We'll finish our meeting as soon as there's time. Right now I need to check on what foolishness Major Bamford is up to. Come along, Clay, we better get started."

Gowdy accepted the disc Clay handed her, put it in the disc drive of her computer, and immediately made a duplicate copy. Clay's original went into a locked file cabinet. Working with the copy, Clay explained the data it contained, and they discussed the Rome meeting. Gowdy quickly grasped the situation. "You have seven computer addresses here. For the Spanish, English, and Italian, we have people who can burrow in and understand what they find. We have no one on our staff who reads the Urdu or Persian languages."

Clay suggested, "Why don't you make copies of these addresses and assign someone to start on each one. What we need is for one of them to come up with details on the meeting and what these guys plan to talk about. A good fix on the location for the meeting would really help."

Gowdy nodded. "You get on the computer over there and write up a guide describing what we want to look for. While you do that, I'll make a disc of each of these sites to hand out to our people. In a few minutes, we can have someone digging into each of the five."

They were busy at their keyboards when the door opened, and Thorsen came in pushing the food cart from his office. Both glanced up briefly. Clay finished first and sent his document to the printer, which started up a few seconds later. As her computer spit out each disc, Gowdy wrote the date on it with a felt pen and identified its target. Gowdy stood up with five discs in her hand, reaching for Clay's printouts. "It will take me a few minutes to explain this project to each of the people and get them started. Clay, tell the general about our little problem in the Middle East." The office door closed behind her as she hurried out into the hallway.

Thorsen gave Clay a quizzical look. "What's this little problem Pat mentioned?"

"Sir, two of the targets I identified are in the Middle East. Pat says she doesn't have anyone on staff who can read the languages used in Iran and Pakistan." Clay grinned. "I believe she wants me to ask you for help in finding the right people to chase those two leads."

"Aren't they using English?"

"Exchanges between countries are in English. We expect that when our people start digging into files in each country, there will be local communications in their own language. If we can't read them, we may miss very important information."

"I see." Thorsen nodded thoughtfully. "Army Intelligence should be able to help us, and it would keep everything in the family. If they can't help, I'll ask the CIA. The problem with the CIA is you never know what they'll do if anything important turns up."

"Of course, sir. It wouldn't really bother me one little bit if the CIA decided to put a hit on the meeting and eliminate all of them. Besides, it would keep our noses clean from the reactions that will result when the politicians start yelling and the media speculates."

"Were you able to identify who will be attending the meeting?"

"Not yet." Clay shrugged. "It may not be the kingpins, although it should be safe to assume that whoever they are, they'll be high-ranking members of the cartels. If decisions are going to be made and agreements negotiated, they have to be senior people."

Thorsen lapsed into silence as he mentally reviewed everything told him so far. When the door opened, he looked around to see Gowdy returning. "You got everything organized?"

"Sure have, except for the two I assume Clay told you about."

"He told me and I'll ask for the loan of people who can help." Thorsen stood up and walked to the food cart. "We may as well eat."

After two days of intensive effort with Thorsen's talented group of computer people and two intelligence officers with Middle Eastern backgrounds, borrowed from the army, they gathered a wealth of information. It completed Clay's work. Once again he had helped them get started by coming up with the targets needed to focus a search for information. While the communications group continued to uncover new data, their attention now focused on analyzing the reams of information residing on computers and feeding their conclusions to the operations people.

Clay felt his excitement building as a plan of action for sending people to Rome started coming together. Like an old warhorse, he wanted to get involved, to charge ahead once again and be in the middle of things. After the seven years he spent deeply engaged in Thorsen's operations, the temptation to volunteer to join in the action once again ate at him. In his mind, he could hear, feel, and smell the action that was going to occur in Rome, conducting surveillance on everyone involved in the meeting and trying to do it covertly without anyone noticing. A very challenging undertaking! Thorsen planned this as purely intelligence gathering, with no physical action against any of the participants. That would come later, after they understood the intentions of the group and could identify the most damaging way to intervene. Clay told himself not to let the old memories tempt him into getting involved. His life had changed, and it was time to go back to ranching.

Clay walked into the general's office. Thomson smiled as he looked up. "Thompson, it's time for me to go back to the ranch."

Clay received a sly look, "Thought you would want to join the team on their excursion to Rome."

Pulling back a chair, Clay sat down across the desk from him. "It's a temptation. That's why it's time for me to leave. My life is different now. Besides, it will be best for me not to know the details. Can you arrange a plane for me in the morning?"

Thompson leaned back in his chair. "Are you sure? Rome's a nice place to visit. All those pretty girls, it would be a holiday for you."

"I'm sure." Clay knew Thompson's game and grinned at him.

"Okay, Clay. What time do you want to leave?"

"Around six."

Thompson reached for the intercom and pushed a button. Maxine answered. "Mrs. Cherrett, please arrange for a plane and crew to be ready at six in the morning to fly Major Bamford to Mountain Home."

"Certainly, General. Should I alert Thomas to pick him up from the hotel at five?"

Thompson looked at Clay, who nodded. "The major agrees with that. Thank you." Leaning back, Thompson remained silent for a moment and then said, "You've been a big help to us once again, Clay."

"Always pleased to do what I can. It keeps me sharp, and while the hours get long and are tiring, the challenges are enjoyable. Anytime there's something you think I can help with, just let me know."

"Okay, Major, you're off the job as of now. What do you think of the two of us walking over to your hotel to have dinner and a drink? We may not see each other for some time."

Smiling at him, Clay stood up. "A great idea, General. Give me a few minutes to say good-bye to the crew and get my briefcase."

The flight went smoothly as far as Cincinnati, where the head winds picked up, with strong gusts that got worse as the plane approached Illinois. Soon the crew started to dodge snow squalls and even stronger winds. The pilot changed course to the south to take advantage of weather reports showing the northern plains suffering from a huge blizzard. Winds were still strong when the plane touched down in Wichita to refuel and get the latest weather data. From Wichita, the pilot chose a route across southern Colorado, until the plane was west of the front range of the Rockies, leaving the storm behind them. The pilot turned northwest and crossed the Great Salt Lake to fly straight on to Mountain Home.

Clay got to his truck in midafternoon and started the five-hour drive back to the ranch. More snow had fallen while he was away in Washington. He kept his speed down, wary of icy spots and not wanting to end up in the ditch. It had been his plan to stop at Johansson's to pick up groceries, except with the delay in the flight; he was now late and drove past town after dark to start the last thirty miles home.

Clay sighed happily when he saw lights on in the house. Alorenzo must still be there, and that meant there would be coffee ready.

Chapter 10

Winter kicked up her heals with more snow and a strong wind building drifts. They were in for a white Christmas, a very white Christmas, with snow already a good two feet deep on the level. The men fed the cattle every day now to supplement the forage they were finding in sheltered places or by pawing through snow. At lower elevations, the streams were still open and running. When a warm spell arrived, the melting snow would cause them to breach their courses everywhere with low banks. In other pastures, where the cattle depended on ponds for drinking water, the men used axes to reopen holes in the ice every morning. At the end of each day, the riding horses were always stabled in barn stalls, where it was warm, to munch on hay and a generous portion of oat chop.

Chopping ice holes in the ponds gave the cattle a source of good water. It also attracted other animals needing to drink. Shoshone Mike came in with a large elk to hang in the barn, where heat from the horses would keep the meat from freezing. The next afternoon, Peggy and Clay leaned against a stall to talk while watching Mike and the men skin out the elk and cut up the meat. Peggy mentioned their son Jason would be home from Boise next week, and Clay's mind went immediately to thoughts of Jennie Mae. Clay commented, "Going to drive into town on Saturday. Anything you need from the store?"

"Don't think so." Peggy shook her head. "I'm going to start baking next week, with Jason coming home." She paused. "Oh yes, I could use some icing sugar and more cocoa."

Getting out his little notebook and pen, Clay wrote Peggy's items down so he wouldn't forget them. "You think of anything else, let me know before I leave."

They watched Alorenzo nail the elk hide to the wall of the chop room, getting it ready for scraping and tanning. Other than feeding cattle every morning, it was a slow time on the ranch, and everyone worked together, making fun out of whatever one of them started doing. The men got in each other's way, all trying to help with the elk hide, joking about which one was doing the most work. Alorenzo finally walked away, leaving the other three to continue without him. He came to join Peggy and Clay. Leaning on the wall, putting Peggy between them, Alorenzo brought out his snuffbox. With a pinch of snuff behind his lower lip, he held the box out to Peggy, a ritual followed ever since Mike brought her to the ranch. Usually, Peggy just told Alorenzo "no thanks." This time she accepted the box and turned toward Clay, who shook his head no. Peggy held the box in her left hand and tapped the lid just the way Alorenzo would. She opened the box and held it to her nose to smell the contents, put the lid back on, and handed it to Alorenzo, who smiled. It was a little game the two of them had played for over twenty years. Alorenzo never failed to include Peggy when she was nearby.

Alorenzo glanced at Clay. "Heard you talking about a trip to town this coming Saturday. Want us to put a blade on one of the John Deere's and plow out the ranch road?"

"Do that, Lorenz. Plow out the yard at the same time. Some of the neighbors will be stopping by to say hello and have a drink with us over the holidays."

* * *

Inside the front door of Johansson's, Clay stomped the snow off his boots, unbuttoned his sheepskin-lined coat, and shrugged out of it as he walked to the counter. There was only one other customer in the store, and Hilda was there helping her in the dry goods section. Lars put aside what he was busy with and came along the counter to where Clay stood. "It's been a while since I've seen you around town, Clay."

"With all this snow, we're feeding cattle every morning." While running a hand through his hair, Clay added, "Most days we have to chop water holes in the ponds to keep the water open."

Lars nodded, understanding. "Come on back. There's a fresh pot of coffee in the office." He led the way with Clay following.

Clay's heart rate stepped up a notch at the thought Jennie might be there; Thanksgiving seemed like a long time ago.

Jennie wasn't there, and Lars turned a chair for Clay to sit in before filling two mugs with steaming coffee. Clay's first sip—hot, black, and strong, just the way coffee should be—tasted good. Lars looked at Clay. "Everyone out at the ranch okay?"

"Yeah, they're all doing fine. Mike came in with a fat elk two days ago. He and Peggy are expecting Jason home from Boise at the end of the week."

"That fits. Jennie Mae phoned last night and told her mother the last class is Tuesday afternoon. She'll be driving home Wednesday." Clay felt a thump in his chest again and sipped coffee to buy time.

"Good coffee, Lars. Almost as strong as what Lorenz makes; his will float a spoon. A man has to be careful drinking it late in the day or he won't get much sleep."

Hilda arrived, poured a little coffee into a mug, added water and cream, and sipped. She looked at Clay over the cup as he said, "Want to invite you folks to come out to the ranch for New Year's."

A hint of a smile creased Hilda's face as she looked at Lars, who nodded yes. Hilda said, "Make you a deal, Clay. You come to church with us Christmas Eve and stay over for turkey the next day, and we will spend New Year's at the ranch."

Hilda's idea was even better. Clay grinned. "Are you trying to reform me, Hilda?"

Hilda didn't smile this time. "You don't need reforming, Clay, just a little improvement in your habits."

"Expect you're right, Hilda." Clay nodded. "You have a deal." His face felt hot when he said, "Would like to get a Christmas present for Jennie, except I don't know what it should be—maybe a sweater or something."

Lars snorted. "Don't go buying clothes for a woman, Clay. You'll never get it right."

Hilda glared at her husband. "You be quiet, Lars. Not all men are as color blind as you are." Hilda considered for a moment. "Jennie Mae loves to read, Clay. Just give me a minute. I'll be right back." Lars smiled, and they finished their coffee. Hilda arrived with a package and handed it to Clay. "Here are two books I ordered for Jennie Mae. You give them to her, and we'll find something else."

"Thank you, Hilda." Clay stuck his hand in a pocket and came out with money. "How much do I owe you?"

"You don't have to pay for them, Clay. Just take them and wrap them up."

Now it was Clay's turn to be firm. "Hilda, I won't take them unless you let me pay the cost. How much were they?

This time Hilda didn't argue. She opened the package, took the receipt out, and handed it to him. It came to thirty-seven dollars and forty cents. Clay peeled off two twenties and handed them to her.

"I'll be right back with your change."

"No you won't; you keep it. You just saved me a lot of worry and probably kept me from looking foolish."

"Okay, Clay. Lars, you go and put together what Clay needs so we don't hold him up."

Driving back to the ranch, Clay felt happy and excited, wondering what excuse he could give to the men for going back to town again so soon.

Clay kept busy on the computer, tracking activities in Seattle and Portland and making plans for the new year. Each day, another piece of the story fell into place. Luong, or Wong, the name he used in e-mails, had expanded his operations. It appeared the operation in Portland was running smoothly with a delivery once each month at 500K. He saw the 500K several times before it registered—the K was not kilograms, it was code for half a million dollars. Now Luong had begun dealing with people in California, a huge market, which would dwarf his present operation. Something was pushing him; he was expanding very rapidly—too rapidly in Clay's opinion. Luong seemed to be running a tight, little operation in Seattle, from which he would be making a large profit. Now he was moving toward handling a much larger volume that would vastly increase the risk of discovery and of getting caught. Luong must be very confident of his setup, and of course, there was always the greed factor. Few people are satisfied, no matter how much money they have. Still, it seemed out of character, besides being risky. It was a quandary that nagged at Clay's mind for days; something or somebody must be pushing Luong. Maybe he wasn't the one in charge?

From Clay's perspective, going back to Seattle to settle the score with them might have him stepping into something much larger than it first appeared. While gathering intelligence, he took time to Google every location that came to his attention in the messages, and he downloaded maps.

* * *

Hilda led everyone down the aisle to the second pew from the front and stood aside so they could enter. Jennie sent Clay in first so she could sit between him and Hilda. Jennie stuck an elbow in Clay's ribs and whispered. "Sorry about that. Mother is showing off." It was Clay's first time in church since the funeral, and Hilda wanted to make sure everyone knew of his attendance. Clay's singing left much to be desired. It didn't matter to him as he stood up and followed along, actually enjoying the music. There were only a few people in the crowd not familiar to him. Probably they were visitors, here for the holiday. Every hand coming his way got shook, and he joined in the happy atmosphere. Jennie wanted to walk home, so they strolled along the road. Jennie took hold of Clay's hand and told him how happy it made her to have him come to share Christmas with them. Lars tooted the car horn as he drove past. The walk seemed short, and all too soon they were seated in the living room, along with a few neighbors of the Johansson's.

Lars drove into the yard in the afternoon. The men got the ladies into the house with all their suitcases, bowls of food, and other necessities. Clay took the car and parked it in the machine shed. When he walked back to the house, he found Alorenzo standing outside the house door. He had been behaving like a little kid, bubbling with excitement ever since he heard Jennie was coming. They hung up their winter clothes in the mudroom, took off their boots, and Clay followed Alorenzo into the kitchen. Alorenzo headed straight for Jennie, grabbed her in a bear hug, and lifted her feet off the floor. "Miss Jennie, you're all growed up. You haven't come out to the ranch for many a year. Why haven't you been comin' to visit us like you did when you were a little thing? What you been doing with yourself?"

Jennie laughed while Lars and Hilda looked on, ignored by Alorenzo like they didn't exist. "It's very nice to see you, Mr. Gonzalez."

Alorenzo didn't like being called Mr. He stepped back, frowning. "Now, Miss Jennie, when you were learning to ride a horse, I tell'd you to call me Lorenz, like other folks do."

Jennie actually blushed. "Yes, you did. It's just that, well, I didn't want to be disrespectful."

Alorenzo growled. "Calling me mister is disrespectful. We've been friends for a long span of years, ever since you were a wee mite." Alorenzo smiled, and his voice softened. "Miss Jennie, you come along to the sitting room and tell me what you been up to."

Jennie looked at everyone, shrugged, and trailed after Alorenzo. Alorenzo had surprised Hilda and Lars, who looked at Clay, so he explained, "Lorenz always kept a soft spot for Jennie. He admired the determined way she tackled everything she did—like learning to ride, helping with the cattle, and her books. He loved to ride alongside her while she talked about one of her books. Said he got schooled just listening to her."

Hilda reverted to her usual form. "You men take these things to the bedrooms while I put the food away. Some of the neighbors will be showing up soon, and they'll want to eat. I've brought turkey to make sandwiches, and Jennie Mae whipped up cookies and a chocolate cake. Now you two get out of my way while I straighten up."

Jennie and Alorenzo sat in big armchairs while she told him about her university courses. She smiled as Clay went past with her suitcase. It occurred to Clay to wonder how much of what Jennie related to him Alorenzo understood—probably not much. It didn't matter; Alorenzo had always doted on her and right now was as happy as he was ever likely to be.

Lars and Clay put things away and got the fireplace going while Hilda rattled pots and dishes in the kitchen. Peggy came in through the door, followed by Mike and Jason. Peggy had both of them loaded down with fresh made bread, rolls, desserts, smoked elk meat, and more turkey. Clay hurried to help them.

Just before dark arrived, a neighbor, old Bill Sayers from across the county road, drove into the yard in his pickup. Mike went out to help him to the house. They would feed Bill and give him a couple shots of Jack. Later, someone would have to drive him home because he didn't see well enough to drive in the dark. Over the next hour or two, the house filled up with neighbors and people who drove out from town. New Year's was the one time during winter when the ranch gave a party. Everyone in the area knew they were welcome to come, and there had been times in the past when some of them slept on the floor because they didn't trust themselves to drive, or at least their wives didn't.

All the lights were on, and the house was full of storytelling, noise, and laughter. Clay only got a few chances to see Jennie, with all these people to visit and talk to. Finally, he wandered into the kitchen, looking for Jennie amongst all the women. She stood talking to one of the neighbor's wives and glanced his way. Picking up the big carving knife, Clay shaved off thin slices of smoked elk meat and laid them on crackers. He poured a cup of coffee and headed for the fireplace to sit on the stone ledge. All the chairs and sofas were taken up, and many of the men were standing around the rooms. As Clay got settled down, a soft, musical voice asked, "Will you share with a girl?" There Jennie stood, holding a glass of Coke and smiling. They sat side by side, eating tangy elk meat crackers and looking at each other between interruptions from friends.

Late in the night, the crowd thinned out. Alorenzo went back to his cabin, and Hilda and Lars crawled into bed, leaving Clay with Jennie. They went around the house checking on things and turning out lights before coming back to the living room to sit side by side on a sofa. Jennie asked, "Are you going to help feed cattle in the morning?"

"Don't have to; the men will do it. Most days, I usually help."

"Lorenz said he would saddle a horse so I could ride along."

Grinning, Clay joked, "In which case I will drag myself out of bed and pretend to be happy."

Jennie laughed at him. "Since when have you started sleeping in?" She paused, with him watching her. "Three more days, and the holidays are over."

Clay didn't like hearing that. "When will you be coming home again?"

"Expect it will not be until Easter break, unless there happens to be an unscheduled break in classes."

"I'm going to miss seeing you."

"You could phone me. Or better yet, drive up to Moscow for a few days." Jennie hurried on. "That is, if you don't mind sleeping on the sofa."

"The sofa would be just fine. I can bring a bedroll and sleep on the floor. Here on the ranch, we sometimes sleep in a lot worse places."

Jennie moved closer and clasped his hand. "It would be real nice if you came for a weekend. During the week, classes keep me very busy." They stared at each other, and suddenly Jennie was in his arms. They kissed for the first time, and Clay squeezed her tight.

Chapter 11

The Asian gang stayed on a regular schedule, which was a surprise to Clay. Searching through a file of their communications, he produced a calendar with the meeting dates for several months marked on it. The shipments coming in by boat were regular, almost always on the second Saturday of each month. Once that became clear to him, he tried to figure out why. In the middle of the night, his brain put it all together and caused him to sit up in bed, wide awake. He must have been dreaming. Anyway, it seemed clear and logical to him now; Saturdays made sense. Most people were off work for the weekend, which resulted in many small boats going out fishing or just taking the family for a ride. In any case, boat traffic increased on the weekends. Statistically, this lowered the likelihood of Luong's boat being noticed. Also, on Saturdays a larger number of people were available to sign up for charter fishing trips, which again enhanced the gang's cover operation. Their boat ran charters every weekend, and on the second Saturday each month, the customers were all members from the gang. Ingenious and so simple; no wonder the boat seemed to go about its business unnoticed. The boat went unnoticed because of always being there and everyone in the area being accustomed to seeing it; there was nothing unusual to attract attention.

On the Tuesday following receipt of the Saturday sea delivery, a shipment went to Portland, Oregon, and somehow the gang was fitting the new California business in with that schedule. Again, simplicity was stamped all over the system used in transporting drugs to Portland. No fancy cars, nothing flashy, and no speeding. All this information Clay had on discs from the computer and from e-mails sent and received at the clubhouse.

The gang was attempting not to keep drugs in their possession any longer than necessary. Within three days, the new supply arriving in Seattle on a Saturday started moving. This seemed to be a logical course of action to reduce the risk to the gang should a police raid hit the fish market where drugs were stored and processed.

As near as Clay could determine, the only time money and product were transported in the same vehicle was on the round trips of the fishing boat. The boat took money packed in a sailor's old, well-worn, wooden trunk on the trip out and brought bales of drugs to the fish market on the trip back. Otherwise, the two were always separated.

It was a tight operation, closely controlled and strictly disciplined. From the Seattle police computer reports, Clay felt sure the beheadings being discussed were linked to the Asian gang. Police reports mentioned the possibility of a connection to the drug underworld, although the police seemed largely unaware of this particular Asian gang. One female police officer, Angie Hoffman, seemed to be the only officer in the Seattle Police Department who seriously believed there was an Asian gang in her district. Even so, most of her comments related to how the gang kept order in the small community encompassing a few city blocks and didn't like strangers being there, particularly at night.

No sign of a money trail provided another major mystery for Clay. Somehow money made from dealing drugs had to get into bank accounts, safety deposit boxes, or investments. You can't keep piling up cash, or in time it becomes a huge problem; it must be laundered to become legal. There were no traces of electronic money transfers, at least not any he could find. Some cash might be filtered through the restaurant and the fish market, the taxes paid and the money deposited in a bank. Only relatively small amounts could be handled in this manner. Possibly they were smuggling cash out of the country and into Asian banks, but how? To do it, someone had to be travelling or running an export business, or somehow shipping manufactured goods to customers overseas. Not even a hint of any such activity had shown up.

To get revenge for the death of his parents, Clay needed to develop a plan. He wanted to hurt them and put them out of business, and he didn't yet have a clear idea of how to do it. He still needed to gather more information on their operations by continuing to monitor communications. Maybe a trip to Portland and Seattle to observe them would help? Something to nail down more of the picture and settle on his course of action. He wanted to make sure the whole operation came to an end as a result of one decisive move from him. Also, when he made trips to Seattle, he needed to get clear without attracting attention.

* * *

A few minutes after eight o'clock on Friday evening, the phone rang, and Sandra stopped on her way to the door to answer it.

After a momentary pause, a voice inquired, "May I speak to Jennie Mae Johansson, please?"

A strong, baritone voice Sandra hadn't heard before, her curiosity immediately piqued. Who could this man be? When men called, they were always looking for her, not Jennie. Sandra felt a strong temptation to inquire why this man wanted to talk to Jennie. She giggled softly to herself; it wouldn't be wise for her to do that. "Hang on a minute." Sandra turned and looked at Jennie, who was busy typing on her computer. "There's a gentleman on the phone who wants to talk to Jennie Mae Johansson."

Jennie looked up in surprise, pushed back her chair, and walked across the room. Jennie took the phone receiver, and Sandra went to the sofa and busied herself straightening the seams in her stockings—not because they needed it. She wanted to hear this conversation. "Hello."

"Hi, Jennie. It's Clay calling."

"Oh, Clay, I'm so pleased you called. How are you?" Sandra noted the happy lilt in Jennie's voice.

"I'm good, except the days are long, and I get lonesome."

Jennie laughingly inquired, "Now why would that be, Mr. Bamford?"

"Because you have a habit of keeping yourself so far from home. Lorenz is always telling me stories about the wee mite who spent her summers at the ranch. He did it again at dinner tonight."

Jennie sat down in the armchair beside the phone table and laughed, pushing her curly blonde hair back from her face with her free hand. "Good for Lorenz. It's only been two weeks, Clay."

"Yeah, I know. Still, it seems a lot longer. We had such a good time over the holidays."

"Yes we did, and I enjoyed it very much. There hasn't been time to read the books you gave me."

"No rush; read them when you get around to it. To be honest with you, Hilda got those books and let me give them to you because I didn't know what you might like."

Jennie already knew about the books and several times wondered if Clay would confess. "My, you are a sneaky man, aren't you?"

"Well, I wanted to get you something, but I don't know how to shop for a lady. Lars warned me to never buy clothes because the size and color will always be wrong."

"That sounds like Dad. Anything you get me will be fine, Clay. If the size isn't right, we can always exchange it."

"Thanks, Jennie. How are your courses going?"

"Everything seems to be going along smoothly. There are a lot of reading and writing assignments to work on, which fills my evenings and a good part of the weekends. I'm enjoying it all. How's everything at the ranch?"

"Okay! It warmed up enough, so the snow is settling, even melting in places where the sun really shines on it. The water is over the stream bank down below the buildings. Wolves pulled down one of the yearlings, so the men are putting out snares on some of the wolf trails and keeping an eye out to get a good shot at them. Wolves always give us more trouble when the snow is deep and it's hard for them to get elk. Cattle are easier prey."

They chatted on, and Sandra waited, wanting to question Jennie to find out who this could be. It took a few minutes until the talking ended.

"I'm going into town in the morning. Anything you want me to tell your parents?" Clay said.

"Just tell them I'm fine. Will you phone again?"

"I sure will. Maybe I'll drive up to Moscow to see you."

"Do that. It would make me very happy. You come any weekend you want to. Good-bye, Clay." Jennie hung up the phone and found Sandra waiting.

"Who is this guy calling you? You never told me you had a boyfriend. Where did you find him?"

Jennie smiled. "I've known Clay all my life; we're old friends—that's all."

Sandra jumped to her feet. "You're lying. How come this old friend hasn't been here to visit you before?" Sandra smirked. "You invited him to come for a weekend. Have you been sleeping with him?"

Jennie's face showed her shock. "My heavens, no. Don't you ever say such a thing. We're longtime friends, and I like him a great deal. I've always liked him, even as a little girl."

Sandra eyed her critically. "You're lying. I think you're in love with this guy."

Jennie blushed with annoyance. She pointed at the door. "You get out of here, and leave me alone. I have piles of homework to finish. Go on, get out." Sandra laughed as she pranced out the door, feeling very satisfied with herself.

Jennie stood still, thinking. She was in love. She had been in love for a long time, and now he seemed to be responding likewise. He seemed so restrained and bashful on their first few dates, and she was waiting for him to become more romantic. She wondered; maybe he only saw her as an old friend. Finally in exasperation, she started holding his hand every time there was any kind of excuse, which seemed appropriate. At Christmas he wanted to see her and had a present for her. The present held two books that she had asked her mother for, and when questioned, Hilda told her what happened. It didn't matter. Jennie was happy, and Clay began loosening up. He drove to town twice to see her after Christmas, and then came New Year's Eve at the ranch. It was a great time, except for a house full of people laughing, talking, and telling stories. After everyone went home, they were finally alone. They sat together on a sofa to watch the fireplace burn itself out, and she decided to be more aggressive, at the same time worrying he might think she was too bold. She moved closer to him and held his hand, then moved closer again until their hips touched. They stared at each other, and to her great joy, he put his arm around her shoulders and kissed her. Filled with happiness, Jennie snuggled right up to him. He held her and kissed her, she knew not how many times, until the fire was down to a few dim coals. Happy and content with the ice between them broken, she gently pushed herself away and told him, "If we're going to feed cattle in the morning, I need to get some sleep."

He let her go, and in a few minutes she settled in her old bed, the one she used all those years on holidays. Jennie lay awake and listened until she heard Clay enter his room next door just before she went to sleep.

Jennie shook her head to clear it and went back to her desk, happily satisfied that they were finally building a relationship.

* * *

For two days, Clay spent his time working on a plan, finally deciding to be in Seattle when the fishing boat made its next trip to bring a drug shipment to the fish market. Something he should have done in October. Of course, at that time, he didn't have any idea the important role the market played in the gang's operation. Now it appeared the gang's operation centered on the market. If a way could be found to cause trouble for them at the market, it might blow everything sky-high. Almost three weeks remained until the second Saturday in February when the next shipment would arrive; there was plenty of time to think about it.

* * *

Friday morning, just at opening time, Clay walked into the store. Hilda was sorting bolts of cloth and putting them in their proper places. Clay leaned one arm on the long cutting table and watched her. Hilda glanced at him, smiling. "What caused you to get all dressed up on a working day, Clay?"

Wearing a new pair of jeans, shined black boots, his going-to-town Stetson, and a clean sheepskin jacket, Clay had shaved, combed, and brushed. "Figured it was time for me to take a day off, Hilda. Just leaving to drive up to Moscow. You got anything you want to send to Jennie?"

Hilda's hands stopped moving, and she stood still for a long moment before turning toward Clay. Hilda's face seemed a mite pale, and her eyes were flared. "Are you going to see Jennie Mae?"

Grinning at her, Clay nodded. "Sure am. She invited me to come for the weekend. Expect to be back on Monday." His purpose in being here was to be up-front with Hilda. Sooner or later, Hilda would find out he had gone to visit Jennie, and Clay didn't want her or anyone else thinking they were sneaking around or doing anything unacceptable. Hilda was a strict, straight-laced mom who set a high standard of conduct. She always allowed Jennie a lot of freedom while expecting her to meet those standards. As far as he knew, Jennie always did.

Hilda frowned. Clay expected her to question him or come up with some kind of lecture. "I can't think of anything we need to send to Jennie Mae." Hilda paused. "Give me a moment while I check with Lars." She hurried along the aisle and disappeared into the store office.

Several minutes went by before they came out of the office together, finding Clay seated on a stool at the counter, talking with a farmer from south of town about cattle prices. Hilda went past Clay and back to her bolts of cloth; Lars stood at the counter and listened until the conversation slowed. "Hilda says you're on your way up to Moscow."

"Sure am, Lars. Expect to be back Monday afternoon."

Lars nodded. "We have nothing to send to Jennie Mae. While you're in Moscow, will you check her car over and make sure the oil isn't low? She often forgets there's more involved than driving a vehicle and filling up the gas tank."

"Will do, Lars! I'll tell her you two are hale and hearty, and everything is good." By now there were people other than the farmer in the store, and Clay knew all their ears were wide open. Clay smiled as the store door closed behind him. By the time he got home on Monday, the whole county would know he went to visit Jennie, and speculation would be raging. Country folks are mostly great neighbors, if you can tolerate them knowing most of what you do; there are very few secrets out in the country.

Clay had two choices: north up Highway 93 to Missoula, Montana, and then west on Highway 12 to Lewiston; or drop down to Mountain Home and go north through Boise to Lewiston and Moscow. The first was shorter by a hundred miles or more, but it was winter now and not the best time to argue with the

Bitterroot Mountains, so he chose Mountain Home. Cruising along the highway, by the time he passed Sun Valley, his mind had begun thinking maybe the time had arrived to replace the GMC. It had some years on it now even though Cal kept it running like new. Close to five hundred miles to Moscow, Idaho. Thinking about the distance made it obvious to him why Jennie didn't come home more often; it was a nine-hour drive. He should have started earlier, except there was no way he wanted the Johansson's getting any wrong ideas.

Pulling to the curb behind Jennie's car, he got out and locked the truck doors before climbing into the box. After unlocking the mounted toolbox and lifting the lid. Clay removed his bag and bedroll and dropped the lid with a bang. With the lid relocked, he climbed down and headed for the apartment building. After looking at the list of names, he found the right call button to push. Jennie answered immediately and unlocked the door for him. When he came out of the stairwell, Jennie stood in the hall waiting. It took his breath away just seeing her. She was stunningly good looking and neat, with a healthy glow seeming to radiate from her. It had been a whole month since he'd seen her.

Jennie pushed the door open and followed him in. Another girl sat on the sofa. Dropping the bedroll against the wall and lowering his bag down beside it, Clay removed his Stetson. Jennie did the introduction. "Clay, this is my roommate, Sandra. Sandra, say hello to my good friend, Clay Bamford."

Sandra came off the sofa in a smooth, fluid movement that put Clay in mind of a puma on the hunt. She stuck out her hand, and they shook. It seemed to Clay like Sandra hung onto his hand a little longer than necessity required. Clay glanced at Jennie, and she stood there watching with a slight smile. Clay stepped back to take a look around the apartment. There were two bedrooms, a bathroom, a kitchen, and this room that obviously served as a living room and study. Jennie said, "You must be hungry, Clay. What would you like to eat?"

"Whatever you have," he said. "Don't go to any trouble on my behalf. If you want, we can go out to eat."

"You've been driving all day. We'll eat in tonight, and tomorrow you can take me out for dinner." Jennie turned toward her roommate. "I plan to cook bacon and eggs for Clay. Do you want to eat with us?"

"You guys go ahead. I'm going out. Probably be late." Sandra smirked at Clay. "You two behave yourselves."

Sitting in the kitchen, they ate and talked, and Jennie poured coffee. Clay told her about his visit to the store, and Jennie laughed until she got tears in her eyes. She dried her eyes while still smiling and told him, "You did the right thing, Clay. Mother is always concerned about my virtue because she thinks university campuses are one big den of pot smoking and sex orgies. She'll be phoning to check on us, even though she's been assured I intend to keep my virtue in place until I'm married."

After a moment, he commented, "You do understand everyone in the whole county will know I came here and will be talking?"

"So what!" Jennie shrugged. "They can talk if they want to. We have nothing to be ashamed of, and as far apart as we are, I can only see you if you drive to Moscow. You come as often as you want to." Impulsively, Jennie stood up and came around the table, took Clay's hand, and said, "Let's sit on the sofa. I want you to kiss me."

Jennie got what she wanted, and Clay's hands stayed on her back. Those hands of his wanted to wander, requiring all Clay's will power to hold them back. Maybe Jennie just wanted him to know what she had.

Clay asked about the courses she was taking. Jennie went to her table and came back with a binder. "These are some of the short stories and essays I've written for assignments. Take a look and tell me what you think." Jennie sat beside Clay, watching him as he started reading. Jennie knew the stories were good. Her professor's told her the writing was crisp, to the point, and moved right along with often a surprising twist toward the end. Probably not the type of stuff Clay would buy in a book store to read, but Jennie watched as he kept reading.

The phone rang startling both of them. Jennie jumped up, exclaiming, "It will be mom." She went to the phone. It was, and Clay half listened while keeping on with the reading. Jennie came back and sat at the other end of the sofa. Clay glanced at her and Jennie blushed. "Mom isn't happy with our arrangement. She doesn't think it's proper for a lady to have a man staying overnight."

Nodding his head in agreement, Clay smiled. "I can go to a motel if Hilda's going to lose sleep over my being here."

Jennie's chin came up firmly, and her big blue eyes flashed. "No, you won't. I like having you here. I want you here, where I can see you and hear your voice. I like it when you kiss me and hold me tight. Maybe a proper lady wouldn't allow that, but I like it. No man ever kissed me until last New Year's and we have never done anything to be ashamed of." Jennie's eyes were damp and glistening.

Seeing that, Clay set the binder full of stories aside and moved down the sofa to take her in his arms. That triggered something in her, and she started crying. One moment she was telling Clay what she liked, and the next she was crying. He held her, not knowing what else he could do or what he should be saying to comfort her. After a few moments, Jennie moved away to fish a tissue out of her pocket and wipe her eyes. "Sorry about that, Clay. Mother upset me. I'm a grown woman of twenty-one years, and my mother doesn't trust my judgment."

"Hilda's very proud of you. It's not you she mistrusts; it's me. Hilda only wants the best for you."

"And what is that, Mr. Bamford? I like being alone with you, having you all to myself. How are we to get to know each other if there are always other people crowding around? The best time of all on New Year's Eve came after everyone left, leaving you, me, and the fire."

"It's that way most of the time at the ranch. Do you think you could stand it every day?"

"I would love it." Suddenly those big, blue eyes were looking right through him. "As long as you're there."

There it was—everything out on the table. Clay knew what he wanted to ask; it just seemed too soon. "We've only known each other for a little over two months."

Jennie's eyes were dry now, her face serious, as she watched Clay carefully. "We've known each other all our lives and we've been friends for longer than I can remember."

They stared at each other, two long steps separating them. "I'm seven years older than you."

"What's seven years? You're you; that's all that matters." A hint of a smile crossed Jennie's face, and she stood there waiting.

The silence lasted. He had to give Jennie credit; she knew when to stay quiet and let a man think. Clay wanted it. He thought about it. There was so much Jennie didn't know about him. Was it fair to her? Hell yes! They would work it out. "Will you marry me?"

Jennie looked at him for a long moment. "Yes, Clay. I want that very much. I love you."

Clay choked up. Finally he had found his future. "Jennie, I love you, I want to marry you, and I just hope the ranch won't be too isolated for you." By the time Clay got the words out, Jennie had her arms around his neck. This time she was doing the kissing, and Clay kissed her back.

Saturday, Jennie took Clay to the university. They walked through the library where she did research and the classrooms where she attended lectures. At noon, while eating cheeseburgers, Clay asked, "Do you know a good jewelry store?

Jennie smiled. "There's no hurry, Clay."

Grinning, Clay insisted, "Do you?"

Jennie's happy smile beamed at him. "There's a jewelry store just a block or so from here."

"Let's go and look at the rings. See if they have anything you like." Now that Jennie had agreed to marry him, Clay wanted to get on with it. There was still the problem of Jennie finishing her degree, which would take until next Christmas. They hadn't talked about that or set a date for the wedding.

Arriving at the store, Jennie took charge, and Clay thought, *'She must be related to Hilda.'* They looked at everything in the store, and Jennie tried on several rings. She didn't seem impressed with any of them.

Walking back to the apartment, Clay suggested, "Your birthday is in March. In the next few weeks, check out all the jewelry stores in town and find a ring you like. I'll come to Moscow for your birthday, and we'll make the engagement official."

Jennie squeezed his hand. "Sounds like a great plan. How much do you want to spend?"

"Find a ring you'll be happy to wear. Don't worry too much about the cost. When you find it, let me know how much, and I'll bring the money with me."

Jennie gave Clay a questioning look. "Some of the rings we looked at were three or four thousand dollars."

The temptation was too great for him. Clay bent down to kiss her, right there in the middle of the sidewalk. "That will be fine, Miss Jennie Mae Johansson."

Jennie liked that, and her face beamed. "Not Miss for long, Mr. Bamford."

Jennie complained about her computer being slow, so he cleaned it up for her. He got rid of a virus, updated her security, and defragged the machine. Two hours of effort by Clay, and the computer returned to its original speed, making Jennie happy. She looked at Clay with a twinkle in her eyes. "My, you are going to be useful around the house. I'd marry you just for the computer support."

Clay left early Monday morning in order to get back to the ranch before dark. With his head crammed full of thoughts of Jennie, Clay drove while thinking about the future, and the miles slipped by unnoticed. It took four days away from the ranch just to spend two in Moscow. After considering a stop at the store, Clay went on past town. Hilda's phoning every evening didn't make Jennie happy. As a consequence, or maybe because she wasn't ready, Jennie never said anything to her mother about their engagement. From Clay's perspective, it was up to Jennie to tell her parents, and he didn't want to face them carrying that secret, just in case they asked a leading question.

Less than an hour after arriving at the ranch, the phone rang. Jennie phoned to check on Clay and make sure he got home safely.

Chapter 12

Two days before the fishing boat would be making its Saturday trip, Clay walked along the waterfront dressed in hiking clothes with a wide-brimmed, white canvas hat, sunglasses, binoculars, camera, a reference bird book, and a backpack. Finding various places to sit for an hour or so to watch the birds, he worked his way along, sometimes down near the water and at other times back from the shore looking up into the trees. There were plenty of land and water birds, far more than he would normally have noticed. Their activities were interesting, and Clay spent a lot of time searching in the bird book to identify them, all the time keeping an eye on the fish market. The boat took out charter groups both Thursday and Friday, mixed groups of men, women, and even a few children, mostly Caucasian. He noted when the boat left and when it arrived back at the dock.

On Friday, Clay arrived with extra food provisions, planning to stay all night for a chance to see the gang's preparations for the Saturday trip and learn how things were done. He expected nothing would be going on from when the fish market closed Friday evening until early Saturday morning.

At eight o'clock, the market closed, and a few minutes later the lights in the fish market went out as everyone left. A dim light showing through a dirty window near the rear of the building and below the front street level drew Bamford's attention. Periodically a shadow passed across the window, so someone remained in there and continued to move around. The floor on this second level matched up with the surface of the dock and was above head height. This was a part of the building giving access to boats tied up alongside the old wooden wharf. People going on charters parked their cars and were taken across the parking lot and up a set of cement steps to the wharf and hence to the boat. Unless there was a basement dug toward the street under the fish market's main floor, the back part of the building couldn't be very large.

Being wintertime, the sun had disappeared in the west several hours ago. Around the building, faint light coming from the one window, combined with a single streetlight located up the street, left everything dim and gray. Bamford's first action was to stow the white hat in the backpack and put on a charcoal gray ball cap that would be invisible in the dark. Walking quickly across the street to the side of the parking lot, he crouched down to survey everything before moving closer. After watching for two days, the terrain had become familiar, and he intended to try for a look through the window to see what the interior held. Moving quietly across the parking lot to the water side, he turned and started toward the warehouse. After no more than twenty steps, the headlights of a car showed on the street. Squeezing between two large rocks, part of a long row of rocks providing a fence at the edge of the lot, Clay crouched down just before a car turned off the street and lit up the rocks as it drove into the parking lot. The rocks formed a fencelike barrier to stop cars from ending up in the ocean. On the ocean side, the ground slanted down steeply to the saltwater, leaving only a narrow ledge along the side of the rocks.

When the car turned toward the wharf to park, its lights lit up the concrete steps leading to the top of the wharf, leaving Clay in the dark to watch. The man who wore Will Bamford's watch got out of the passenger door and removed a red duffle bag from the backseat. He walked toward the steps, allowing Clay a good look at him before the car lights went out. The car driver turned the engine off and followed.

As they climbed the four concrete steps, Clay moved quickly, at a trot, toward the car. Coming up to the rear of the car, he listened for any sound from inside before silently moving along the rear fender to check for anyone sitting in the car. It proved to be empty. He hurried toward the window in the side of the building, but it was set too high in the wall, way above his head, allowing no way to get a look through it. Crouched low, he moved silently to the corner of the building and peeked around. No one was in sight. The steps were made of concrete, so noise wasn't a problem as he ascended to the wharf, which had a surface of heavy planks. Two small windows, one set on each side of large double doors, were the only openings in the rear wall. The large doorway obviously provided access for moving freight and other large items in and out of the building.

Even a gopher wants more than one way to escape from its hole, so Clay crossed the wharf to check for steps on the other side. There weren't any, just a ladder on that side of the wharf that disappeared downward in the dark.

Crouched low, Clay moved to a window and slowly raised his head to look in. There were three men inside, all Asian. The room was as wide as the main building and about twenty feet deep, with a door in the far wall. It seemed obvious the door gave access to stairs going up to the main floor. The men were busy moving banded packets of hundred-dollar bills from the duffle bag into an old, well-used seaman's chest. Clay estimated each packet of bills contained $5,000, and there were a lot of packets. In total, it must have amounted to several hundred thousand dollars.

Ducking down in the darkness for safety and after allowing time for his eyes to adjust, Clay quickly scanned the area, finding no indication of anyone being nearby. He returned to the window just in time to watch them finish the money transfer and lock the chest. Nothing fancy about it, just a simple padlock and two leather straps to buckle on either side of the lock. Two men took hold of leather handles on each end, moved the chest over to the wall, and shoved it under a table while the other man from the clubhouse watched. Very simple, and the chest was hardly noticeable sitting there with all the boat parts, ropes, and fishing gear stored in the room.

The third man, who appeared to be a seaman, went to the far end of the room and turned off a light switch. It appeared they were preparing to leave for the night. Ducking below the windows, Clay scurried down the cement steps and past the car to the rocks. From the dark, he watched the far side of the double door open and a light switch go off before the three men came out. Using a flashlight for light to see the lock, the seaman closed the door, and snapped another padlock in place. Standing on the wharf, all three lit up cigarettes and talked for several minutes before coming down the steps and standing beside the car. While the men talked in Vietnamese, Clay gleaned nothing from the conversation. The seaman turned and walked away toward the street while the two men got into their car and drove out of the parking lot.

On a hunch, Clay decided to see where the seaman went. Walking away, he couldn't go very far and probably lived somewhere nearby. Streetlights were far apart, and darkness was Clay's best friend. The seaman turned away from the ocean at the first corner. After waiting a few seconds to give him time, Clay ran to the corner and watched the man pass through the light shining from a window. Following along the opposite side of the street, the seaman led him for two blocks before turning in at a large, rambling, old house. Clay watched from across the street for several minutes until a light came on in a room on the upper floor. No way of knowing for sure that it was the seaman, but it seemed likely. Crossing the street, he looked at a sign on the gate advertising rooms to rent, with a phone number. The seaman would be starting early in the morning, so it was highly likely he'd stay in for the night.

Approaching the warehouse from the opposite side, Clay worked his way through the darkness to stand at the foot of the ladder he had discovered earlier. Grabbing a rung and giving it a tentative shake, it held and seemed to be solid. Taking hold of both vertical sides of the ladder, Clay tested it again before climbing to the top and peering over the edge of the wharf. The fishing boat gently swayed and creaked as small waves in the water moved it. Otherwise everything seemed quiet, and no one appeared to be around. Stepping onto the wharf, he went to inspect the padlock on the door. Clay was amazed; all that money inside, and the door was locked with an old-fashioned padlock, probably used for many years, which would present no problem to his entry. The temptation to enter felt strong, but this wasn't the right time. This was a reconnaissance trip, and there were more pieces of the puzzle to check. Wanting to check the door on the front of the building, Clay moved along the darkest side of the warehouse to the street. After watching for several minutes and seeing no sign of anyone, he stepped out and walked to the door set back from the street in an alcove, a common enough arrangement on many buildings built in the 1800s.

In the alcove around the door, it was pitch dark. Locating the door lock by feel, he knelt down and turned on a small flashlight for only a few seconds, enough to see what it looked like. It was an old-fashioned door lock found almost universally in old buildings across many of the western states. A skeleton key would open it easily, or a few seconds with a lock pick.

Returning to the street, Clay crossed the road and went to where the backpack lay hidden in a small copse of trees. He had six blocks to walk to where the rental car was parked. Wearing the backpack, he hiked along the dark street. Outdoors, it was always dark on the ranch, except for the few nights when the moon shone brightly. Long ago he had become comfortable in the dark. Sure, he had to be careful where he walked in the dark of night, or he might trip or bump into something. Sounds were the big thing. Natural sounds that he hardly noticed during the day could be scary at night if he didn't recognize what they were.

Walking along thinking about these things, a part of Clay's brain remained constantly aware of his surroundings. Two blocks short of the rental car, his senses alerted him to movement in the shadows of the next building ahead. Three figures became barely discernible. Thoughts of crossing the street to avoid them entered his mind and were quickly discarded. What good would it do if they had ulterior motives? They'd just follow him.

Angling to the outside of the sidewalk, he maintained his pace without breaking step or giving any sign of knowing the men were there. Coming abreast of them, he had almost decided it was all innocent when one of them yelled. "Hey, you!"

Stopping and turning to face them, Clay watched. They came out of the black darkness into the gray light of the sidewalk and spread out in an arc, facing him. To try to defuse things before it went too far, and using a soft Texas drawl, Clay asked, "How you doin', boys?"

The one in the middle yelled, "Shut up, mister. We want that backpack and your money."

It seemed like they were teenagers, maybe late teens. If they were carrying weapons, nothing was visible. "You all sure you want to do that, boys?"

The man on Bamford's right stepped forward. "Don't call us boys. Now give me your backpack." He reached one hand out toward Clay.

They weren't going to back off, so to upset them, make them angry and reckless, Clay drawled, "Why don't you boys run on home to your mommas so they can look after you? You shouldn't be out this late at night. One of you might catch a death of a cold in this damp air."

- 145 -

The man in the middle yelled, "To hell with you," and both men leaped toward him, getting in each other's way. With his left hand, Clay swung the backpack in a wide arc and heard a solid clunk as it collided with a head. The man he hit staggered back, and Clay turned to the left while his right hand chopped into the side of the second man's neck. The second man dropped to the sidewalk. The left turn put him in position to face the third one who now carried an open switchblade in his hand.

Taking a step back and watching him warily, a Texas drawl suggested, "Put the knife down and get out of here." The man kept coming. Gauging the distance carefully until he felt it was right, Clay stepped forward with his left foot, the knife came up, and Clay kicked the man hard in the kneecap with the toe of a hiking boot. This one hadn't spoken through the whole encounter. Now he yowled in pain, dropped his knife, and collapsed on the concrete. With one boot, Clay slid the knife across the sidewalk into the street. The yelling caused a light to come on up above in a second-story window.

All three men were down, and Clay's breathing wasn't even hard. Showed what training could do. These street ruffians were probably considered tough in their little part of the city. Now they had run into someone who really was tough. Maybe the fight would bring some reality to them, and they'd change their ways. The locals wouldn't have to worry about them for some time, at least until they recovered. Shouldering his backpack, Clay walked away.

Saturday morning brought a change in his plan. Instead of going back to the warehouse to see the fishing boat put to sea, Clay cleaned out his backpack and disposed of it. The camera with its long lens was broken from encountering a hard head. After taking out the memory card and wiping the camera clean of prints, it got lost in the ocean. The bird book went through the grating on a curbside storm drain. All that remained were the binoculars, which he still had a need for. The hiking clothes went into three separate Dumpsters. If the police got involved with last night's three street toughs and started questioning people about a man with a backpack, there would be nothing to point them at Clay.

In midafternoon, with just a few hours left until dark, Clay drove to the fish market and left his rental car in the parking lot, now almost full of cars. Inside, he walked the aisles looking carefully at all the fish and seafood items offered for sale. Twice the aisles took him to the back of the warehouse, which provided a good look at a flight of stairs going down to a wooden door that probably gave access to the storeroom; it should be the same door he had seen from the wharf. If his assumption was true, he could access the lower room right through here. There were two walk-in freezers on each side of the stairs. The old wooden floor creaked as he stepped on it, and it gave slightly as it took Clay's weight. It must have been a hundred years old or more. Seattle had been a seaport for more years than that.

With a small salmon and a package of frozen prawns wrapped in heavy, waxed, brown butcher's paper, Clay wandered back to the car and put the fish in the trunk. Visiting the fish market had managed to waste most of the remaining daylight. Driving the car west along Commodore Way, Clay took his time, found an easy turnaround, and drove back to the fish market. Daylight was fading when he parked under a large tree that provided a good view of the wharf and proved ideal to watch for the fishing boat.

As before, the fishing boat pulled in just before dark and tied up to the wharf. The men unloaded fishing gear. There didn't seem to be any fish. Just before dark, they used the ship's hoist to lift three large bales, one at a time, onto a four-wheeled dolly from the storeroom. The dolly made three trips to roll the bales into the building. The ship shut down, and everyone disappeared inside the warehouse. The last man closed the double doors and, if they were smart, locked them from the inside.

The fish store would be open for another two hours. The temptation to get a look into the storeroom ate at Clay. He wanted to go down there and see what was happening. His common sense told him there were too many people around the market, and at least six men were in the storeroom. From the communications on the tapes he had made, they should be starting to process the bulk shipment into smaller allotments for distribution to dealers.

After considering for several minutes, Clay accepted it was too risky and probably unnecessary to see what they were doing. One of the men might come out and stumble on him snooping around, which would blow the whole operation.

Drugs were flowing to a network of street distributers, probably in small batches. The next large shipment to Portland should leave there on Tuesday. Clay decided to leave Seattle the next morning and be waiting in Portland.

* * *

Carrying a copy of the *Seattle Times* into the hotel dining room, Clay stood looking around until a waitress showed him to a seat. The place was busy, bustling with activity. Sunday morning chatter, the clink of dishes, and the good smell of coffee permeated the air. While waiting for his food to arrive, he started reading through the newspaper. On page five, he found an article describing three men who were injured in a street fight, two nineteen-year-olds and a twenty-year-old. One suffered a broken clavicle bone in his left shoulder and badly bruised neck/shoulder muscles. The twenty-year-old had a severe concussion from a blow to the right front of his head. The other nineteen year old received a serious injury described as a badly shattered left kneecap. The Seattle police charged all three with possession of marijuana. The reporter went on at some length speculating in the article that the three men had been involved in a fight over drugs, although he quoted the man with the damaged knee, who claimed they were attacked by one big man with a strange accent.

Monday afternoon, Clay did a recon on the parking lot at Smith Lake Park and located a place suitable for observing the drug transaction that should take place the next day at about noon. Tuesday morning, he moved into position with binoculars, a camera, and notepad. It would have been nice to have long-range microphone gear to overhear any conversations.

Five minutes before noon, a green van drove into the lot and parked at the far end, followed shortly after by a bright blue Cadillac that backed into a parking stall at the near end, facing away from Clay. Using binoculars, he wrote down both license plate numbers. The vehicles sat there idling, and no one got out. Maybe they were on a lunch break? He laughed softly to himself and waited. Ten minutes later, an orange U-Haul arrived and parked one stall away from the van. A familiar white Chevy parked near the Cadillac. Again Clay recorded the licenses, and this time he took photos.

Wasting no time, a man exited the passenger door of the U-Haul, joined by two men from the van. They opened the rear door of the U-Haul, and each came out carrying a large cardboard box, which they loaded into the van. The camera snapped pictures at a rapid rate.

Clay's eyes automatically switched to the passenger door of the Chevy when it opened. The watch-wearing Asian from the club got out and removed a red duffle bag from the backseat. The Asian walked toward the Cadillac where a large black man removed two brown-paper-wrapped packages from the Cadillac's trunk and dropped them into the bag. While this happened, the other vehicles started moving to leave the parking lot.

The Asian stooped to close the zipper on his moneybag as the Cadillac sped away. The bag went in the car trunk, and the white Chevy drove slowly to the exit. Glancing at his watch, it had taken six minutes—smooth, fast, and efficient. He had to admire them for that.

After they were gone, Clay headed for the airport, returned the rental car, and checked in for a flight to Salt Lake. Tomorrow he would arrive home; not bad for a week's work. Next month, these Asians would start wishing they had never troubled a Bamford.

Chapter 13

Wednesday evening after they finished eating dinner and talking, Alorenzo went home, and Clay called Jennie. She answered immediately. "Hello."

"Hello, Miss Jennie Mae Johansson, how are you?

"Clay! Why haven't you called? It's been a week and a half, and I called you twice. No one answered."

"Now, Jennie, there's a ranch to run, cattle to feed, and when everything is done, a house to clean, food to cook, and clothes needing washing. There's no time around here to waste gossiping on the phone."

Jennie's merry laugh came clearly through the phone, "In due course, I'll take care of all the house work for you, unless you change your mind."

"Never change my mind, girl; I'm one of those stubborn Bamfords. Have you thought of a date for us to tie the knot?"

"Of course, the upcoming wedding is the most important thing in my life, and I haven't told anyone about it. There are three times suitable from my perspective. The first is next Christmas, after I finish my degree. Or, secondly in August before I return to attend fall term. Thirdly, we could get married in May after the current term ends. What do you think?"

Grinning at the phone, Clay understood the subtlety of Jennies wording and answered her, "Don't need to think. Let's set the wedding for May."

Jennie's voice took on the musical, fun tone it always did when she teased him. "My, Mr. Bamford, don't you think that's a little early? We haven't even announced our engagement. Every tongue in the county will be wagging over the quick wedding, and everyone will count the months."

Jennie's statement gave Clay a chance to laugh. "Doesn't matter what they think or say. Why should we waste time? Besides, I need to get my brand on you before some rustler steals you away."

"Are you sure, Mr. Bamford?"

"Okay, Jennie. What do you think we should do?"

"Why, Mr. Bamford, my preference would be to go to a justice of the peace tomorrow, but it wouldn't be acceptable, so I do believe we should make May work. That way we'll have the summer months together."

"You are a little devil, Jennie." Clay's voice grated, although there was a happy lilt to it. "You wanted May all along and put me through this long discussion just for spite, didn't you?"

"Not for spite, Clay. I wanted to find out what you wanted. If you had picked the wrong time, I planned to cry and carry on until you changed your mind. Since you made the right choice, you'll be spared the crying."

They laughed happily together for a minute before Clay told her, "You should phone your parents tonight and tell them we're engaged and when you want to have the wedding."

"You're a mind reader. Calling them is the next item on my list of things to discuss with you. Number three is: do you have time to go into town tomorrow to talk to Mom and Dad about the wedding arrangements—invitations, reserving the church, space for a reception, etc.?"

"What do I know about such things? Well, okay, I'll go see them if you give me the high sign everything is agreeable with them. More than likely, Hilda will take over and look after everything anyway."

"Yes, she will, Clay. It's my intention to insist everything must have your approval before she finalizes anything. It's awkward with me being so far away and unable to get directly involved."

"Don't worry about the details, honey. The wedding will go fine, and we'll be married. It's all that matters."

"Thank you. I'll call back in a few minutes after I talk to Mom and Dad."

"You do that. I'll be waiting."

"Good-bye, Clay. I love you." The phone went dead, and Clay hung up.

Lars sat watching TV, and Hilda was busy nearby stitching the hem on one of her dresses when the phone rang. "Are you going to get that, Lars?"

Lars turned off the TV and answered the phone to hear Jennie Mae's voice. "Hi, Dad, how are you?"

"Your mom and I are fine." Lars glanced at Hilda as she stood up. "Why are you calling midweek?"

"Dad, can you call Mom to the phone so both of you can hear the announcement I have to tell you?"

"Of course, Jennie Mae." Lars turned. "She wants both of us to hear some announcement she's going give us." Hilda hurried to the sideboard where the phone sat, and they held the receiver between their heads so both could hear.

Hilda started right in. "What is it, Jennie Mae?"

"I have a little announcement to make. Clay asked me to marry him, and we're planning to have the wedding in May." After a long silence, Jennie said, "Mom, Dad, are you there?

Lars looked at Hilda; her eyes were wide, and a hand was up covering her mouth. She replied, "Yes, we heard you, Jennie Mae. When did all this happen?"

"When Clay came here two weeks ago. It's why he came to see me, and I said yes. We were talking on the phone a few minutes ago and decided we didn't want to wait until after my graduation, so we've decided on May for the wedding."

Hilda, still feeling the shock, managed, "That seems rather hurried, Jennie Mae."

Jennie laughed at her mom. "I told Clay it would start tongues wagging, and all the old women would be counting the months. He said to hell with them, we should do what works for us." Hilda looked at Lars, again at a loss for words. "For your information, Mother, my virtue is still firmly in place and will remain so until the wedding."

Lars watched Hilda relax before he replied, "We never doubted that, Jennie Mae. It's just, well, you surprised us."

"Please accept my apology for that, Dad. If it wasn't so far to drive, I'd have come home to tell you. Clay is such a wonderful man, so strong and sure of himself. You'll find this hard to believe: he hesitated when it came to asking me to marry him because he was worried I'd get lonely living on the ranch, so far from town."

Hilda finally found her tongue. "What about all the wedding arrangements, dear? There are so many things to get lined up and planned."

"Mom, Clay plans to drive into town tomorrow to sit down with you and Dad, so be prepared when he arrives. Clay can talk to the minister, make reservations, and things like that. If you don't mind, Mom, please take time to think about all the wedding details. It's a helpless feeling being way up here in Moscow."

Hilda took off running. "You stop worrying. We'll discuss everything with Clay, and I'll get some of my lady friends to help make plans—invitations, music, food, and all those things."

"Thank you very much, Mom. I'd better let you go now, and we'll talk again on Saturday night."

Hilda and Lars said, "Good-bye," together and hung up the phone. They stood there looking at each other, not sure what to say. "Lars, it's so soon. Do you think they really know what they're doing? They've only dated since Thanksgiving."

"Our daughter knows exactly what she's doing. Clay's no kid. He's been around more than most and is as level headed as anyone we know. Their friendship goes back many years. Their marriage will work out very well."

"Now when there's time to think about it and the surprise is over, you're probably right. What great news." Hilda sighed. "Oh, Lars, I'm so happy Jennie Mae picked Clay." Hilda reached for the phone and began dialing.

"What are you doing?" Lars asked, bewildered.

"I've got to share the news with all my friends. Now you go and sit down. Hello, Elsie, it's Hilda calling. You won't believe the news I just heard from …"

They finished breakfast and were drinking an extra cup of coffee when Clay said to Alorenzo, "Go and put on a clean pair of jeans. I want you to come to town with me."

Alorenzo eyed Clay in surprise. "Ain't been to town for a long, long time."

Clay nodded. "True, but today is a special day. Miss Jennie and I decided to get married, and she's sending me into town to talk with Lars and Hilda. Need you along for support."

Alorenzo sat with his face frozen for a moment as he digested the news, and it slowly changed to a huge grin. "Miss Jennie is coming to live here, to be Mrs. Bamford?"

"You're damn right, Lorenz." Clay smiled. "Want you to keep an eye on the arrangements I make, so everything is right for her."

Alorenzo jumped out of his chair. "Damn right I will. Got clean jeans all ironed up." He started for the door and stopped, hurrying back with his hand out. "Best news this old man has heard in a long time. A Mrs. Bamford—just what this ranch is a needin'."

At ten thirty, Alorenzo followed Clay into a crowded Johansson's, carrying his Winchester across his arm. Over many years, he had never gone anywhere without it. By now the whole town would be talking about the wedding. People in the store smiled at Clay, and many spoke to him. A few faces frowned as they looked in surprise at Alorenzo carrying his Winchester around the store. Hilda came hurrying from behind the counter to meet Clay and hugged him; he gently kissed her on the cheek. Lars leaned across the counter to shake hands. "We got some mighty good news last evening, Clay. Jennie Mae sounded very happy. Got to admit it kind of surprised us."

"Sorry about that, Lars. Reckon I fell in love with Jennie back at Thanksgiving and just didn't know how to ask her. Finally built up enough courage to go ahead and ask. Damned if she didn't say yes. Guess the truth is I've been in love with her for a long time, just didn't rightly realize it until then."

"We couldn't be happier, Clay. Hilda hardly slept a wink last night, what with thinking and writing lists. She's going to be pushing you for help."

"That's why Jennie sent me in here, Lars."

Hilda grabbed his arm. "Come back to the office, Clay, so we can talk." As they walked to the office, Alorenzo followed a few steps behind, giving everyone watching the impression he was guarding Clay's back. It was a thought that caused a few smiles; as if Clay Bamford needed protection.

Sheriff Tom Odleson walked into the store twenty minutes after the meeting started, having received a phone call. Odleson immediately spotted Alorenzo leaning against the wall outside the office door with a rifle across his left arm, giving the impression he was a security guard. Odleson stopped at the counter. "How are you today, Lars?"

"Everything's going along fine, Sheriff." Lars nodded his head toward the office. "A meeting is going on back there to lay out plans for a wedding. I'm doing my best to stay out of the way."

Odleson smiled. "You always were a smart man, Lars. You think it would be okay if I went back there to congratulate Clay?" This last part was in a louder voice to make sure Alorenzo heard it.

Lars waved a hand toward the office and raised his voice. "You go ahead, Sheriff. Clay will be happy to see you."

Odleson stopped outside the door and spoke to Alorenzo. "Good to see you, Lorenz. A rumor's circulating around town saying Clay has plans to get married."

Alorenzo's brown, weather-beaten face broke into a wide smile. "Yes, sir, Tom. We is going to get us a Mrs. Bamford come spring time." Alorenzo's voice boomed loudly, reaching every part of the store, turning heads and causing smiles. Many of the shoppers had only heard of Alorenzo Gonzales and had never actually seen him, simply because many years had gone by since the last time he had been off the ranch. Today more stories about the old bull rider would get started. Clay walked out of the office, and Hilda stopped in the doorway.

Odleson held out his hand. "Congratulations, Clay. This talk about a wedding came as a surprise to me; always figured no woman would want to live with you."

"Thanks, Tom. Jennie surprised the heck out of me when she said yes. Guess she'll have her hands full, trying to reform me."

"Everything will be fine. Jennie is a mighty smart lady, and she's getting herself a good man." Odleson wanted to involve Alorenzo. He turned his head. "You agree, Lorenz?"

"Yes, sir, Tom." Alorenzo's voice boomed again. "Miss Jennie can ride and rope, and she knows cattle and such. She can shoot a rifle too—learned with this here Winchester of mine. Shoots mighty straight, Miss Jennie does."

Odleson asked quietly, "That Winchester loaded, Lorenz?"

Alorenzo's voice boomed again, "Sure is, Tom." Alorenzo grinned at the sheriff. "A gun what ain't loaded is no good to anyone."

"No one's supposed to carry a loaded gun around town, Lorenz." Odleson shrugged. "Not safe for all these town folks."

"That so! All my life, never came to town without my Winchester. What if some varmint shows up? A man needs to do what needs doing."

Odleson turned back to Clay. "Going to be in town for long?"

Clay understood the suggestion coming from Odleson. "Hilda is sending Lorenz along with me to talk to the preacher and make a reservation for the church and hall. Afterward we may stop at the Ranchers before heading home."

"Mind me tagging along? May be able to help out here and there."

"Be glad to have you." Clay turned to Alorenzo. "Will you take Tom out to the truck? I need to check a couple of things with Hilda and will be right there." Clay stood beside Hilda as they watched the two men walk across the store. Clay shrugged. "Tom wants me to get Lorenz and his rifle out of town. If it's okay with you, we'll go and talk to the preacher. I'll come back on Saturday to see what else you need me to help with."

"You go ahead. By Saturday most of the plans will be worked out. Lars and I are really happy you and Jennie Mae are going to be married."

Clay glanced at her. "Thank you, Hilda."

* * *

Luong An Chie'n sat in his office in a quandary. For several months, the larger operation had run smoothly. Deliveries to Portland were routine, and the first shipment to California in January went off without a hitch, the transfer of product for cash taking place in Yreka, California. Where it went from there was of no concern to him.

Using a U-Haul rental to Portland seemed foolproof. For the longer trip to Yreka, Luong purchased a two-year-old Ford truck with an enclosed van style box on the back and created a fictitious used-furniture business. Signs painted on both sides of the large, square truck box in big letters proclaimed Used Furniture and Antiques.

Luong considered this to be brilliant. Used furniture purchased at an auction and paid for with cash packed the truck box. On the five-hundred-mile trip south, with two men taking turns driving, they made it there and back in two days. When the men met the buyer in Yreka, a few items of old furniture were removed and placed on the ground for the benefit of anyone driving past. The drugs, in wooden crates, were removed and transferred, the packages of money loaded, and the furniture replaced. The truck was always full of furniture, and its contents never changed. Each trip to California netted $1 million for Luong with the added potential of unlimited growth in the future.

Quang waited and took charge of the money when the truck passed through Portland on the return trip. It worked very well, and Quang brought the money to Luong, which kept the drivers distant and unaware of him or his office.

All the cash now piling up in the vault on the first floor of this old bank building was creating a dilemma. Stacks and stacks, in row after row, of packets of hundred-dollar bills. Each packet contained one hundred bills, wrapped with a rubber band to hold it together—$10,000 per packet.

Shelves in the vault were filling up quickly, creating a storage problem that worried Luong. He needed to find a solution to the problem in the near future. It almost seemed like the operation had become too successful. Luong quickly discarded the thought.

It had frustrated him for days now, thinking about the new storage problem, and he still didn't have a solution. Wearily Luong stood up and stretched. His wife expected him to go to the fish market with her list of items the restaurant needed, and it would require a couple of hours to take care of.

Luong drove to the wharf, parked his white Chevy in the space closest to the door, and walked in. He handed his wife's list to one of the salesmen. "Fill this order quickly."

While waiting, Luong walked along the aisles, inspecting the operation. Nearing the back, he looked along the doors of the four walk-in freezers across the back wall. Suddenly an idea came to him, and his face lit up. Last summer they installed a new freezer to take the place of a long unused one, no longer efficient. He hurried to the office of his second cousin, who ran the market, and said, "Show me the old walk-in freezer that stopped working."

The two men walked to the large freezer door and opened it. Luong peered inside. Empty boxes and assorted items rarely used littered the freezer floor. It wouldn't be hard to get them out of the way. The inside space contained a far larger volume than the vault in the old bank building. Ideal! Luong excitedly turned. "Cousin, have this freezer cleaned out immediately. I have need for it."

Second Cousin nodded, and Luong continued, "I will come tomorrow to see it. We need to consider the installation of good locks on the door and find someone to install shelves along the walls. See if you can find a craftsman to do the work for us."

Luong paced around the market, smiling at employees and customers. A simple solution to his most pressing problem had come so easily. As he waited patiently for his wife's food order to be filled, several of the employees began to wonder what could possibly have happened to change Luong's normally abrupt and rushed attitude.

Two men carried the seafood order out to Luong's car and packed it in the truck. He drove away feeling happy and knowing it had been a very good day.

Chapter 14

As much as Clay wished to talk to Jennie, he kept putting the temptation aside. With plans to make another trip to Seattle, which he figured would take a week, he didn't want Jennie to start expecting phone calls every day or two. He did dial the phone for the Winehousers. "Hi, Sadie, it's Clay calling."

"How very nice, Clay. How is everything at the ranch?"

"It's winter, and the snow is deep. It's starting to melt somewhat now, and with longer days, most of it will be gone soon unless we get another storm. How's Edgar?"

"Edgar is fine, Clay. He's out for dinner tonight with a group of other judges discussing whatever judges talk about. Very boring I'm sure."

"Wouldn't know about that, Sadie. I called to let you know I'm planning to get married."

"Oh, Clay, I'm so pleased to hear that. Who's the lady?"

"Do you remember the Johansson's who own the store in town? She's their daughter, Jennie Mae Johansson. Jennie is working on her master's degree at the University of Idaho."

"Oh, how very nice that sounds! Do you have a date set for the wedding?"

"We picked the first Saturday in May. The invitations should be in the mail next week."

"The moment Edgar gets home, we'll start planning our trip."

"Very good, Sadie. It will be good to have both of you here and introduce you to Jennie. Please pass on my best to Edgar."

"Thank you for calling, Clay. Edgar will be very pleased. Good-bye."

Clay regularly monitored the Seattle Police Department computer center. It had required a significant amount of time and work to finally gain access to the police mainframe. This time he searched for a report on the three hoodlums who tried to mug him. When he found the report, he spent time reading it in detail. The officers involved were all new names to him, which wasn't unexpected; this was a different area of the city. The reporting officer suggested the three men were lying about one man attacking them. How could one man take on three street toughs and create all the damage they suffered?

There was nothing in the reports to point at Clay Bamford. One more trip and Clay hoped to have Seattle and these troubles behind him.

In the morning, Clay dialed the Washington number for the general. "Thorson here."

"Good morning, General. Don't want to waste your time— just alert you that I plan to be married the first Saturday in May."

"Good for you. Are you sending me an invitation?"

"The invitations are almost ready to go in the mail. Hope you'll be able to come, and bring anyone you want with you."

"Hell, son, everyone will want to come. We'll try to keep the numbers down. By the way, the little operation you helped us with went exceedingly well. You'll be filled in when I come west."

"See you then." Clay hung up.

Next week, Clay planned to leave for Seattle. Clay decided he would take the truck to Cal and have him check it over. After eating breakfast and talking to Alorenzo, he drove to town and walked into the garage. Cal looked up from the invoice he was busy filling in. "Morning, Clay."

Clay grinned. "Got the coffee ready?"

"Just got coffee started. Can you wait a few minutes?" Clay nodded. "There's talk all over town that you and Jennie Mae are planning to get married."

"That's right, Cal. Caught her at a weak moment and managed to talk her into it. It's a long drive up to Moscow, and I plan to go see her. You got time to check the truck over for me? The brakes need doing, and there might be a leaky seal in the differential. Oil is dripping from somewhere."

"I'll open the big door right now, and you drive onto the hoist so we can take a look." Cal went to work the chain drive to lift the overhead door while Clay started the truck. Cal moved to the front of the hoist and held up his hand when the truck arrived at the right position over the hoist. Cal positioned the frame lifts, operated the air valve, and they watched the hoist rise until there was room to walk under it.

Clay watched as Cal checked the differential. "You do have a seal leaking, right here where the drive shaft connects to the differential." Cal grabbed the drive shaft and wiggled it. "The U-joints are loose; they need to be replaced." Cal walked clear of the hoist, wiping his hands on a red rag. "Go check the coffee while I put the big door down."

They sat in old wooden armchairs, sipping coffee and talking. After a while, Cal looked at Clay without his head turning. "Everyone in Challis is talking about Alorenzo packing his Winchester around town."

Clay looked across his coffee mug. "Reckon it was a mistake, me bringing Lorenz to town. He's always been like a second dad to me and got all excited when he heard about the wedding. He thinks the world of Jennie."

"No harm done, Clay. There aren't many old timers like Alorenzo left now—guys who go back to the rough days. I told

Sheriff Odleson it was a mighty good thing for people to see Alorenzo. He's a sample of our history, and people around here ought to be aware of it. Soon, guys like him will all be gone. Jennie Mae is a writer. After you marry her, you should encourage her to get Alorenzo talking and write down what he says about the early days."

Clay nodded thoughtfully, thinking about it. "All those years Jennie was at the ranch on holidays, she spent many an hour talking to Lorenz. She should have a head full of stories he told her. Probably he cleaned them up because she was so young at the time." Clay took off his Stetson to run a hand through his hair. "Not a bad idea, Cal." Clay finished his coffee and went to the sink to wash the mug before turning it upside down to dry. "Fix up the truck, Cal. Have to go to the store to help finish invitations and whatever else Hilda has lined up for me to do."

Clay's handwriting tended to be big and bold. Hilda watched him addressing envelopes, telling herself, *'The people getting those invitations will know it was a man who sent them.'* She went back to working on her share of the guest list, between interruptions from almost every customer who entered the store. People were seeing a whole new side of Clay, with him sitting at the table doing what Hilda told him to do. Elsie Olson, Hilda's good friend and one of Clay's former teachers, arrived. "Clayton, Hilda tells me you twisted Jennie Mae's arm until she agreed to marry you."

Clay looked up. "Now, Mrs. Olson, no way is that true." Tipping his chair back, Clay put down his pen. "Fact is, back there in high school, you made such a perfect man out of me Jennie's fairly foaming at the mouth to get married. After fighting her off for months, I finally gave in."

Both women laughed, enjoying his response. "One thing you weren't taught, Clayton, was to tell lies. Hilda, I do believe he's worse than Lars at making up tall tales."

"One thing I can tell you, Elsie: Jennie Mae thinks Clay is a pretty good man."

"Ha! Young girls are easily fooled. Don't let it go to your head, Clayton."

A new voice joined the conversation. "Are you ladies beating up on Clay?" All three turned to see Sheriff Odleson watching them. "Hilda, do you think you could give Clay enough time off to go to the Ranchers and eat a sandwich with me?"

Hilda feigned a frown. "Yes, I suppose so, if you promise to get him back here on time. You go along with Tom, Clay. We'll work on these this afternoon."

Elsie sat down in the chair Clay vacated, and they watched the two men cross the store to the front door. Without turning her head, Elsie commented, "Always was a good boy, and now Clay is a fine man."

"Yes he is, Elsie. There's a certain, I don't know what, just something about him, like there's a caged tiger inside him that could explode if it got loose."

"Much the same as Will, and don't forget—Clayton received his military training, which made him even tougher than he would have been otherwise. Still, he's a gentleman. Always has been, even when he was a boy."

"Jennie Mae says the same thing. The other night she told me on the phone she finally asked him if he ever planned to kiss her before he did."

"From what I hear, Hilda, not many young men are so self-restrained these days."

The phone rang, and Lars pushed the speaker button to hear Cal's voice. "Lars, could I speak to Clay?"

"Sorry, Cal, he left a few minutes ago with the sheriff."

"When he comes back, will you ask him to call me? There's more wrong with his truck than he thought. I won't have it finished until tomorrow."

"I'll tell him, Cal."

Clay worked all afternoon on preparations for the wedding and agreed to stay overnight with Lars and Hilda. He and Lars watched the evening news on TV while Hilda cooked dinner. Just after eight, Lars suggested, "Clay, why don't you call Jennie Mae and bring her up to date on the wedding plans."

Clay walked to the sideboard and dialed the phone. "Hi, Jen, how are you tonight?" Lars and Hilda both wished they could hear Jennie Mae's side of the conversation. "No, I'm staying in town overnight with your parents.

"Of course I should be back at the ranch. Hilda won't let me go until all the arrangements for the wedding are finished." Lars and Hilda smiled at each other.

"Can't even straighten my fingers, they're so cramped from holding a pen." Clay listened for several minutes. "You're right, honey. Got so used to him carrying his Winchester, I just didn't think about it. Lorenz got so excited about you coming to live on the ranch; I thought bringing him along to town would calm him down.

"Yeah, maybe.

"Look, Jen, I know you plan to write novels and short stories after you graduate. Have a suggestion for you. Lorenz is one of the last of his generation. He used to tell you stories when you were a kid, and if you spend time talking to him, you could write up sort of a history of the early days. You know, back when he was riding bulls. Times were very different from what they are now, and most of it will be lost when he dies."

Clay laughed. "Yes, Miss Jeanie Mae Johansson, I expected you would keep digging until you found out. Cal is repairing the truck, and it won't be ready until tomorrow.

"Now, Jen, you can't expect me to know about things like that. You better talk to Hilda. Talk to you in a few days." Clay turned and held out the phone. Hilda came to take it.

Clay went back to his armchair. He glanced at Lars. "Jennie is always full of questions."

"Get used to it, Clay. Women see the world different than we men do. Jennie Mae has always had a high level of curiosity about everything. You best be careful what you say to her; it may show up in one of her books."

Clay smiled. "I'll keep all my secrets, secret." They could hear Hilda talking in the background without paying attention. Lars knew she would tell them anything they needed to know; the rest didn't matter.

Clay paid Cal's bill with cash and found the truck ran smoother with the seal replaced, new U-joints, new ball-joints, and the brakes repaired. He drove into the ranch yard early in the afternoon. Seeing activity around the barn, he went over there to park.

A steer hung from the barn rafters for butchering. Mike explained, "We found him this morning with a broken leg. From the tracks, we figure one leg went through the ice on the pond while he was running. Something must have scared him. We didn't see any tracks, although there might have been a puma up in the rocks."

"Let's go out in the morning and take a look. If there's a puma hanging around, we can try to scare him off. One of us might manage to get a shot at him." Clay glanced at Alorenzo. "Are wolves starting to cause any trouble?"

"Some fresh tracks scattered around, Clay. With thinning out snow they could've moved up country to chase elk. A bear come out of Rocky Gorge. He ambled around some. Most likely out of hibernation now. He'll be hungry." Alorenzo shrugged. "Rode around some having a look, didn't see him. You plan on comin' along tomorrow?"

"Hell, yes. Hilda kept me tied to a table with a pen in my hand all yesterday. Need the feel of a good horse and plenty of fresh air to get me back normal." All the men chuckled.

Mike added, "We figure to let this carcass hang for a couple of days before we cut up the meat."

Clay nodded his agreement. "About time we started checking all our gear. It won't be long now until the cows start dropping calves. If this weather holds, we may be able to move the steers before the cows get started. Started working on a list of things we need from town. March is here now …" Clay paused. "Damn, I should have phoned those two boys to see if they'll be coming back for the spring and summer. May as well get them back. There could be calves in two weeks or so."

Clayed grinned at the three men. "You guys are at fault; you should have reminded me."

Shoshone Mike smiled, a bit of a rare thing for him. "Never did figure on you getting in a tizzy over a little thing like having a wedding. When Peggy agreed to marry me, we just went down to the courthouse and got it over with."

"Yeah, Jennie and I talked about that. The difference is you didn't have a Hilda Johansson to contend with. She's set in her ways on how things should be done. Well, I'm going to the house and unload the truck."

"You need help, Clay?"

"I'll be fine, Lorenz. You stay here and keep these two out of trouble."

Clay worked alongside the men for several days. Searching in the rocks, they found puma tracks in the snow and followed them for a ways until satisfied the animal had left the area. Trouble was a Puma could quickly circle around and be right back, so they would have to keep an eye pealed for him. The bear made tracks over a wide area, and they spent a day trying to find him, with no luck.

With Alorenzo taking the lead, Clay followed him as they trailed up the valley for several miles watching for signs of a wolf. Every track they found seemed old. The snow was melting fast, except in the shade. Before long there would be green shoots in the grass.

Wednesday afternoon, Clay packed what gear he wanted to take with him. He and Alorenzo ate dinner, and Clay told him he planned to be away for a few days. Alorenzo nodded. When he was alone, Clay phoned Jennie. He told her how quickly things were changing. That calving would start in a few days, and they were hoping to get the steers moved up to the high country. The two temporary cowboys were back on the payroll. Jennie, as always, chatted happily, listened and questioned him, teased him, and wanted to know if he was coming to visit for her birthday.

When the talking ended, Clay turned out the lights, picked up his bag, and went to the truck to begin the trip west.

Chapter 15

In a dark blue Dodge SUV rented under a different driver's license, this one registered in Virginia, Clay drove out of Portland on his way to Seattle, setting the cruise control at five miles per hour under the speed limit. He was in no hurry. He wanted to be parked with a view of the fish market before dark to witness the arrival of the duffle bag full of money.

A bundle of the *Oregonian* daily newspaper picked off a street corner in Portland at first light this morning sat in the back of the SUV. There would be a number of upset homeowners when they didn't receive their daily paper. He admonished himself for inconveniencing them.

Following Highway I-5 north to the exit for the town of Tukwila, Clay exited and drove to the Hamptons Inn, a mile or so east of the Seattle-Tacoma Airport, where he registered for two nights. Located on the third floor, the room provided an excellent view of the city and the sky. Clay stood at the window watching the sky and wondered if the sun ever shone in Seattle. This was his third trip to the area, and each time the sky was overcast, which seemed to be normal. Today it was raining, not hard but steadily. If the west wind kept blowing off Puget Sound, it would be cold and wet around the fish market tonight. Looking at his digital watch, it showed two o'clock—time to grab a cheeseburger and get going.

Finding the way onto Highway 518, the drive was only a couple of miles west to connect with 509 and a further six miles north to the bridge over the Duwamish Waterway and onto Highway 99. Eight miles later, Bamford parked the SUV at the curb, half a block from the fish market.

With a slouchy, blue rain hat pulled down over his ears, gray tinted sunglasses, which weren't really needed, and wearing a long, gray rain slicker, Clay walked to the fish market to recon the place. To see if everything seemed normal other than fewer shoppers being out in the rain.

Wandering slowly along the aisles inspecting fish, a large tuna caught his eye. While standing there looking at it, a short, little Asian lady hurried up to his side. "You want tuna, mister. Tuna fresh—just come today. Good tuna steak make you wife happy."

"She sent me here to get a salmon to roast in the oven, to feed our guests." Pointing at the tuna, Clay added, "Never seen a fish as large as this one before."

The small lady squinted up at Clay. "This tuna little big. Sometime we have big tuna." She spread her arms as far as she could.

Feigning surprise, Clay inquired, "You get tuna bigger than this one?"

She nodded her head yes. "Salmon over there, mister." She pointed to the next aisle, and his eyes followed where her finger pointed.

"Thank you. I want to look around before buying the salmon."

She persisted. "How much pounds you want. Get for you."

"My wife said fifteen pounds."

"Hokay mister, I have it ready for you. You come there." Again she pointed at the salmon stall.

"Be there in a couple of minutes. Just want to see what else there is." The lady nodded again, and Clay wandered toward the back of the store, stopping here and there to look at seafood, much of which was totally strange to him. After growing up on beef, Clay had no idea what much of it was.

At the end of the aisle where the door to the downstairs room became visible, Clay stopped for a look. Removing his sunglasses, he fished out a tissue and pretended to be cleaning them. He blew on each lens and wiped them carefully with the tissue while his eyes scanned around. The door to the back seemed the same. Looking at the big freezer doors, something new caught Clay's eye. One of the doors had two padlocks on it, the others didn't, and workers were going in and out of the unlocked doors carrying fish and trays of seafood. The locks struck Clay as curious. He couldn't remember seeing locks the last time he visited the market, and he had looked carefully at everything. Returning the tissue to a pocket of his slicker before putting his glasses on, Clay continued across the back of the room and up the last aisle to the salmon counter.

The small lady had a salmon in the concave, metal tray of a hanging weigh scale. Clay glanced at the weight dial; the dial read slightly over seventeen pounds. She watched him. "No find fifteen pound. You like this one?"

Clay looked at the dial again, wondering if this was her variation of putting a thumb on the scale. Most likely the lady intended to up the sale by a small margin. Taking his time to consider, he asked, "What's the price for this one?"

Her answer came quickly. "One dolla, seventy cent, each pound." She punched numbers into a calculator and held it up for Clay to see. "Twenty-eight dolla and ninety cents.'

Clay handed her a twenty and a ten. She put the bills in one pocket of her apron and started taking change from another. Clay smiled. "You keep the change."

The lady smiled and bobbed her head in agreement as she pulled waxed butcher's paper off a role and wrapped the fish. When she handed the fish to Clay, she advised him, "You come, bring wife. Wife shop much."

Walking away, he wondered if the extra dollar and ten cents would go to the store or end up in her pocket. Back at the SUV, Clay unlocked the doors, opened the rear hatch, and put the salmon in. Shrugging out of the raincoat, he spread it over the bundle of newspapers to dry, closed the hatch, and walked around to the driver's door. With the windshield wipers swinging, he drove past the fish market and went several blocks west before turning around to come back.

Parking under the same large tree as the time before and settling in to wait for the money to arrive, he mentally reviewed everything once again. There were two key parts to his plan, which he hoped would cause a war in the gang's drug operation. Tonight was Friday, and he planned to take the money meant to pay for the drug supply coming in Saturday. On Tuesday, the plan was to grab the money coming back to Seattle from sales to Portland and south. Not knowing if people on the ship checked the money upon delivery or transported the chest back to Mexico unopened worried Clay. If they checked immediately, there would be trouble tomorrow; if not, it would take a few days. This operation had been up and running successfully for months now, and with past experience, it seemed reasonable to assume a certain level of trust would be in place. Therefore, he was betting on the money getting checked after it arrived in Mexico.

Consoling himself once again, he sat in the SUV thinking, *'You can only do what you can do, and observe the results.'* Chuckling to himself, he made a correction to his statement. If everything went as expected, it would take a few days before the fireworks started; by then, this cowboy planned to be far from here.

With the car radio turned on, he listened and caught the five-thirty news. This rain was forecast to continue overnight, with the temperature dropping to thirty-nine degrees. Highly unlikely there would be people wandering around in the dark in this weather, taking a walk or whatever they might choose to do.

Within a few minutes of the last time, the white Chevy arrived. The duffle bag disappeared into the back room of the fish market, and darkness descended. When everything closed at eight, all the windows went black as everyone left. The Chevy had left over an hour before. Not many customers came in the rain to purchase seafood, and it surprised him the market hadn't closed earlier.

After waiting for two long hours in the dark, with no activity around the fish market, the time to prepare arrived. Pulling a black wool sweater on for the cold, Clay laced up a pair of dark runners, with hard rubber soles that wouldn't squeak. A fighting knife with its slim, seven-inch, double-edged blade, which tapered to a sharp point, went in a scabbard at the small of his back. The small flashlight worked, and extra batteries were in one pocket of the black canvas jacket. An inside pocket held a leather case containing a set of lock picks. Several sizes of skeleton keys on a ring were in the left side jacket pocket.

Donning a dark baseball cap and the jacket, he checked everything again to make sure nothing was missing. With the bundle of newspapers under one arm and the car locked, he followed the sidewalk down a slight incline to the front door of the fish market. Standing back in the dark door alcove that served as an entrance, he watched and waited several minutes. Satisfied no one was hanging around, he checked the time. It took only seconds to find the right skeleton key to open the door, and once inside, he reset the lock. Using the faint light coming through the windows, Clay walked softly to the top of the stairs and descended into the dark.

Keeping the flashlight partially hooded with one gloved hand to minimize the amount of light, it took several tries with different keys to unlock the door. In the interest of speed, the key stayed in place, hanging from the lock.

A different sea chest from the last time sat right where they had put the other one a month before. After pulling the chest out from under the table and selecting a pick, Clay went to work on the lock. It took longer than expected, and soon his forehead started getting wet with sweat. As the seconds ticked by, the tension built. Finally the lock opened. Trained to always be methodical helped to prevent him from forgetting anything; the case of picks went back in a jacket pocket. He took a second to remove the hat and wipe his forehead with the back of one gloved hand. The two buckles took seconds, and the lid lifted easily. With the flashlight on, he removed the wooden drawer sitting across the top of the chest and checked the stacks of hundred-dollar bills. Pulling a long canvas bag from inside his jacket, Clay transferred the packets of bills from the sea chest into the bag and cinched up the top. Finally he placed the bundle of newspaper in the chest to replace the weight of the money and put the wooden drawer back in. The newspapers seemed heavier to him than the money but not significantly different.

Relocking the chest and sliding it back to exactly where he found it, Clay pushed the light button on his watch. Just over five minutes. Not bad. Quickly shining the flashlight on the floor, everything seemed normal, except for where water had dripped off his jacket. He expected it would dry quickly on the old, well-worn wooden floor.

With the door relocked and the keys back in the left side pocket, he climbed the steps to the main floor. After placing the canvas bag on the wooden floor, he watched out the windows for a moment. The lights of a car passing on the street briefly lit up the front windows before darkness returned. While waiting in the SUV, the locked freezer kept returning to his mind. Why was the door locked when the others weren't? What could be in the freezer with high enough value to require locks? It must be drugs, and a quick look would confirm it. A faint glow from a streetlight came through the windows, enough for Clay to use picks and work on the padlocks. They were brand-new, and each opened on the first try. Grabbing the heavy, cast-iron door latch and pulling, the door swung open easily. It was a thick, heavy, wooden door with serrated edges. It had a round, flat knob attached to a steel rod that ran through the door so it could be opened from the inside; that seemed like a scary idea. Moving a chair into place to keep the door from closing on its own, Clay turned on his small flashlight to have a look around. Three walls of wooden shelves, mostly empty. Along the back wall, there were six leather suitcases stacked on the shelves, each about ten inches thick. The suitcases appeared to be new. Mentally congratulating himself for being right, he pulled out one suitcase and set it on the floor. It wasn't locked, and a clasp at each end held the lid closed. The clasps opened easily, and the lid went up, causing Clay to suck in a large breath at what he saw. It wasn't drugs, as he had so smugly thought. Money, row after row of packets of hundred-dollar bills, each held together with a wide elastic band.

It didn't take much thought on his part. Causing mistrust, anger, and fighting within the gang had been his objective right from the start. Closing the suitcase and putting it under his left arm, he grabbed another for his left hand and went out into the store for the canvas bag. Leaving the front door unlocked, he trotted along the sidewalk to the SUV and deposited everything in the back. Running got him back to the front door in seconds. He moved the last four suitcases to the front door before going back to lock the freezer.

Sweating from all the exertion in a very short time, Clay was feeling hot and thinking, *Shouldn't have worn this heavy sweater.* With the flashlight, a quick check showed the chair and everything else back in their original places and looked normal. The door to the back room had already been locked. Moving the suitcases out into the alcove, Clay carefully relocked the front door before putting the keys away and picking up the cases, one under each arm with one hanging from each hand. Stepping to the edge of the sidewalk, he stood still for several moments to check the darkness; everything was quiet. This time he walked up the slight slope to the SUV.

With the luggage neatly arranged and covered with the rain slicker, Clay got into the car and immediately locked the doors. He decided to sit still and rest while cooling off and to consider the possible consequences of his actions. All this money disappearing should deal a tremendous blow to the gang and cause an explosion locally. When the Mexicans learned they were paid with newspapers instead of money, a second explosion and resulting war should erupt.

The only concern was that the missing money in the sea chest might be discovered before Wednesday. The rest of the plan still involved dealing with the Portland operation, and he had a letter to mail.

Taking off his gloves, he was reassured there were no fingerprints left behind—not that it really mattered; it was highly unlikely the gang would call the police. After starting the Dodge SUV, Clay drove sedately and carefully away, back to the Hamptons.

At one in the morning, sitting cross-legged on the hotel room bed, Clay looked at one packet of bills he had removed from the bag. He started counting, thinking there would be fifty bills— another major wrong, for the second time tonight. There were a hundred one-hundred-dollar bills in the packet.

While counting the packets as they went into the bag and mentally calculating half a million dollars, now the total had doubled. If each of those suitcases contained the same amount, $7 million in cash sat out there in the parking lot along with a seventeen-pound salmon. Damn, something had to be done about the salmon before it started to spoil and smelled up the car.

Lying in bed, Clay reconsidered his plan for Saturday. Should it be changed? No! He wanted to see if the fishing boat came back and everything remained normal. If it did, he would carry on with his plan and stay around for Tuesday. If there was a problem, he would leave for the ranch Saturday night.

Saturday afternoon, the sky cleared. According to radio reports, the temperature came in at fifty-two degrees, which the announcer assured listeners was about normal for March. Late in the afternoon, the fishing boat arrived. It tied up to the dock and unloaded a cargo of six bales, twice as much as last time. Good! Now he would make a round trip to Portland to stow the suitcases in the metal toolbox in the back of the GMC. He wasn't comfortable driving around with so much money in the SUV.

Even though another night at the Hamptons was paid for, all Bamford's gear was packed and ready to go, so the time to leave had arrived. Tonight, he would sleep in Portland.

An SUV wasn't an old car to be parked anywhere near the Asian gang's clubhouse. Late in the afternoon, Clay left the car at the motel where he rented a room. He walked the mile to where the white Chevy was usually parked. Maybe the guy lived here or somewhere nearby; he didn't know and didn't care.

There were few streetlights in this neighborhood, and rarely did anyone go out on the streets after dark. Clay waited in the deep darkness under a large oak tree with wide, spreading branches where no one could see him. His dark clothes made him invisible in the dark of night, especially when he didn't move around. Standing beside the tree trunk allowed him to blend in, appearing as just part of the tree to any casual observer. If the Asian followed his usual pattern, he would park along this street and walk past the oak tree on his way to the clubhouse. Hopefully he would be alone; if he wasn't, so be it.

By his watch it was eight forty-five when car lights came toward him. From behind the tree, he watched as the car pulled to the curb and parked. Both front doors opened. The Rolex-wearing Asian got out of the car along with his driver. He opened the trunk and removed a large, red duffle bag, which appeared to be heavy. They walked toward Clay, talking about the successful day and how pleased Luong would be. The way they were walking, the driver would be closest to the tree. As they came abreast of him, Clay stepped out and, with the butt of his left hand, drove the driver's head sharply up and back. The bones in the driver's neck snapped, making a clear, fairly loud sound. The real enemy started to turn to see what was happening, and Bamford's right knee hit him hard in the groin. As he bent over, the long, thin knife came down inches from the left side of his neck and went in deep. Clay's hand moved the knife to slice toward the man's neck, severing the main arteries and the bundle of nerve fibers controlling the heart. The Asian was dead before he hit the sidewalk. No sound occurred other than the breaking neck bones, which wouldn't be audible even a few feet away.

Leaning down, he cleaned the knife on the Asian's jacket, glanced at the Rolex knowing taking it would be asking for trouble, before he took hold of the heavy duffle bag and walked along the street past the white Chevy. Back at the motel, everything went in the SUV, and Clay drove away, heading for a mailbox a few blocks along the street. Wearing gloves, he removed an envelope from a plastic shopping bag on the passenger seat and dropped the envelope through the mail slot.

The work in Seattle had been completed. All that remained was the drive to Portland. He would return the SUV to the Budget rental agency at the airport and drive east in the truck. He glanced at his watch, which showed nine thirty. He should arrive in Portland just after midnight, followed by a night drive to Pendleton.

* * *

At fifty miles an hour, Clay drove into Pendleton at seven in the morning to register for a room at the Hamptons Inn, using his own name. The lady at the desk asked, "What in the world are you doing coming in this early in the morning?"

Grinning at her, Clay gave her his story. "Came to Pendleton to look at some bulls I might buy for the ranch. Need to do that and get back home by tomorrow."

"Well, you came to the right place. You fool ranchers never seem to know when to slow down. There's always another day coming, you know."

Smiling at her, Clay gently disagreed. "Another day brings its own work, which needs to be done." Pulling out cash from his pocket, he paid with the comment, "Expect I'll be gone afore tomorrow morning."

"You drive tired, you're likely to kill yourself."

Clay walked away, commenting, "Maybe."

In his room, Clay stripped and took a long shower, shaved, and relaxed on the bed. At eight, he called Jennie. "Is this Miss Jeannie Mae Johansson?"

She responded with her happy way of laughing as she replied, "Clay Bamford, you know it's me."

"How are you, honey?"

"I'm fine. Why aren't you out feeding cattle?

"Because I'm in Pendleton."

"What in the world are you doing there?"

"You know the ranch needs to replace bulls on a regular basis, or have you forgotten everything you learned? I know it's a few days early, but if you say it's all right, I'm going to drive to Moscow later today to see you."

"Yes, Clay, come. Oh, what a nice surprise. How long can you stay?"

"This is Wednesday, and if you can stand me, I'll stay until Sunday. Have you found a ring?"

"There are several. They're expensive, and the cost is worrisome. You'll have to look at them."

Clay shrugged happily. "What kind of money are we talking about?"

"It embarrasses me to tell you. The highest priced set is forty-two hundred dollars."

"You go to the store this morning and tell them to size it properly to fit your finger, and we'll be in tomorrow to pay for it."

"Are you sure, Clay?"

"Honey, I told you before I never change my mind, being a stubborn Bamford and all."

"Oh, Clay, thank you. It's so beautiful. I hope you'll be pleased."

"If you like it, I'll like it. What about a wedding dress? Should we go and look at dresses?"

"It would be nice to have your help, even though grooms aren't supposed to see the dress before the wedding."

"Okay, honey, I should be there by dinnertime."

"Good-bye, Clay. I love you."

With that done, Clay pulled the covers up to his chest and prepared to catch some sleep. Just before fading away, a thought came to him. *'Didn't lie to her about being in Pendleton, only avoided her question. Jennie is always running over with questions.'*

Waking at noon and feeling refreshed, he showered and dressed in his normal clothes. At the desk, he paid for the call to Moscow and told the same lady that he would be looking at bulls the rest of the day and didn't expect to be back.

Before leaving Pendleton, Clay gassed up the Dodge GMC and got himself a large cup of coffee and two donuts, covered in chocolate.

* * *

At 7:20 a.m., the duty desk took a call from the 911 operator. "There's an eleven-year-old boy on the phone who's reporting two bodies on the sidewalk. I told him to stay there until the police arrive. Here's the address …"

Moments later, a radio call went to Officer Hoffman. "Hoffman here."

"Ange, dispatch here. We have a report of two dead bodies in your district, one and a half blocks south of the Asian clubhouse."

Angie Hoffman swore before she pushed the button to reply. "On my way. If they're dead, I'm going to need help."

"Right, Ange, will send another car." Hoffman switched on the flashers and stepped on the gas.

Her partner, Ted Hanson, asked, "You want the siren on?"

Angie glanced at him. "If they're dead, there's no sense in waking up everyone in the area." She turned right at the service station, and as the car lights came around, she immediately saw a small figure standing on the sidewalk. As the car pulled alongside, Angie could see two bodies. She told her partner, "Take your shotgun and keep watch while I check these two."

Angie walked to the two bodies and checked each for a pulse and knew they were dead, so she concentrated first on the little boy. "How are you, son?"

His little hand still clutched a cell phone. His voice quavered. "I called 911 like my teacher said. They told me I couldn't turn off my phone, and my battery will die."

Hoffman knelt down beside the boy and put an arm around him. He was shaking. "Everything is all right now, son. Let me have your phone." He handed it to her, and Angie asked, "Nine-one-one, are you there?"

"Yes we are."

"This is Officer Angie Hoffman. I'm going to turn the phone off now."

"Roger, Hoffman."

Angie looked at the boy. "How would you like to sit in my car where it's warm?"

"I'm late for school. My teacher will be angry with me."

"We'll talk to your teacher; everything will be fine. Come along now and warm up. In a few minutes, we'll drive you to school." Settling the boy in the backseat, Hoffman hurried to look at the two bodies. She noted both were Asian. One man's head lay at a crazy angle, and she quickly concluded his neck was broken. Looking the second man over, there was no obvious sign of what caused his death, but she noted a blood smear on his jacket. Angie walked to the car and reached for the radio. "Dispatch, Hoffman here."

"What you got, Ange?"

"Two dead men, both Asian, probably Vietnamese, ages— around twenty. One with a badly broken neck. No sign of violence on the other. This must be another homicide. You better send Brand and Heftner, along with the tech crew."

"Right, Ange. Roberts is right here and is leaving now."

"Thanks, Dispatch." Angie sighed. She took out her notebook and pen and wrote up her observations and conclusions. She got out of the car and moved to the backseat to interview the little boy. Angie was still sitting there when another patrol car pulled in ahead of her car, and a few minutes later, Roberts arrived.

Sergeant Roberts walked around the scene, looking at the two bodies from all angles before going to stand beside Hanson. "Where's Hoffman?"

"She's in the car talking to the little boy who found these men. He was cold and scared."

Roberts leaned down and looked into the backseat. He straightened and asked, "Hoffman checked these men?"

"Yes, sir. She checked for a pulse and left everything as is."

"Good. Homicide is on the way to take charge. You stop anyone coming from this side. I'll get the other officers to look after the rest."

Vehicles started arriving, and quickly the view for anyone going past on the street was blocked. Brand and Heftner came to stand beside Roberts while the techies did their thing. They all turned to look when Hoffman got out of the backseat and came around the rear of her squad car. She walked to Roberts. "Sir, there's a scared, little boy in the car. He's late for school. Do you want to talk to him?"

"You questioned him? You know where he lives?" Hoffman nodded. "I don't need to talk to him."

"Sir, he lives with his grandmother. I'm going to take him to see her before we go to talk to his teacher. Will you come along, sir?"

"Of course, Angie. Brand and Heftner can work without us."

The little boy directed Angie along the street, past the service station for one block, and pointed at a corner grocery. He said proudly, "My gamma's store."

The police car pulled to the curb, facing the wrong direction. Angie got out and held the back door open so the little boy could exit. Angie closed the door and turned to find a small Asian lady standing inside the grocery store door watching. As the boy got out, the store door opened, and Grandma came out. A stream of Vietnamese flew between her and the boy. It seemed obvious to Angie the boy was being upbraided. She rested one hand on his head. That stopped Grandma. Grandma looked at the officers, her face grim, and stated, "What does grandson do? Him good boy, go to school, work hard. Him no make trouble."

Angie smiled, trying to ease her concern. "Yes, he's a good boy."

Grandma seemed to relax somewhat. "You say good boy. Why good boy in policeman car?"

Angie worried the lady wouldn't understand in English, so she knelt down and asked the boy, "Can you explain to your grandmother?" Again the Vietnamese words flew. Angie stood and watched Grandma's face. At first, Grandma seemed relieved. Then Angie was sure she saw fear. She wondered—the police or something else? Angie watched as the boy pointed at her and said something to his grandma.

Grandma's eyes shifted from the boy and stared at Angie. "Grandson say you talk him teacher, him no get school trouble."

Angie smiled again. "Yes, I will explain to his teacher. Is it okay if we take him to school now?"

Grandma looked stern. "Yes, grandson go school, you take. Him very good boy, no makes trouble."

Angie nodded agreement and patted the boy on the head. "Do you want to sit in the front seat with me?" She was rewarded with a happy grin and a nod.

At the school, both officers followed as the boy led them along hallways to his classroom. Sergeant Roberts knocked on the door and watched through the door window as a female teacher came to open it. Roberts asked, "May we come in?"

"Yes, of course, please do. Is there a problem?" She stepped back and waited. Roberts entered, followed by the boy and Angie. The teacher's face tightened up, and she exclaimed, "Tuan, where have you been? You're late. What in the world have you been up to?"

Roberts interrupted her. "I will explain, ma'am, to you and the class. My name is Sergeant Ian Roberts of the Seattle City Police Department, and this is Officer Angie Hoffman. Your student, ma'am, is a very brave boy who provided a great service to this city and the police department. He is a boy all of you should be proud of." Angie observed Tuan straighten his shoulders and stand taller. "This morning on his way to school, he discovered a crime scene and called 911 to report it, using his cell phone. He stayed on the phone and guarded the scene until Officer Hoffman arrived. He is to be commended for his bravery and as a good citizen of this city.

"Thank you, ma'am, for allowing us to interrupt. We are on duty and must return to the crime scene to continue with our work now." Roberts reached out to shake hands with the teacher, turned, and offered his hand to Tuan. "Thank you for being such a great help to us."

Hoffman drove them back to the crime scene. The bodies were being loaded to go to the medical examiner as they arrived. They walked over to stand beside Heftner. Roberts asked, "What do you think happened, Barry?"

"It appears they were ambushed. Come over here and have a look." Heftner led them to the large tree and stopped several feet away. "See how the leaves and grass are trampled down on this side of the tree? It appears someone waited here for quite some time for them to come along. We think it's possible the white car up the street belonged to them. Brand impounded the car so we can have the lab check it for prints."

Heftner turned to a technician. "Bring the bag with the watch in it and show Ian."

Roberts took the bag and held the evidence as he looked at the watch. "Expensive looking watch, Barry."

"That's right, Ian—a Rolex. You remember the Bamford case from last summer?"

"Hell, yes. You think this is the missing Rolex?"

Heftner grinned. "Judge Winehouser told us Bamford's Rolex had a diamond set in one side. Take a look."

Chapter 16

Toward the end of her shift, Constable Angie Hoffman returned to the police station and found an envelope waiting for her. Nothing strange about the envelope; it was the name and address which were strange. It read *Policemans Hoffman* and underneath, *Seattle Police*. The printing appeared to have been done by a small, pinched, and uneven hand. Angie started to pick the envelope up and stopped. She sat looking at the envelope thoughtfully, realizing it bothered her. After hesitating a moment, she put on a pair of gloves and picked up the envelope by the edges. With it in her left hand, she walked along the hallway to the Sergeant Roberts's office and knocked on the frame of the open door. Roberts looked up and beckoned her in. "Sir, this strange-looking envelope came for me. I'm not sure whether I should open it."

Roberts stood up and came around his desk. "Hold it up so I can see."

Hoffman lifted her arm, and Roberts studied the writing, "It does appear to be strange." He paced away a few steps, turned, and came back. "I have a feeling someone is trying to communicate with you. Someone for whom English isn't a first language, or else the person doesn't want to be identified." He rubbed his chin. "Come on, let's take it down to the lab and have them look at it."

As they walked side by side, Roberts asked, "Do you have an informer I don't know about?"

"No, sir."

"Okay, we'll find out what the lab technicians can tell us."

The first thing they learned came after a technician looked at it with a magnifying glass. He told them, "The stamp was cancelled by the Seattle post office, so it was mailed here in the city." He looked up. "We'll check it for prints, but since it's been handled by both the post office and our own mail people, there's a slim chance of learning anything."

Roberts told him, "You may as well open it and see what the contents are. There may be good prints on the paper inside."

The technician picked up a linoleum knife with his gloved hand and carefully slit open the end opposite the stamp. With tweezers, he pulled the sheet of paper out and laid it on the desk, stating, "Just one folded page of lined paper. Looks like it may have come from a kid's school workbook." Touching only the corners, the technician unfolded the paper and turned it so they could all read. It was the same writing as on the envelope.

> *Policemans Hoffman*
> *much hurry*
> *much people di*
> *drugs*
> *careful se all nook*
> *kid club cumputer mail*
> *fish sel mart fisher boat*

Hoffman read it twice, as did the men. She stepped back and looked at Roberts. "*Kid club* could be the Asian Youth Club in my district, and it says to look in every nook, which probably means nook and cranny. I wonder if the youth club owns a computer with an e-mail account."

Roberts muttered, "*Much people di*. Angie, this may be a warning there's a drug war coming. It may tie in with the two men killed this morning."

They stared at each other for moment. "This message must have come from someone who knows you, someone you talked to. Could it be one of the Asian residents of your district?"

Hoffman slowly shook her head. "I don't know, sir. I've talked to a large number of the local people, ever since being assigned to the district. It's been hard to break through the language and cultural barriers." Hoffman shrugged.

Roberts said, "Think about it, Angie. There may be something in your memory, if you can jog it." Roberts turned back to the technician. "We need copies of this message before you check for prints or anything that may give us a clue to the source."

"Half a dozen copies do it?" Roberts nodded yes. "Be right back."

Holding the copies he received in one hand, Roberts reiterated, "Test the message with everything your lab has available. We need any information you can find for us. Come on, Angie, we're going to brief the chief."

An hour later, Chief Otto Kruger assembled Detectives Heftner and Brand along with Roberts, Hoffman, and Hanson. He started the meeting. "The Nark boys will be here in a few minutes. Quickly, guys, bring me up to date. Heftner, Brand, you guys start."

Both held their notebooks open. Heftner talked while looking at his notes. "The two guys found this morning, both Vietnamese, one twenty-one, the other nineteen. The coroner and the lab are doing their thing, and we have to wait for the reports." He looked up. "Chief, those two men died fast and quiet. It looks suspiciously like a professional hit to me. No noise, no clues, nothing for us to go on. Chief, you remember the Bamford case from last year that hit a dead end? Well, it looks like at least one of these guys was linked to the killing of William Bamford."

"How so?"

"You will recall one of the first things Hoffman told us about the Bamford case; *'she reported the man's watch missing.'* Well, we now have a Rolex that fits the description Judge Winehouser gave us. It came off the left wrist of the oldest of these men."

Kruger ran a hand over his hair, thinking. "What would a Rolex like that be worth?"

Brand smiled. "We plan to check on it, Chief. My guess is several thousand dollars, maybe as much as five."

"Hard to understand why the killer didn't take it?"

Heftner replied, "This wasn't a robbery, Chief. The men were executed. The guy did his job and walked away without leaving any sign of who he is. As neat as anything I've ever come across. He may not be physically big, but for damn sure he's strong. That's why we think he's a professional sent in to do a job. We need to figure out why. My bet is we'll never find any sign of who he is or that he ever came to Seattle." Heftner shrugged. "Maybe ex-CIA?"

The silence lasted several moments before Kruger said, "Ian, hand out your copies of the letter and explain the contents to the men." As Roberts stood up, the door opened, and three detectives from the Narcotics Branch came in. Kruger gestured. "Find chairs, guys. We're just getting to your part in this."

Roberts made the rounds, handing out copies of the letter, and returned to his seat. "What I have just given you is a copy of a letter delivered through the US mail this afternoon to Officer Angie Hoffman. We believe it may be from a resident living in her district. Angie received it two hours ago. The original is in the lab for analysis. First thing, Angie believes the words *kid club* may refer to the Asian Youth Club in her area. The line above is probably emphasizing the police should search the club building very carefully. Other than those facts, the word *drugs* is clear, and there seems to be an implication of a drug war. Read the last line. Does it make sense to anyone?"

Kruger waited, watching everyone. A Nark detective looked at Kruger. "Chief, it seems to me the last two lines are four separate items, and line three refers to all of them separately. The last one is probably a fishing boat. The problem is there are hundreds of fishing boats in this area, big and small."

Brand suggested, "Mart may be a store or a supermarket, like a shopping center."

Another detective said, "Turn the words around. What about a store that sells fish?

Kruger parried, "There must be hundreds of grocery stores in the Greater Seattle area selling fish."

The detective came back with, "True, Chief, but what about stores selling only fish?"

Kruger leaned back, looking at the man. "You've got something there. Right after this meeting concludes put together a list of every store specializing in selling fish. Okay, let's talk about drugs." Kruger sighed. "The first half of this letter seems to be all about drugs. Is there anything new going on? Changes out on the street, any problems, fights, anything at all?"

The same detective responded, "My informants tell me there's an endless supply of high-quality cocaine available. None of them seem to know where it comes from. Last week, I talked over the phone to a detective in Portland, and he said the same thing. In fact, he said Portland is being flooded with high-quality cocaine. It gives me the feeling there's a new supplier operating along the West Coast."

Roberts muttered, "Damn druggies. I hope there's a special place in hell for them."

Kruger smiled before asking, "Is there anything else?"

Hoffman suggested. "Sir, this note arriving today may be tied in with the two men murdered last night. The letter is postdated yesterday and arrived today. It's telling us to hurry because something's going to happen. Maybe it's already started."

Kruger frowned. "Angie, are you suggesting those two men were part of a drug ring?"

"Could be, sir. Both are faces I recognize from the street near the club, and this letter implies the club is involved."

Kruger turned to Roberts. "Sarg, do we have enough information to lay a raid on the clubhouse?"

"It's thin, Chief. All we really have is this letter, and we can't be sure it's even referring to that club. On the other hand, if everything being inferred at this meeting is true and something big is coming down, the sooner we hit the place the better. Get there before they move or destroy everything.

"Okay, Ian, I'll talk to the DA and ask for a search warrant. The murders are probably on the six o'clock news right now and will ruffle feathers up above. You make a plan, figure out who and what you need to hit the place and the timing. The rest of you stay on this. Put together everything you can, fast. Hoffman, you and Hanson step up your patrols; show people in the area the police are present."

Chapter 17

Jennie Mae Johansson stood inside the front door of the apartment building waiting when Clay's GMC truck drove up, her face radiating happiness, fighting to hold back her tears. How long it had been—yes, six weeks since his last visit. She watched him get out of the truck and put on his Stetson, lock the door, and walk around the front of the truck to the passenger side. He removed his leather travel bag and a large, plastic shopping bag, locked the door, and came toward her. When he saw her waiting, his face broke into a huge grin. She opened the glass door and held it for him before letting it swing closed.

Clay put down his luggage and looked at her. Jennie smiled. "Are you going to kiss me?" Jennie thought she'd be crushed as he grabbed her tight, her breasts firmly against his chest. Never before had their bodies been this close together. Clay kissed her, and Jennie's heart raced wildly as she thought, *'Oh my, what have I done? Was I too forward? Clay hasn't even said hello.'* Clay kissed her again, and Jennie clung to him. She didn't know how many minutes went by or how many times they kissed, until at last, she put her hands on his chest and gently pushed away. Clay slowly, reluctantly let her go. "I'm so happy to see you. It's been a long time since you were here. How are you?"

"I've missed you, girl. It's nice talking to you on the phone, but holding you close is much better."

Jennie blushed, still aware of how close they had been. She tried to calm herself. "Have you eaten, Clay?"

"Not since noon. Do you want to go out somewhere?"

Clay still stared at her, and Jennie hurriedly said, "That would be nice," thinking maybe this wasn't a good time to stay in the apartment. Going out to eat would allow both of them to cool down. They climbed the stairs to the apartment, and Clay put his gear against the wall. Jennie got a winter jacket to wear and led the way to her car, which was more maneuverable and easier to park than the GMC. Jennie drove while being acutely aware Clay had only said a few words.

He surprised her by asking, "Do we have time to go by the store and see your ring?"

Jennie felt her concern drain away. "The store should still be open. Let's do that." She speeded up and luckily found a parking spot right in front of the store. Jennie walked through the door, with her big cowboy behind her, heading straight to the glass cabinet where the ring belonged. It wasn't there. A voice asked, "Are you looking for your ring, Miss Johansson?

"Yes, I am. My future husband wants to have a look at the rings." Jennie linked her arm with Clay's. "Mr. Snowdun, this is my husband-to-be, Mr. Clayton Bamford."

"It's a great pleasure to meet you, Mr. Bamford. Miss Johansson possesses a very discerning eye when it comes to jewelry. Just give me a moment to get the rings." Clay idly looked at the showcases, and in a minute the jeweler hurried back. "May I inform you, Miss Johansson, that the ring is now properly sized to fit your finger? Please try it on." Snowdun opened the velvet case, and Jennie reached for the engagement ring, slid in on, and held her hand out so Clay could look at it closely.

Clay wondered how many carats in size it was but refrained from asking. Instead, he moved the ring on Jennie's finger. "How does it feel?"

Jennie smiled happily. "Just right. It was only slightly too large in any case."

Clay looked at Jennie's happy face before checking the ring again. His hand disappeared inside his jacket and came out holding a large leather wallet. Looking at Snowdun, he inquired, "How much do we owe you?"

The question surprised Snowdun. Young Miss Johansson chose the rings carefully, inspecting them thoroughly under his jeweler's light, and she hadn't told Mr. Bamford the price. He opened the case again and retrieved the small, white price tag. "The price on this set of rings is $4,170."

Jennie took her eyes off the engagement ring and watched as Clay counted out forty-two hundred-dollar bills. Both she and Snowdun observed a substantial number of bills remaining in the wallet.

Clay didn't notice them looking; he was remembering the clerk in Lewiston. Clay had explained what he wanted, and the clerk searched for a wallet large enough to accommodate his request. When he filled the wallet with bills, the clerk's eyes grew large. Clay explained that, as a cattle buyer, most ranchers he dealt with wanted cash when they sold a herd, which necessitated him carrying large sums of money.

Jennie touched his arm as Clay put the wallet away. He looked at her, and Jennie's eyes were damp and glistening in the light. He didn't understand. "What's wrong, Jennie?"

"Nothing's wrong, Clay. I'm just so happy, I can't help it. You'll have to get used to my silly ways." Clay put his arm around her shoulders and squeezed.

Snowdun checked the wedding ring and closed the velvet case, commenting, "I will just wrap this case for you, Miss Johansson. Only be a minute."

Jennie suggested they eat Italian food, and Clay agreed. They ate and talked. Jennie kept looking at her finger, and Clay enjoyed watching her. Returning to the apartment, Jennie was her normal, talkative self, every bit a lady. It gave Clay a happy feeling just listening to her. Finally she asked, "Would you mind if I called Mother? I can't wait to tell her about this ring." Clay nodded his agreement.

Hilda answered the phone, and Jennie was bubbling with happiness. "Mother, you won't believe the beautiful ring Clay gave me. I wish you could be here to see it. After we got the ring, we went to an Italian restaurant and ate a great meal. Of course, I did most of the talking. Poor Clay, he's going to get tired of me and all the noise I make. How is Dad?"

"My goodness, Jennie, you must learn to talk one sentence at a time. I can't even remember everything you said."

"I'm sorry, Mom. Clay gave me a ring, and I can't stop looking at it."

"Is Clay there?"

"Yes, he is. He got here just before the stores closed."

"You tell him all the invitations went in the mail three days ago. What are you going to do about a dress?"

"Clay is going with me to shop for a dress."

"A white one, I hope."

"Yes, Mother. Nothing is changed, and it won't."

"I'm only teasing, Jennie Mae. This past month, I've come to know Clay much better. You're a very lucky lady."

"Thank you, Mom. Say hello to Dad. Good-bye."

Jennie came to sit beside Clay and snuggled up to him with her head resting on his shoulder. Clay told her, "After we're married, you should have a more reliable vehicle. Is it all right if I buy an SUV for you?"

"Clay, you must stop spoiling me. Are you sure the ranch can afford a new vehicle?"

"Well, I don't know for sure. We may have to sell off the herd to pay for it!" Jennie elbowed him in the ribs, and they laughed together.

At bedtime, Clay took a brand-new blanket out of the shopping bag and said, "I forgot my bedroll."

When Clay left for home on Sunday morning, Jennie's wedding dress was paid for and was being modified to fit her. She argued with him, saying it wasn't right for him to be paying. Clay actually laughed at her. "Woman, we're almost married, and from now on we share everything—at least for the next fifty years."

* * *

For two days, the surveillance team assigned by Roberts watched the clubhouse from a vacant building across the street, photographing everyone who approached the building. They tapped the phone line, and tonight two men would enter the building to place radio transmitter bugs. Friday afternoon, a Vietnamese man left the building and got into a white Chevy. By radio, the team alerted two ghost cars to follow the Chevy.

The ghost cars followed the Chevy to the fish market on the east side of Elliot Bay. Everything, along with the presence of a commercial fishing boat, went into a report to Roberts, and another surveillance team was quickly organized.

Friday, Brand and Heftner sat through yet another detailed autopsy done on the two murder victims. At the beginning, they were told both men had been in good physical health. The one with the broken neck died in seconds from major trauma, suffered from a forceful blow to the lower jaw that lifted his head and forced it back to an extreme angle, shattering the neck vertebra and severing his spinal column.

The second man died after being stabbed with a thin, very sharp knife that penetrated downward between the neck and the sternum, slicing the arteries and the nerves running from the brain to the heart. The result was instant death, with very little bleeding, because the heart stopped immediately. Dr. Keith

Herman looked over his glasses at the detectives. "Any questions I can answer for you?"

Brand asked, "Have you ever seen injuries like these before?"

The good doctor smiled. "I was expecting you to ask that. I've seen neck injuries similar to this one, although not near as damaging. It's conjecture on my part, but I suggest a very strong, well-trained man applied very considerable force, probably with the butt of his hand, and followed through until the vertebra shattered. Obviously it all happened very rapidly. Never have I seen a stab wound like the one on the second man, but obviously any medical doctor would understand the consequences of such an occurrence. Consequently, I did a little research. This was a tactic taught to and used by British Army commandos against German forces during the Second World War. It's a very effective, silent technique for dispatching sentries or others of a like nature."

"Doctor, are you suggesting that a commando from the 1940s is responsible for this?"

Herman laughed. "Hardly, Detective Brand. Any man from those days would be rather elderly now. It may be something the British Army still teaches their men, and not all men stay in the army until retirement. Who can know where they end up subsequently?"

"Thank you, Doctor. As always, you have expanded our knowledge while giving us much needed information."

Brand and Heftner left muttering to each other. "Ex-CIA, military training, British commandos. Heft, do you think someone would send a hit man all the way from England?"

"Anything is possible, Justin. Maybe an ex-commando is working in the United States. A damn good cover if you ask me."

A few steps later, Brand suddenly stopped and stood still. Heftner waited. "Heft, didn't Winehouser tell us Will Bamford's son served in the US Army?"

"He did, and we can certainly check our notes. Are you suggesting the kid came out here from Idaho and killed these guys? Hell, Justin, we've worked our butts off and never came close to finding these guys. There's no way he could have found them. This whole thing must be related to drugs."

"Yeah, you're most likely right." Brand didn't sound convinced.

At the fish market, the surveillance team watched a large number of people coming to shop. Saturday morning, the boat crew began preparing to go to sea. Several Styrofoam coolers were loaded, followed by fishing rods, rain gear, and five people, including one woman who appeared to be day fisherman. Again cars came and went in a steady stream as people shopped for fish and seafood. Midafternoon, the boat returned and unloaded its passengers. They stood around watching as two crewmen cleaned salmon at a table where running water washed all the fish waste into the bay. Hordes of seagulls swarmed around, swooping and diving in a fight over the discarded fish parts. Sunday, the surveillance was called off.

* * *

Monday, they planned to start moving the steer herd up country to higher pastures where the rich grass would fatten the animals. By fall, each steer would average around seven hundred pounds and would be ready for sale to a feedlot. Clay discussed the move with the hands and Peggy, who always rode a horse, helping herd the animals. Everyone spent the afternoon checking gear and inspecting riding stock. As they worked, he took a ribbing from the men about his spending so much time in town, fussing over the wedding. He grinned at the jokes and answered questions.

Peggy asked how Jennie was doing. Clay hung the rope he had coiled on a post and considered how to answer. "Guess it's been hard on her. She's so far away and is doing everything over the phone. She and her mom have argued over details. Hilda has strong opinions on everything, but Jennie can be tough when her mind is made up."

"Has she bought a dress?"

"She has, and it's being restitched, or whatever you ladies call that, so it will fit properly. Jennie says it will be ready in a week or two."

The men were all listening. Shoshone Mike said, "Hey, Peg, if the dress is ready in a week, we should move the wedding ahead. Can't wait to have someone around here that knows cattle."

Peggy pretended to be angry. "Be quiet, Mike. Jennie needs to finish her schooling. You know nothin' about weddings. You rushed me off to the courthouse to get wed."

Mike scratched his head and gave Peggy a sly look. "Couldn't wait to get you into bed. You were a mighty handsome woman them days."

Peggy smiled. "Keep talking that way and you'll spend the rest of your years sleeping on the floor."

Mike grinned. "See what's comin' your way, Clay? These gals are all sugary and nice until you marry them. Afterward, they ain't the same no more."

"Clay, don't you listen to this no-account. Jennie is a fine girl, and I'm looking forward to her being on the ranch."

"Thank you, Peggy. Mike's problem is he's been lying around all winter. Some of the fat he put on must have settled in his head." Everyone roared with laughter at Mike's expense.

Sunday evening, Clay checked the Seattle Police computer. He intended to be out on the range for several days moving steers and wouldn't get another chance until he came back. Daily reports on surveillance of the gang's clubhouse were being posted, including transcripts of conversations from both phone taps and bugs. Clay immediately thought, *'I hope they got court approval for the recordings so they can be used in court.'* He reread the report on the killing of the two men. Detective Heftner suggested a professional hit man might be responsible, and Brand entered a comment speculating the hit man could be ex-military, and this needed to be checked. This comment gave Clay pause; it hit close to the truth.

Clay carefully reviewed everything from his recent foray to Seattle. He had been extremely careful, using his years of training and experience, and felt sure there was nothing that could be traced back to him. One possible error might have been taking the truck to Portland. At no time did he drive or park the truck anywhere where the license plate could be recorded on surveillance cameras. The only possible danger might be someone who noticed the plate and would remember the number. Dumb things like that did happen. Common sense said his being in Portland, even if discovered, didn't link him to Seattle. He mused about the philosophy of the situation, well aware that doubt, fear of discovery, or guilt often led normal people to react in ways that gave them away. Well, he felt no doubt or guilt. In the encounter with the street toughs, his actions were only to put them out of commission, not kill them. They got what they deserved. As for the Asians, they received fair retribution for their actions, and the companion should have picked a better class of people to associate with.

Growing up here on the ranch, it was engrained in him that Bamfords looked after other Bamfords and everything that belonged to them. It was a long family tradition that went all the way back to Old Bob Bamford. While he was growing up, Clay heard many stories of how thieves and criminals were handled. The ranch took care of its own affairs, and cattle rustlers who were caught were shot or hung. After all, in those days it was a long trip from the ranch to a courthouse, and no one was inclined to waste time when it was obvious the person was guilty. You had to be tough, living so far from help, and it wasn't just with thieves; there were broken bones, sicknesses, and body damage done by the cattle, and from time to time, someone came down with a serious cold. The only medicines they had were aspirin and Jack Daniels or whatever the people could make up at home. Clay had absorbed the family credo and accepted it as being right as long as you were fair.

Clay mused about it being a necessity of life far out here in the mountains, which time had outdated now, with good roads and all. Still his army training taught a similar approach, and the actions he became involved in only reinforced his beliefs. At the same time, Clay believed in helping his neighbors and cared for all the people who worked on the ranch. He didn't see anything wrong with it. There were a lot fewer problems in the past when more people around the area were like his family. Fair, honest, and tougher than an old, sundried boot.

Now Will Bamford could sleep in peace, knowing justice had been done.

Chapter 18

Detective Brand phoned and made an appointment to meet with Judge Winehouser. He took the Rolex along. When they were seated in Winehousers office, Brand placed the watch on the judge's desk. "Please inspect this watch and tell me if you can identify it."

Winehouser took his time. He looked carefully at the watch, turning it around and over to see every part of it. When he looked up, he spoke quietly but firmly. "All I can tell you is this watch appears to be identical to the one Will Bamford wore."

"Thank you, Judge." Winehouser pushed the watch across his desk so Brand could put it back in the evidence bag.

"Have you found Will's murderer?"

"The man wearing this watch got himself killed half a block away from where we found William and Mary Bamford."

"I see. So you have found the murderer."

"We believe so, Judge. To be honest, there's no way to prove it with what we know today. Does the family want this Rolex back when it's released?"

"We will phone our nephew tonight and ask him. Oh! We may not be able to reach him. Clay phoned his aunt a few days ago to tell us he's getting married. He also mentioned they would be starting to move cattle to the summer range, and he and all the hands would be away from the home ranch for ten days or so. Clay may still be out in the mountains. In any case, we'll try tonight.

"Frankly, Brand, when we talk to him, I won't surprise me if he says no. Clay didn't want the motor home back. Said it would be a bad memory for him. His aunt and I are very pleased to learn he's going to be married. It's lonely living out there so far from people, and that big ranch keeps him tied down. They have some five thousand head of cattle to care for; it's a large operation. Accept my apology for rambling on like that, Justin; we've both been worried about Clay."

"Apologizing isn't necessary. Is the lady someone he met in the army?"

"Not at all. She's a local girl, a few years younger than Clay. They've known each other for years. She's working on a graduate degree at the University of Idaho."

"Thank you, Judge." Brand stood up. "I won't take any more of your time."

Sergeant Ian Roberts walked into the chief's office. "We just received a report of two more beheadings."

Chief Kruger leaned back in his chair. "Are they druggies, Ian?"

Roberts shrugged. "One of them for sure worked as a street pusher in the downtown area. We have nothing on the other man yet."

"It adds up to four men dead in two weeks, Ian." Kruger's chair came forward, and his hands went on the desk. "Do you think there's a war going on?"

"I don't know, Otto. The letter Angie received said many people would die."

Chief Kruger scowled. "Roberts, I think it's time we laid a raid at the clubhouse and the fish market out on Elliot Bay. Set up a meeting this morning to review all the facts. I want everyone there."

Kruger didn't want to raid the fish market with it full of innocent customers, so the raids were scheduled for nine o'clock Tuesday morning. Two separate operations.

Right on the nine o'clock schedule Roberts walked to the front door of the club house with two men who were equipped to break the lock. He turned the doorknob, and to his surprise, the door opened. Roberts held the door as his men rushed in. Three young Asian men were having a great time playing a game of pool on a table in the large central room which occupied most of the ground floor. Half of Roberts's team was assigned to this floor. They quickly cuffed the three men, patted them down—finding no weapons—and told them to sit against the wall. Hoffman took on responsibility for guarding them. Roberts pointed at the three doors in the back wall. Two men opened each door to check the rooms. One was a utility room containing a furnace, utility meters, cleaning supplies, and a few boxes of junk. The middle room seemed to be used for storage of tables, chairs, old blinds, and such. A large bank vault attracted immediate interest, and Roberts was requested to come and take a look. Roberts donned a pair of gloves and tried the handle. The door was locked. He turned and walked to Hoffman's three prisoners and asked, "Who knows the combination to the vault?" He received blank stares. Abruptly and without hesitation, he backhanded the nearest man on the cheek. "Don't give me that shit and stop wasting my time. Who has the combination?"

The frightened man stammered, "Luong is the man who knows the lock."

Roberts glared. "Where can we find this Luong?"

"Me not know." Roberts raised his gloved fist. "Luong not here. Him not here two days now."

Without taking his eyes off the men, Roberts instructed an officer, "Find the technicians and tell them to bring in a locksmith immediately to open the vault."

The third room proved to be a narrow hallway leading to a back entrance located on the alley. There were antique coat hooks along one wall, a pair of well-used shoes, and a worn wooden floor leading to the back door.

Roberts went up the creaking wooden steps to the top floor. The team had already finished inspecting the rooms and reported, "No one here. There are two rooms at the front with beds and not much else. This large room here is an office. At the back, there are four rooms that were probably offices at one time. Now they're full of boxes and junk. It'll take time to sort through it all."

"Okay, get men started going through everything. Show me the office?" Two things immediately interested Roberts, a computer in one corner on a small table and the desk. He pointed. "Get the techies up here to remove the computer for analysis. What's in the desk?"

A rookie officer answered, "The drawers are locked."

Roberts frowned. "Open the damn thing. When we leave here, every nook and cranny will have been inspected, just like the letter Hoffman received told us. Take the drawers out and put all the contents on top of the desk so the technicians get a good look at all of it."

Now with the building secured, men were assigned to inspect each room, inch by inch—floors, walls, ceilings, contents, nothing to be overlooked for any reason. Roberts ordered the sniffer dogs brought in.

A police patrol boat arrived first to block the wharf at the fish market. Uniformed officers jumped from the deck to the wharf. Two ran to the back doors of the warehouse and flung them open while two took charge of the fishing boat and its crew. Inspector Reeser, followed by eight officers, entered through the street door and spread out. Two men and six women worked busily sorting fish and arranging merchandize for the usual ten o'clock opening. Reeser asked, "Who's in charge here?" No one answered, but he saw several women look toward one of the men. Reeser walked to him, glowering. "Are you the manager?"

The Asian man bowed slightly. "Yes, me manager. What do police want?"

Reeser pointed at what appeared to be an office. "Take all your people in there and stay there. Move. Now." One of Reeser's men hurried into the cubbyhole of an office, which contained only a desk, chair, and filing cabinets. The officer unplugged the phone and took it with him as the people crowded in. He took up a position outside the door to stand as a guard on the group.

Reeser looked around. "Open those freezer doors." One freezer was full of packages of frozen seafood, shrimp, scallops, fish filets, and on and on. The second freezer worked as a cooler to store a great variety of fish. An officer approached Reeser and pointed. "The freezer over there on the far end has two padlocks on the door."

Reeser scowled. "Locked! Now that's interesting. Call in a technician with a bolt cutter and open it." Reeser went to look, wondering, *'What kinds of fish are so valuable they need to be stored under lock?'* His anticipation soared, expecting a major discovery.

When the technician arrived, Reeser said, "This door has to be checked for prints. Can you open it without disturbing those?"

After looking at the door handle, the technician replied, "Yes, sir. It will be necessary to make sure none of the men touch the door after I open it."

"Go ahead." An officer came up the steps from the back door. He stopped when his head cleared the floor. "Inspector, we have drugs."

Reeser's face lit up. "Do you have everything secured?"

"Yes, sir. There were two men in the place. We have them cuffed and lying on the floor. Should I call in the lab boys now?"

"Absolutely, and make sure they take pictures of everything first. See if the Nark detectives are outside and get them in. They can start by questioning those two men."

Reeser paced to the wall and came back, thinking about how good he was going to look in the reports. The technician opened the first padlock with a set of picks and removed the lock with a gloved hand. A minute later, the second lock came off. Using a bar as a lever, he pried the ten-inch cast-iron handle out. The door swung open.

With great anticipation, Reeser went into the freezer to look, expecting to find drugs. He muttered, "Shelves—nothing but shelves. The damn freezer is empty." He turned to an officer, disappointment obvious on his face. "Get a crew in here to check for prints and traces of drugs. This door wasn't kept locked without a reason."

Reeser walked away and followed behind the men going down the stairs.

When the vault door opened, Roberts and the locksmith brought in to help needed a minute to accept what they were seeing. Stack after stack of hundred-dollar bills. Roberts took one step inside and surveyed the huge amount of money. Turning to leave, he commented, "Must be millions of dollars in here." Roberts asked the locksmith, "Do you have the combination written down?"

"Right here in my notebook."

"Good! Now close the door and lock it. Stay here until the financial types arrive from the head office to take charge of all this money." Roberts went out to his car, radioed the station, and asked for a connection to the chief so he could file a verbal report.

Both the mayor of Seattle and the district attorney pressured Chief Kruger to arrange a press conference. Both men saw a great opportunity to gain publicity and advance their political careers. Reluctantly, Kruger finally agreed. When the media gathered, both men made speeches taking credit for the success achieved in fighting crime in Seattle. On a long, well-lit table, the police displayed plastic bags of cocaine, stacks of money, and dozens of photos taken at the Asian clubhouse and the fish market before the police moved in. Officers at the tables explained and answered questions for everyone who showed interest. Kruger remained adamant nothing would be said concerning the computer, records, and files being examined in the labs, in order to protect any information being recovered. He already knew from preliminary reports this investigation would spread to other cities and jurisdictions. The FBI would become involved because of the movement of drugs across state borders, which automatically made it a federal case. He couldn't hold off much longer in notifying the FBI, who would demand control of all the records. Kruger wanted his people to extract any information useful to the Seattle police before the files were handed over.

News stories covering the discovery of a major drug ring by the Seattle police made news in all the national media.

Out on the ranch moving cattle, Clay was far from any news source and unaware of the results achieved by the letter sent to Officer Hoffman.

* * *

Judge Winehouser phoned Brand to explain they had called the ranch each evening for three days, and still there was no answer. Brand and Heftner believed they were looking for someone with military training. The only one remotely connected to the case who fit was Clayton Bamford. They went to Chief Kruger and explained their reasoning and requested permission to fly to Boise, Idaho, rent a car, and drive to Challis to investigate. Kruger considered it a ridiculous idea but was somewhat amused. "You two want to go on a fishing trip. Is this trip necessary or are you really after trout? I've heard the fishing is real good in Idaho."

Heftner replied, keeping his face serious, "Sir, we have very little to go on in this case, except for two facts. First, everything points to a professional hit man. Secondly, according to Doctor Herman, the way the men were killed appeared to be the result of military training, possibly the British Army. We requested access to the army's personnel file on Clayton Bamford's training and were flatly rejected. Their reply never changed: 'The file is classified.' Each time we repeated the question coming from a different angle, they gave the same answer."

Kruger considered this for a moment. "What this tells us is Bamford received some very special training, new tactics, or something else the military is not going to disclose. Look, I understand your frustration. Simply put, you don't have enough to go on to justify this police department getting into a fight with the U. S. Army over a file. What do you expect to learn in Idaho?"

"We don't know, sir. Judge Winehouser has tried to contact his nephew repeatedly, and there's no answer. The judge thinks it's rather normal because of the time of year. He says everybody on the ranch is busy moving cattle. Just suppose it's something else? It's a thin lead, but it's also the only one we have."

The fingers of Kruger's left hand repeatedly tapped the desktop while he stared at the men. "Okay, I'll approve your trip. One condition—you fly out on Sunday using your own time, take your look around, and get your butts back here. Is that clear?"

"Yes, sir, thank you."

Kruger waved a hand. "Get out of my office before I come to my senses."

Chapter 19

Odleson walked out of his office after hearing someone ask the receptionist if the sheriff was in. Odleson quickly appraised the two men, one standing in front of the reception desk, and the other several paces away and slightly turned toward the sheriff's office. The second one spotted Odleson immediately. Odleson quickly noted both men looked to be fortyish, wearing suits that were somewhat wrinkled. No one around here wore a suit except to go to church, funerals, and such, so these two had to be city men. The receptionist told them, "I'm sorry. This is Monday, the sheriff's day off. Is there anything I can help you with?"

Odleson interrupted, "It is okay, Shelly. Good morning. I'm Sheriff Tom Odleson. Is there something I can do for you?"

Both men squared around, looking at him with hard, inquisitive eyes. The closest man asked, "Can we talk to you for a few minutes, Sheriff?"

"Certainly, please come and sit in my office. Would you like coffee?" Both shook their heads no, so Odleson turned and walked back to his office and around the desk. The men laid business cards on the desk, and Odleson picked them up before sitting down. "Grab a chair, fellas." Tom took time to study the cards. Then he lined them up on the desk and stated, "You gentlemen are a long way from home. What brought you to our mountains?"

Brand replied, "Last summer, two people from this area, named Bamford, died in Seattle. It was a clear case of murder and robbery. The case was given to us to investigate, and we're still working on it."

Heftner removed a plastic bag from his coat pocket and laid it on the desk. "Have you ever seen this watch before?"

Odleson picked it up, removed the watch, and examined it closely. When he looked up, his eyes were noncommittal. "Over the years, I've only seen one Rolex watch. Will Bamford wore one his son Clay gave him."

Heftner questioned, "Is this the same watch?"

Odleson shrugged. "Can't rightly say. Looks about the same to me." Heftner sensed the sheriff was reluctant, possibly didn't trust them. Confirmation came a minute later when Sheriff Odleson said, "Talked to some fella from your police force last summer, don't remember ..."

Brand said, "Sergeant Ian Roberts called you."

"Yes it was." Odleson smiled. "Couldn't rightly recall the name." Both detectives knew they had just been tested. They watched the sheriff relax and become friendlier. "The only person I know who might identify this watch for you is Clay Bamford."

Brand jumped on the opening the sheriff gave them. "Can you tell us where to find Bamford?"

"Thirty odd miles out to the ranch." Odleson paused. "Good chance you might not get there on your own, so I better drive you. This is always a busy time of the year for all the local ranchers. At the 2B, they'll be moving cattle to summer pasture and settling them in."

Heftner inquired, "What's the 2B?"

Odleson smiled. "Old Bob Bamford came in and started the ranch back in the 1850s during the gold rush days. Two-B stands for his initials." Odleson stood up. "If you want to go to the ranch, we might as well get things underway."

Brand said, "Why don't you ride with us, Sheriff."

Odleson nodded his head in agreement and told Shelly as he left, "I'm going to show these gentlemen around. See you in the morning."

The car started moving, and Odleson suggested, "Take the next left. We might as well stop by the store in case Clay happens to be in town."

Lars Johansson looked up from his seat at the counter when the front door opened. He watched Odleson and two strange men approach before saying, "Morning, Tom."

"Howdy, Lars. Clay doesn't happen to be around?"

"Hell no! Clay spent most of the last month or so in here taking orders from Hilda over the wedding." Hilda walked up behind Lars. "Now Clay's busy out at the ranch with spring arriving. Expect he's having second thoughts about the wedding with the mother-in-law he's going to get."

Hilda stopped a few feet behind Lars and stood with her hands on her hips. Odleson grinned. "Reckon so, Lars. I recall coming in here one day, and Hilda had Clay chained to a table writing on envelopes. Long days on the ranch will seem like holidays to him."

"Tom, don't you believe anything this old coot tells you. It's getting so he lies most of the time." Lars grinned at the sound of Hilda's voice. "Clay and I are getting along just fine. You have two sons, Tom, while we only have Jennie Mae. Daughters are special, you know, and it always worried me where she would find a man good enough for her. Well, no way she could ever do better than Clay."

"How's Jennie doing with her studies, Hilda?"

"She's happier than a robin in springtime. You know Clay, how strong and direct he is. Well, Jennie Mae told us about their engagement. A month ago Wednesday, Jennie Mae phoned so happy I could see her smile all the way up the phone line. Clay was there visiting her, and she had her ring. Clay stayed until the weekend, which bothered me no end; a single lady shouldn't have a man staying overnight. Jennie Mae assured me Clay brought his bedroll and would sleep on the living room floor."

Odleson nodded in agreement. "You should never worry about Clay. He's just like Will was—fair but tougher than hell on men, and very shy and respectful with ladies. Lars, has Clay been in the store lately?"

"He was here Friday morning right after we opened. He filled his pickup with supplies for the line camps and hurried to get back to the ranch. While I put together his list of items, he looked around over in dry goods. Turns out he wanted to get something nice for Peggy. Clay said without Will, they're a man short on the ranch, and Peggy has been wearing out two horses a day chasing steers." Lars laughed. "Clay said if he had two Peggy's on the ranch, he wouldn't have to do a thing himself."

"Thanks, Lars. Peggy has always had a reputation as a worker. I'm going to drive out to see Clay. You got anything you need to send out?"

"Nothing, Tom."

Odleson lifted one hand and turned away.

Odleson sat in the front seat with Brand, who did the driving. Heftner asked from the backseat, "Who's this Peggy they were telling you about?"

"Peggy's married to Shoshone Mike, who's fourth generation on the ranch. She's the type who never sits still when there's some kind of work needing to be done."

Odleson answered questions about the area and the history as they traveled along first the highway and then the county road. As they neared the ranch turnoff, he said, "See those tall gate posts up ahead? That's where the ranch starts. Turn in there." Brand turned the car and drove slowly along the three-mile ranch road leading to the headquarter site of the 2B Ranch. They were passing black Angus cows, grazing behind tight barbed-wire fences, although none of this seemed of interest or to mean anything to the city men.

For Odleson, whenever he visited, everything he saw brought back memories of when, as a teenager, he worked on the ranch during summer vacations to earn spending money. While working, he also learned how tough, honest, hardworking ranchers and cowhands lived, partied, and treated their neighbors.

Odleson carried an unhappy feeling about this visit to the ranch; still his responsibilities included cooperating with the big-city detectives. People on this ranch were known to him, some of them for most of his fifty-three years. Many times over the past years, Odleson had come here, and he had an open invitation to stop for dinner whenever his duties brought him this way. An invitation he often happily took advantage of. Clay ran the ranch alone now, except for the hired hands, and he wasn't inclined to talk more than necessary. Clay and Odleson's second son were the same age, and the boys were in the same grade all through school.

They drove into the ranch yard, and everything stood empty and quiet. Clay's nine-year-old GMC half ton sat parked in the open-fronted machine shed, alongside tractors and a grain truck. There were horses standing around in the corral, and the windmill blades turned lazily in the midday breeze. Stepping out of the car, Odleson called, "Hello! Anyone home?" His voice echoed back from the buildings. The large ranch house had an addition under construction, although no one seemed to be working so far today. Strung out in a line with the main house was a row of small houses with either one or two bedrooms. They were used as living quarters for the hired hands. Tom lived in similar accommodations during the summers while working for Will Bamford. Looking around, Tom noticed most of the older buildings had been replaced.

Odleson called out again. There was no sign of activity anywhere he could see. He decided to walk across the yard to look for anyone who might be in the barn, or maybe out behind it where they couldn't hear him. He remembered well how work was never done on a ranch, especially one with a cattle herd as large as the 2B had.

Looking around with interest, Odleson crossed the ranch yard. The Bamfords always kept everything in top-notch condition, and it pleased Odleson to see nothing had changed since Clay's parents had been murdered. Some of the buildings were recently painted, so Clay continued a pattern established by his grandparents and parents. Tom would have been surprised at anything else.

Both detectives followed him across the ranch yard as he went to the corral gate to check the ground. There were recent horse tracks in the damp soil near the watering trough, so people were around. The large double doors on the barn were rolled back. When Odleson walked through the wide doorway, he found the barn empty. Odleson led the city men through the long barn and out the back door to a spot where they could see a series of pens, corrals, and chutes where the cattle were worked and their health problems or injuries treated. After a good look around, he turned to the detectives. "There are fresh tracks, so Clay is around, but everyone must be out on the range right now. We'll have to wait for a while to see if he comes back. If they're busy, it may be dark before they quit for the day. We may as well go up to house, and I'll rustle up some coffee for us."

Odleson pushed the doorbell button, and after no one answered, he rapped loudly on the door before opening it and leading the way into the large mudroom where everyone removed dirty clothes and boots. It was a Mary Bamford rule, made years before, which she strictly enforced. No dirty clothes or footwear ever allowed in the rest of the house. All the ranch hands obeyed, although Odleson recalled Will mildly complaining about it, all the while following his wife's wishes.

The inside walls of the room were lined with hooks for clothing, and a wide assortment of jackets, coats, coveralls, and Stetsons hung from them. Several pairs of well-used boots, both high-heeled riding boots and flat-heeled walking boots, lined one wall. This was of immediate interest to the Seattle men. Heftner said, "Sheriff, there sure are a lot of boots here. I don't see any dress shoes or runners."

Odleson looked at the boots and rubbed his chin. "Ranch people don't wear such things—not practical. These are riding and walking boots. What else does anyone want? Down there at the end are Clay's dress boots, which he wears when he goes to town or gets dressed up."

Heftner looked from the boots to the sheriff and back. "You mean to tell me these people only own boots?"

Odleson smiled. "Not just the Bamfords. All their neighbors are the same. I don't ever recall seeing a Bamford wearing anything but boots, unless maybe it was Mary. If my recall is correct, it seems like she might have owned a pair of lady's dress shoes. If she did, they didn't get out of her closet very often."

"What do they wear to go dancing, or to church, or a funeral?"

Tom laughed loudly. "Dress boots. Most ranchers wouldn't be seen wearing anything else, and it goes the same way with the ladies as well."

Odleson sat down on a bench to remove his boots and commented, "You fellas take off your shoes. No footwear is allowed beyond this room." His comment caused the city men to shake their heads.

They entered a spotlessly clean kitchen with the floor scrubbed and no dishes sitting on the table or counters. The only thing seemingly out of place was a copy of the *Boise Statesman* newspaper neatly folded on the large table. Odleson went to the table and checked the date on the paper. "At Johansson's, they told us Clay came in to pick up supplies on Friday. This paper is dated Thursday, so that jibes."

The detectives inspected a gun rack on the kitchen wall which held three Winchester 30/30 rifles, a Remington 270 with a scope, two .12-gauge shotguns, and a .22-caliber lever action rifle.

Boxes of ammunition were stacked on shelves below the guns. Heftner looked at the empty places that showed obvious signs of wear from being used. "Looks like a number of guns are missing from this rack."

Odleson came to look. "They aren't missing. Clay and the other men will each have a Winchester on their saddles. You have to understand; out here guns are tools they use almost every day. There are wolves, coyotes, pumas, and bears, which all go after cattle, and every once in a while one of the cattle breaks a leg, or something else happens. Country folks use guns as part of their everyday life."

"Sheriff, we'd like to take a look around the house." Odleson looked at Brand, not liking the idea. Well there was probably nothing to hide. He shrugged. "Go ahead; be careful not to disturb things. Clay is the type who will notice any changes immediately."

They walked into the family room with its leather-covered furniture and large fireplace and through the archway into the living room where they stopped to look at the glass-enclosed cabinets built into one wall. The cabinets contained old guns, family pictures, ribbons and trophies from cattle shows, and an assortment of newspaper clippings, knickknacks, and other keepsakes. Pictures of men in uniform caught the eye of Brand, and he looked carefully at both the pictures and military ribbons displayed. "Sheriff, who are these fellows wearing uniforms?"

Odleson came to look and pointed. "These two men on the left are Clay's great-uncles. This one I think was killed in the Great War. These next four are Will and his three brothers, all of whom, except Will, were killed in Vietnam. The Purple Heart belonged to Will. The last two pictures are Clay and his brother, Robert. Robert was ten years older than Clay and died during Desert Storm. The last picture is Clay, shown here in his army uniform."

Brand frowned. "He didn't receive any medals?"

Odleson smiled. "He isn't displaying them; that's all. I expect he'll leave putting them out to his children. Mary told me one time about Clay coming home with a whole pocket full of ribbons and putting them away; he didn't want to talk about them."

Following the two detectives into the ranch office, Odleson watched as Brand looked through the desk, and Heftner opened drawers in file cabinets. Heftner removed a file and started leafing through it, and Odleson walked over to see what interested him. It was utility bills. Heftner checked phone bills, running his finger down the list of calls made. He half turned. "Justin, there are calls here to both Seattle and Washington, DC. Come and have a look."

After a moment's study, Brand took out his notebook and leafed through it. "That Seattle number is for the Winehousers. I thought I recognized it."

Odleson became uneasy with the snooping. "The Winehousers are Clay's aunt and uncle."

"Yeah we know," Brand explained. "We talked to Judge Winehouser a number of times."

Heftner kept going through the file, checking other phone bills. "That Washington number has shown up three times this year. Sheriff, who would Bamford know and be calling in the capital?"

Odleson shrugged. "I have no idea. Probably someone he knows from the military. What are you fellows looking for?"

Heftner closed the file and looked hard at Odleson. "We have a drug war going in Seattle. Two men were killed last month, and the coroner says the methods used were a tactic taught in the military. Clay Bamford is the only person even remotely connected to this case who has been through military training."

Odleson's face showed shock. "You think Clay is involved in drugs and may have done it? You guys are crazy." Odleson frowned and stepped back, his voice becoming curt. "Show me your search warrant."

"We don't have one, Sheriff." Brand's face displayed his embarrassment. "Bamford is the only lead we have; we just want to get a feel, to see if a serious investigation is justified."

Both detectives recognized the sheriff's anger, which he was trying hard to keep under control. The silence lasted several minutes until Odleson told them, "Put all these files away. We're going to the kitchen to have coffee and talk this over."

Still upset when he walked into the kitchen, Odleson went about making coffee. Brand pulled out a chair and sat down at the large table. Heftner wandered around. Odleson found the coffeepot, added four heaping spoons of coffee from the canister, filled it with water, and placed it on a front burner of the stove to boil. He got coffee mugs out of the cupboard and brought them to the table. Odleson paced around the kitchen, not talking, waiting on the coffee to boil. When the coffee came to a boil, he filled the mugs and took the pot back to the stove. Standing at the table, he sipped from his mug while Brand called, "Heft, the coffee's ready."

Heftner started toward the kitchen and stopped to look out another window. He turned hurriedly. "Sheriff, there's a man sitting on a horse out in the yard, and he's holding a rifle."

Odleson carried his mug with him as he went to look. When he saw old Alorenzo Gonzales sitting his horse some seventy feet away, staring between the strange car and the house, he muttered, "Shit."

"What is it, Sheriff?"

Odleson gave the detectives a worried look. "That old man out there was born on this ranch a very long time ago, upwards of eighty years. In fact, he was hurt in a rodeo accident and his head hasn't been right ever since. Mary Bamford always looked after him, and the family has kept him here ever since. After Mary's death, he began showing his age and became highly protective of everything associated with this ranch. Four, five weeks ago, Clay brought him to town, and he followed Clay around, carrying that Winchester like he was on guard duty."

Odleson sighed. "On his good days, he's mostly as normal as everyone else, but when the bad days come along, things don't make sense to him. Now, I'm going out there, and you fellas have to come along. Lorenz is looking at the car, and he's going to know it's not mine, so he's expecting to see strangers. Get your shoes on."

Odleson pulled his boots on and picked up his coffee mug before walking to the door. There he stopped and half turned. "I'll do the talking. You guys keep your hands out in plain sight and don't make a move toward a pocket or your suit coats. If Lorenz takes a notion, he can put a bullet between your eyes just pointing that Winchester of his without even lifting it off the saddle horn."

Odleson opened the door with his left hand and stepped out holding the coffee mug in his right. He moved across the porch to the railing on the open side as the two men followed him. He could hear their shoes on the wooden porch while his attention focused on Gonzales. "Howdy, Lorenz. Is Clay anywhere around today?"

Gonzales's cutting horse shifted to bring the rifle to bear on the men. The city men might not know what happened, but Odleson did. The old man and his horse were a team. Gonzales wore a flat-crowned Stetson with almost no curl in the brim. His hard, gray eyes were looking past a large bushy, white mustache. A red kerchief around his neck showed above an open, brown, canvas jacket hanging below his waist. The silence stretched out as Gonzales stared at the three men, and the detectives shifted their feet nervously. Odleson took a sip of coffee and whispered from behind the mug, "You fellas stand still."

Odleson lowered his mug and started to speak, but Gonzales cut him off, his voice gruff and demanding. "What you people doing snooping in Mary's house?"

Odleson raised his left hand. "We weren't snooping, Lorenz. We came out to the ranch to talk to Clay, and I felt like a cup of coffee."

"Who are you anyways? This here is private property, and you all are trespassin'. I caught you breaking into Mary's house. Heard tell of people who break into folks' houses. No better than hydry-fobic skunks; that's what you are."

"Don't you remember me, Lorenz? It's Tom Odleson, the county sheriff." Tom kept his voice calm and just loud enough to carry the distance to the old man. "Why, when I was a youngster working here on the ranch, you taught me to ride."

Gonzales growled, "Don't see a badge."

Odleson sensed a change in the voice; the roughness seemed to be easing. "This is a day off for me, Lorenz. Came out to have a visit with Clay."

Gonzales lifted his left hand and rubbed it over his forehead before shaking his head, as if trying to clear away a fog. He looked bewildered for a long moment. "You say you're looking for Clay. Hell, Tom, he took off two days back, with the pack horses loaded up with supplies, to make a circuit of the summer camps. Said he would be gone a week, maybe more. Used to be my job for many a year, except I'm not up to riding the rough country these days; starting to get old. Not much left for me to do except to see Clay home here with a wife of his own. When he brings her home to look after him, reckon my work will be done. You hear, Tom? Wee Mite is going to marry Clay? Been telling him to get off the ranch and go to town for a look at the ladies if he's going to find a wife. Not right, a young man living alone. All he does is work day after day. Only goes to town when we run low on needed supplies. Now we're all lined up to get us a Mrs. Bamford. Hell, we ought to have young'uns running around the yard while I'm still here to look after them, teach them to ride and about cattle and such."

The Winchester was still pointed at them, and Odleson thought Alorenzo might have forgotten about it, but he couldn't be sure.

"You want me to make coffee for you, Tom?"

"We had coffee, Lorenz. When Clay gets back, you tell him I stopped by to say hello. Tell him the next time he's in town to come see me."

"Will do, Tom. Sure you don't want me to make a pot of coffee? I got me a new bottle of Jack that Clay brought home for me."

"It's getting a bit on the late side, Lorenz. If I don't get home soon, Janet will start worrying about me."

"Okay, Tom. A man should be considering of his wife. You come sometime, and we'll go riding, just like when you were a kid."

"I'd enjoy that, Lorenz. I surely would. It's been a long time since we went riding together." Odleson put the coffee mug down, raised his hand in farewell, and walked to the rental car, closely followed by the detectives. Inside the car, he warned Brand, "Take it easy and don't rush. Drive this car slow." The car backed slowly around and drove out of the yard. As they left the yard, the old man raised his hand, and Odleson waved back. The car reached the county road before the silence ended.

Gonzales sat on his horse watching the car leave, throwing up a plume of dust as it disappeared along the road. He had been out in the calving pasture checking the animals when the car arrived. Not a local vehicle belonging to one of the ranch's neighbors. Rarely did strangers show up on the ranch, and Lorenz turned his horse for home, taking his time. Not much harm anyone could do. Being on the far side of the creek, the route he followed to the crossing point on the creek actually took him further from the buildings, so it took more than an hour before he rode into the yard.

Clay disappeared off the ranch several times in recent months, on some business of his own, one time being gone for close to three weeks. Each time, he cautioned Alorenzo not to tell anyone he was away. Alorenzo knew his Bamfords and the way they looked after their own; he didn't need to be told. Someone killed Will and Mary, and Clay intended to even the score in his own way, just as Bamfords had always done ever since old Bob started the ranch.

These strangers, no matter who they were, likely had something to do with Clay's absences. No one was going to mess with the boy if Alorenzo could prevent it. When he arrived in the yard, he positioned his horse out of pistol range of the house, pulled the Winchester from the saddle boot under his right leg, and waited for whoever it was to make a move.

Now with them gone, he sat and considered everything as the car diminished in size toward the horizon. Those two men with Tom were policemen. Alorenzo felt sure of it. The feeling grew as he watched them, dressed in their fancy suits. Big-city cops. Alorenzo shook his head and rested his hands on the saddle horn, muttering softly to himself. "Did what I could to throw them a false trail. That boy of ours is out to make them pay for what happened to you and Mary. Clay's a throwback, Will, one of the old breed—a man to be proud of. If it happened here on the ranch, we would have buried them in some ravine like old Bob did. That would have been the end of it. Folks think I'm crazy, Will. Some days I reckon I am; those bad days don't happen so often anymore. This old man is hanging on, Will, waiting for Clay to get settled. Afterward, I reckon we'll be back together again."

Sitting up straight, Gonzales rode his horse to the porch, shoved the Winchester into the boot, dismounted, and dropped the reins over the railing. Slowly he gathered up the coffee mugs to carry to the kitchen. Running water in the sink, he washed and dried the mugs and coffeepot, returning them to their proper shelves. Using the washcloth, he cleaned the countertop and table. When he had everything back as it should be, he took one last look around before walking through the house to check. The door to the ranch office stood ajar. It never got left open unless Clay sat in there working. So, those fellows were snooping for something. Gonzales pulled the door closed before going on through the house and walking around the porch, back to his horse.

Both detectives slowly relaxed; this had been a scary event. Obviously dealing with country people was much different from the city. Odleson stayed quiet, busy with his own thoughts. Heftner said from the backseat, "Sheriff, I'm damn happy you were with us. That old man is scary."

"You were right to be scared. I'm glad you weren't alone. It's better this way, instead of me trying to figure out what happened to you two."

Heftner asked, "Do you think he would have shot us?"

"On one of his good days, he would have run you off the place. Lorenz wasn't right in the head today. He'd have shot you, just like they did when he was a youngster. Back in those days, when guys ran off a few head of cattle, they tracked them down, shot them where they caught them, and brought the cattle home. Will toned old Lorenz down, started changing things, always bringing the thieves to town hogtied and scared; at least as far as I know, they always did. Clay would never shoot anyone unless they shot at him first. These days, not many animals are lost to riders. Thieves come in semis, pulling cattle liners, and run off with a whole truckload at a time. The Bamfords don't lose cattle to truckers because there's only one road into the ranch, with the buildings blocking access."

Brand parked in front of the sheriff's office. "Heft, we can't hang around here for a week waiting for Bamford to finish his trip. We may as well drive back to Boise and catch the next flight to Seattle."

Heftner replied from the backseat, "I agree, Justin. It was nice meeting you, Sheriff. Your jurisdiction is a totally different world from ours. I learned a lot today about life out here in your mountains, and one of them is that I don't belong."

Odleson turned to look at Heftner. "Given time, you would adapt. Hell, I feel the same way when I find myself in a city. Do you want to leave the watch here so when Clay shows up he can take a look at it?"

"The watch is evidence in a murder case, maybe even two murder cases. We have to sign it back into evidence storage. Does young Bamford ever come to Seattle?"

"I've never known of him going to Seattle." Odleson frowned. "When Clay was eleven or twelve, Will and Mary took him to visit the Winehousers—some kind of family celebration. Afterward I recall asking the lad how he liked the big city. He didn't; Clay told me there were people and noise everywhere and no horses." Odleson laughed. "Clay said even the air smelled bad."

Brand started the car engine. "Thanks for your help, Sheriff, and for saving our necks."

Odleson shook their hands and opened the car door. Heftner moved to the front seat. Both men waved before the car started moving. Odleson sighed. Another day off ruined for him.

Chapter 20

Smelling of wood smoke and sweat, with a week's growth of stubble hiding his face, a good feeling came over Clay, being almost back to the ranch headquarters. The packhorses were feeling it too, and instead of following behind, they now bunched around him, maybe thinking they could hurry things along. The valley narrowed, leading to the neck where the north fence of the calving pastures was built to stop cattle from drifting. Dismounting at the fence, he swung the gate open, and the horses went on through, turning to watch Clay push the gate back into place.

One week left until Easter, followed in three weeks by the wedding. Ten days had gone by since he last talked to Jennie. Phoning her was at the top of his list—to hear her voice, find out how her studies were going, and get any last-minute instructions on the wedding. Hilda Johansson fussed much more than her daughter; of course, with Jennie being the only daughter, this would be the only wedding Hilda got to host.

The narrow neck took a turn, and the horses were into the herd of mother cows. New calves were scattered here and there, following their grazing mothers. Standing up in the stirrups made it easier for Clay to see riders lower down in the valley a half-mile away. Alorenzo and the summer men were out checking cows. Holding his horse to a steady walk through the herd, hoping not to overly disturb the cows, Clay guided his horse toward the riders. A third rider came into sight, coming from the trees along the creek, and it had to be Alorenzo. As he came closer and could see the lower ground, he saw the GMC parked on the trail. *Odd for the truck to be out,* he thought.

As Clay started thinking about it, Alorenzo spotted him. Not hard for him to do really with seven horses following along. Alorenzo touched a spur to his horse and came loping up the long slope to meet him. His cutting horse pivoted neatly and settled in alongside, matching the pace of Clay's horse. Alorenzo sat up high in the saddle looking almighty pleased. "Good to see you, Lorenz."

"Welcome home, boy. Looks like you could use a shave."

Clay eyed Alorenzo, wondering why he was acting so pert. "Forgot to take a razor with me."

Alorenzo grinned. "Looks like maybe the boys should throw you in the crick and scrub you off."

Clay found it hard not to wonder what was going on. Alorenzo seldom reacted like this, looking so damn cocky, like he had pulled a fast one on Clay.

Alorenzo pointed a finger over his horse's ears. "Look yonder, boy."

Clay's head swiveled, looking for the men. A flash of sunlight reflecting from the truck windows focused his eyes. The driver's door opened, and there Jennie was, standing tall and slim, her blonde hair blowing in the breeze. "You go ahead, Clay. I'll bring the horses on in." Alorenzo grinned, feeling almighty happy with himself.

It didn't take long to get to her, just enough time to get over the tight feeling in his throat. Swinging down with the horse still moving, for sure Clay wasn't much to see after days of riding rough country and sleeping outdoors. Jennie's smile broadened as Clay stared at her. "How are you, Clay? You had me worried. No one answered the phone, and you seemed to be gone for so long." Jennie fingered the ring on her left hand as she waited.

"Damn, it's good to see you, Jen. Planned on phoning you this evening to see how you were doing."

This time Jennie didn't wait on Clay; she stepped forward to hug him, standing up on her toes to get kissed. Stepping back, Jennie wrinkled her face at Clay. "Hope you're not planning to keep those whiskers?" They laughed while Clay shook his head no.

Alorenzo arrived with the horses kicking up dust and said, "I'll bring your horse into the yard; you ride along with Miss Jennie."

Jennie drove slowly along the pasture trail into the yard and right to the house where she shut off the truck. "Are you hungry, Clay?"

"Didn't stop at noon, so I'm ready for dinner."

"You go shower and get shaved." Jennie sounded just like Hilda. "I'll get a meal started." As they got out of the truck, Alorenzo arrived at the barn with the horses. Jennie pointed at the house with her left arm extended and waved her right in a circle. Alorenzo raised one arm in reply.

Clay came back to the kitchen all cleaned up and wearing fresh clothes. Jennie bustled around, busy cooking. Alorenzo sat at the table talking to Tom Odleson, both with mugs of steaming coffee. "Good to see you, Tom."

Odleson swung around in his chair. "Howdy, Clay. Jennie told me she hadn't seen hide nor hair of you around here, and she sent a smelly tramp to take a shower."

"Yeah, I tossed him out." Jennie came to stand beside Clay and put her arm across his back. She took a deep breath. "You smell and look much better now."

Alorenzo chuckled. "Tom tells me he came out here to protect you, boy."

Clay's eyes switched to look at Tom, who grinned. "The truth is I stopped by the store, and Lars told me Jennie took off for the ranch, all hot under the collar because you wouldn't answer the phone. Figured you might need to be fixed up after taking a beating."

"More than likely the beating is deserved." Clay watched Jennie go back to her cooking. "You just visiting, Tom?"

"Mostly!" Tom shrugged. "A pair of detectives from Seattle was here a week ago Monday packing a Rolex watch they wanted you to look at. They found it on some drug dealer who got himself killed and thought it might tie in with Will."

Jennie brought Clay a mug of strong, black coffee. "Thanks, Jen." Clay pulled out a chair at the end of the table where he could sit to talk and continue to watch Jennie. "If it's Dad's Rolex, it will have a small diamond set into the opposite side of the case from the stem."

Tom got out his notebook and wrote down the description. "If it has that, I'll ask them to send it to you when it's released as evidence."

"No, don't do that, Tom. I'd just as soon forget about what happened out there. Tell them to sell it and give the money to their favorite charity."

"That's understandable, Clay." Tom went back to writing in his notebook. Clay's eyes followed Jennie as she moved around.

After they ate, everyone went to tour the addition being added to the house. It was all closed in now with the roof and siding on. The dry walling was completed, and the contractor had started painting the various rooms. Back in the kitchen, Clay laid out brochures received from the Suburban dealer in which were clearly marked the colors and upholstery available immediately. Clay suggested to Jennie, "The dealer said if you choose from the colors marked, he can have one ready for you right away; otherwise he will have to order it in for us. He suggested it would be best to make a first and second choice in case your first choice is sold out."

Jennie took her time before looking up. "A dark color would be best for the wintertime, for visibility in snow. This dark blue or the bright red might be best. What do you think, Clay?"

Clay had hoped Jennie would pick blue, although she chose a darker blue than her bright eyes. "Let's take the blue. If you agree, I'll phone the dealer in the morning and tell him to get it ready." Jennie nodded in agreement.

Jennie looked out the window. The daylight was almost gone now, and it would soon be dark. "Clay, I made a promise to Mom to be back before dark. She's going to start worrying, so I'd better get going."

Odleson said, "Jennie, you phone Hilda and tell her not to worry. I'll follow you back to town."

"Thank you, Tom." Jennie went to the phone and dialed. The men talked quietly until Jennie called. "Clay, Mom wants to talk to you." Hilda invited Clay to dinner on Good Friday, because Jennie would leave to return to Moscow on Sunday morning.

Early Thursday morning, they left for the drive to Idaho Falls in Jennie's car. When they arrived at the small town of Arco, Jennie asked Clay to pull off the highway where there was a good view of the high rock cliff east of town. It was one of Jennie's favorite sights. The yearly numbers painted on the rock wall by each high school graduating class went all the way back to 1922. A tradition started so long ago and still carried on each year by the new grads. Some of the latest graduates might be great-grandchildren of those from 1922.

At the Idaho dealership, they traded in the car and took delivery of a brand-new GMC Suburban, fully loaded and ready for Jennie's trip back to Moscow. Jennie happily drove the Suburban home with Clay riding in the passenger seat. Two weeks later, Jennie would be coming home for the wedding and to spend the summer on the ranch.

* * *

Heftner told Chief Kruger, "We just got a telephone call from Sheriff Odleson, over in Idaho. He talked to Clay Bamford who told him Will Bamford's Rolex watch has a small diamond in the side of the case opposite the stem. We just came from the evidence room, and the Rolex that drug dealer wore belonged to Will Bamford."

"Looks like you've tied the two cases together." Kruger stood up to pace around. "It doesn't really prove the deceased Asian killed Bamford. He could have bought the watch off the person who did."

Heftner shrugged. "You're right, Chief, but it's the first break we've gotten in the Bamford case. Maybe something else will turn up."

"Good work, fellas." Kruger scowled. "Don't start thinking you're getting another trip out to that ranch to return the watch."

Both detectives laughed. Brand said, "There's no way we want to go back there."

Heftner added, "The sheriff told us Clay Bamford doesn't want the watch back; it would be a bad memory he doesn't need. Bamford sent word the department should sell the watch and give the money to any charity we choose."

Kruger mused, "The Police Benevolent Fund could use the money. We'll have to mail release forms to Bamford for signing before the sale can be made."

Brand grinned. "We were holding out on you, Chief. Bamford sent word Judge Winehouser can give us any approvals we need." Kruger scowled again, and both detectives laughed at him.

* * *

Calves were dropping at a fast rate, often two hundred or more in a day, and it kept all four men on the run. Alorenzo kept busy moving the cows who already had new calves out of the calving pasture, to make it easier to spot new arrivals. The hours were long every day, the only consolation being that at this rate it would be mostly over before the wedding. Everyone on the ranch got an invite to attend the wedding and join the only family left on the Bamford side, the Winehousers, and they all intended to be there.

Firing up the computer to check the Seattle police files, it only took a few minutes to satisfy his curiosity. Clay's bug in the computer at the clubhouse had been removed right after he returned from Seattle. As expected, the police confiscated the computer when they raided the place. Having already seen reports on raids at the clubhouse and the fish market, now he looked for a report by the two detectives who travelled to Idaho. When the report came up on screen, there was nothing to concern him. A good portion of the report was about the old cowboy on the Bamford ranch, his rifle, and his mental problems, which gave Clay a good laugh. It was obvious Alorenzo didn't know what Clay might be up to, but he was doing his best to protect Clay's back.

With the computer turned off, Clay sat in the dark and thought about all the money now cached on the ranch. At some point, Jennie would have to be let in on the secret, to know how and why the money was taken from the drug gang that killed Will and Mary. This was not the time, not yet; it would be better to wait until enough time went by to let the whole mess slip into the past and be forgotten.

* * *

On Tuesday afternoon, Alorenzo sat patiently on the porch steps waiting for Edgar and Sadie to arrive at the ranch. When the car came, he hurried to open the passenger door. Sadie watched Alorenzo approach, having first met him at Mary and Will's wedding over forty years before. She was a single girl then, and to this day Alorenzo referred to her as Miss Sadie. Alorenzo opened the car door, and Sadie swung her feet out and stood up with her hand out. Alorenzo took it ever so gently, not even closing his hand. "Welcome, Miss Sadie. You go on to the house. Coffee is ready. Clay drove out to the pasture. He'll be along shortly."

"Thank you, Lorenz." Sadie noticed the new construction. "Has Clay built on to the house?"

Alorenzo turned to look. "Well now, the boy started out to build an office for Miss Jennie. Miss Jennie writes books, you know." Sadie noticed the pride in Alorenzo's voice and maybe a hint of awe. "He got started and ended with most of a new house before he stopped. You'd be best off to get him to explain."

Edgar listened to the conversation before coming around the car. The men shook hands. "Howdy, Edgar. Clay figured you'd be getting here soon."

"Very nice to see you again, Lorenz. How are you doing?"

Alorenzo ran a finger over his mustache to smooth it and nodded. "Most days this old fella gets by; other days my head hurts bad. Don't remember much from the bad days."

Edgar nodded, remembering what Brand told him. "Are you keeping Clay in line?"

"He's good boy, that Clay. Works hard, smart too. After him and Miss Jennie are hitched, we'll have a Mrs. Bamford to look out for us."

Sadie interrupted, "If you open the trunk, Edgar, I'll take a bag to the house."

Edgar removed the car keys from his suit coat pocket. "You go ahead, Sadie. I'll bring the luggage in."

Alorenzo refocused on her. "You go along now, Miss Sadie. Make yourself at home. Reckon Edgar and me can drag your bags in."

The luggage went straight to a bedroom. Alorenzo seated them at the kitchen table and brought mugs, cream, and sugar. He poured coffee and took the pot back to the stove. Alorenzo returned with a bottle of Jack Daniels to add whiskey to Edgar's and his mugs, before looking at Sadie. She shook her head no, and Alorenzo set the bottle in the middle of the table, handy to all of them. Sadie tried her coffee, glancing at Edgar, who never partook of liquor before dinner in the evening, except here at the ranch where this long-standing custom existed. When visitors arrived, the Jack came out.

Jennie arrived in time to help with dinner, bringing her parents to Clay's family gathering. Everyone in the den stood up when Jennie came through the door, followed by Lars and Hilda. The Winehousers last saw Jennie as a young teenager during a visit seven years before; now they were looking at a beautiful, articulate, well-educated young woman. Sadie hurriedly followed Clay from the den to greet the Johansson's. "Jennie Mae, the last time I saw you, you were a long-legged, gangly teenager. Look at you now, such a beautiful lady. No wonder Clay fell in love with you."

"Thank you, Mrs. Winehouser." Jennie glanced at Clay and laughed. "Clay never said anything about my appearance. He only told me, 'With your education, you should make a good bookkeeper for the ranch.'" Clay grinned and put his arm around Jennie's shoulders.

Sadie turned to Clay with a sly grin. "Shame on you, Clayton Bamford, I can't believe you are so blind." Sadie took Jennie's arm. "Come along with me. Edgar will want to talk to you and see this fabulous ring." Jennie glanced into the den at Edgar and Alorenzo sitting in large, leather armchairs. She walked to Alorenzo. "How are you, Lorenz?"

Lorenz hurriedly pushed himself up, using his hands on the chair arms. "Miss Jennie, you is looking so good today. You know this fella? He's Clay's uncle, all the way from Seattle."

Jennie stuck out her hand. "It's very nice to see you again, Mr. Winehouser. Thank you for coming all this way for the wedding."

Edgar held on to her hand. "When you were a little girl, it was only proper that you called me mister. Now you're grown up and joining the family. You must call me Edgar, and my wife is Sadie."

"Thank you, Edgar. I'm very pleased to be joining your family. Do you remember my parents?"

"Of course I do. Lars, how are you?" The men began talking, and the ladies adjourned to the kitchen to cook dinner.

Dinner over, the ladies were chatting as they cleaned up the kitchen. When the phone rang, Jennie glanced around for Clay. He was busy pouring Jack for the men gathered in the den. Jennie picked up the phone. "Bamford Ranch."

"Is Major Bamford there please? General Thorsen is holding for him."

Hilda observed the startled look on Jennie's face and wondered. Jennie hesitated a moment before replying, "Yes, of course. I'll get him for you."

"Thank you." Jennie put the phone down and walked to the den. Hilda and Sadie watched and listened, wondering what was happening. They heard Jennie tell Clay, "A General Thorsen is on the phone. He wants to talk to Major Bamford."

Clay took Jennie's arm and walked her to the kitchen where he picked up the phone. Clay put his arm around Jennie's shoulders, holding the phone between them so Jennie could listen. "Hello, Thompson."

"One moment please while I put the call through, Major."

"Hello, Clay." It was Thorsen's soft voice.

Clay grinned. "Thompson, are you going to make it for the wedding?"

General Thorsen laughed. "We sure are. The air force is going to chopper us in Friday afternoon. Can you pick us up at the Challis school yard at thirteen hundred?"

"Of course, General. How many are coming with you?"

"Thomas and Maxine. Maxine made room reservations at a motel in Challis."

"Thompson, you are not staying at a motel."

"Now, son, it's time you understood. Generals don't take orders from majors. What are you suggesting?"

Clay laughed. "There's room here at the ranch, and we'll even feed you."

"Sounds great, Clay. Is that old, gun-carrying cowboy still around?"

"Lorenz is still here, and he'll pour you a whiskey when you arrive."

"You ask him if he has an old, gentle horse that can't go faster than a walk for me to try out."

"Will do, Thompson. See you Friday." Clay replaced the receiver.

Jennie held onto his arm, a question in her eyes. "Who's General Thorsen?"

"He was my commanding officer in Washington during my time in the army. He's also a good friend. He's flying to Idaho from Washington for our wedding?" Obviously Jennie found this surprising. Clay smiled and leaned down to kiss her cheek. "He will fly into Mountain Home Air Force Base in the morning, and an air force helicopter will bring him to Challis. The chopper will probably come back for him right after the wedding."

"He must be a very important man?"

"You could say that, honey. Someday I will explain everything to you."

Thursday afternoon, Clay and Edgar drove Sadie into town so she could attend an afternoon tea arranged by several of Jennie's former teachers. They were late. Clay escorted his aunt to the door and knocked. Mrs. Olsen opened the door and scowled at him. "Clayton, didn't I teach you to always be prompt?" She didn't wait for an answer. "You come in so the ladies can see you. This must be Aunt Sadie. Come in, come in; we are so pleased to have you."

Clay followed the ladies along the short hallway. Mrs. Olsen raised her voice. "Everyone, this is Mary's sister, Sadie. She came from Seattle for Jennie Mae's wedding. You all know Clayton. I told him to come in and say hello." Clay removed his Stetson and smiled broadly. Just when it looked like he was about to say something, Mrs. Olsen cut him off.

"Jennie Mae, you tell us how this scoundrel proposed to you; we all know what a longwinded talker he is."

Jennie hurried across the room, kissed Sadie on the cheek, and hugged Clay. She turned around to face the ladies with a smug look on her face. "How did he propose? To tell you the truth, I'm not sure he ever did. We dated for a while, and all that time he never kissed me. Finally I asked him if he ever figured to kiss me. Well, he did, although he seemed to be afraid of me."

One of the ladies yelled, "Keep him like that, Jennie Mae."

Jennie looked up at Clay and linked arms with him. "In February, Clay drove up to Moscow to see me. Not his usual talkative self, but finally he got around to asking if I thought I could stand living on the ranch so far from town. I told him I certainly could, and he said, 'We better go buy you a ring.' Having no experience at these things, I assumed that was a proposal." The room erupted in laughter. Clay leaned down, kissed Jennie's cheek, put on his hat, and turned to leave. Jennie called after him. "I'll drive Aunt Sadie back to the ranch." Clay nodded as he opened the door.

On Friday, Jennie drove Clay to the schoolyard and parked the SUV outside the chain-link fence that separated the two schools. They got out and leaned against the front grill to wait. Immediately the principal of the primary school came from the building on their left to greet them. "The wedding is tomorrow. May I wish both of you all the best for the future."

"That's very kind of you, Mr. Wiggins. Clay and I appreciate your thinking of us."

"You're welcome, Jennie Mae. Remember, I watched both of you grow up, and after all, this is a small community. Clay, we heard there's a helicopter coming here to bring people for the wedding. The children are all excited. Do you think they could have a look at the machine?"

"Certainly, I'll ask the captain. It's a military machine, and they may be sensitive about letting people see everything." Clay rubbed his chin with one hand. "Of course, it would be a great opportunity for them to do public relations work, which I will point out to him."

"Thank you, Clay. What time are you expecting them to arrive?"

"The schedule calls for them to arrive here at one o'clock, and the air force takes pride in being on time. Why don't you bring the kids out to watch the helicopter land, hear the noise, and see the cloud of dust it stirs up?"

"Excellent idea, Clay. We'll have the whole school here in a few minutes." Wiggins hurried away.

Jennie held Clay's hand. "That was very nice of you. The children will be excited."

"Well, I still remember the first time I saw a helicopter. It seemed like magic that the thing could get off the ground. Some of these kids have probably seen helicopters in the area fighting fires or doing other things."

The double doors on the school burst open, and a stream of kids rushed out. Most of them rode a school bus to school, and it seemed like they all knew each other. They crowded around the Suburban and sorted themselves out with the smallest at the front and the tallest behind. Mr. Wiggins stood in front. "Now all of you remember, do not go near the helicopter because those rotating blades are dangerous. Mr. Bamford promised to ask the pilot if we can have a closer look after it has unloaded." Wiggins was interrupted by the sound of the helicopter approaching. The kids scanned the southern horizon and soon were pointing.

The twin-rotor helicopter came in over the high school and hovered over the schoolyard before flying a slow circle around the buildings. The kids turned in coordination with the machine, watching as the helicopter flew its circle around the schools before approaching and settling to the ground in the middle of a grassy area between the two school buildings. The wind from the rotor blew the kids hair, dust swirled, and they laughed happily.

The engines slowed to a stop, the noise gradually disappeared, and the dust settled. As the blades stopped turning, a door opened and slowly lowered to the ground, revealing a set of steps. When an air force sergeant appeared in the doorway, Clay took Jennie's hand and walked through the gate in the chain-link fence and across the schoolyard, arriving at the helicopter just as General Thorsen stepped to the ground, holding out his hand. Maxine Cherrett came next, and the sergeant put out his hand to help her with the last step to the ground, which was close to two feet high. Thomas came out carrying his cane and received help from the sergeant.

With both feet solidly on the ground, Thomas straightened and faced Clay. "Major Bamford, sir, it's good to see you again."

With the introductions over, Clay said, "Jennie, please take our guests to the car." Jennie led them away, fully engaged in answering questions, and Clay turned to the sergeant. "Sergeant, most of the children attending this school have never seen a helicopter before. Please ask the captain if they can have a closer look. It would be a highlight of their school year."

"Certainly, Major, I will ask the captain immediately." The sergeant returned with the captain, who assured Clay they would show the machine to the students.

The sergeant unloaded luggage. He and Clay lugged the cases to the vehicle, and Clay stowed the suitcases in the back of the Suburban. When Jennie drove away, the crew was being kept busy conducting a helicopter tour for a large group of interested and excited children.

Chapter 21

Jennie drove the Suburban along the road while answering questions. "For the past week, I've been home from the University of Idaho in Moscow and must return in the fall for four months to complete my degree."

From the backseat, Maxine inquired, "What are you studying?"

"I'm working on a master's degree in the Creative Writing program."

Maxine sat in the middle of the backseat between Thomas and Clay. Thompson, from the passenger seat, asked, "And what do you plan to do after you graduate?"

"Write. All my life, my plan has been to write, hoping to become a successful novelist." Jennie added with a grin, "Of course, Lorenz tells me it will be my responsibility to look after everyone. He doesn't seem to recognize me as being the youngest person on the ranch with the least amount of experience. He expects me to automatically become as capable as Clay's mother was."

"Just a matter of time, I'm sure, Jennie."

Jennie flashed a brief smile at the general.

In the backseat, Clay suddenly became aware of the large leadership role being expected from Jennie. Such a thought had never occurred to him, and he vowed to ease the way for her in every way he could.

Jennie turned in at the gate and proceeded toward the ranch, pointing at yearling heifers in the pastures on both sides of the road, explaining, "These are replacement heifers that will be bred for the first time this summer, to be added to the mother cow herd."

Clay watched the heifers and reflected silently. *All those years Jennie vacationed at the ranch, she obviously listened and observed the operation, absorbing much more than anyone thought a young girl from town would understand.*

With Maxine in tow, Jennie led the way into the house while the men unloaded luggage. They walked through the house, and Jennie stopped at a door. "This is the bedroom where I slept each summer while vacationing at the ranch, if you would care to use it. The linen has been changed, and there are fresh towels for you."

"Thank you, Jennie, this will do very well. You have known Clay for quite some time then?"

"Oh yes, from as far back as I can remember. Clay's mother always invited me to spend the summer here. Mary taught me to cook. The men showed me how to ride, rope cattle, and handle a Winchester. I learned to swim in the stream on hot days. As soon as my legs were long enough to push the truck pedals down, Clay let me drive him around." Jennie reflected. "It certainly wasn't the smoothest ride for him with me practicing, but soon my driving became good enough to drive Mary when she took lunch out to the fields."

"Hello, Jennie."

Both women turned.

"Aunt Sadie, come and meet Maxine Cherrett, a good friend of Clay's who has come for the wedding. Maxine, this is Clay's Aunt Sadie from Seattle."

The two women were of an age, although Maxine seemed younger. Clay arrived with Maxine's luggage, and Jennie opened the door for him. Jennie hurried off to show Thompson and

Thomas to the rooms set aside for them. Clay observed the way Jennie took charge of everything, recognizing she was going to fit in just fine, with very little help required from him.

Edgar and Alorenzo returned from riding to sit their horses and look at the three men standing on the porch. Thompson, wearing well-washed army fatigues and boots, looked like he was prepared to go on maneuvers. Clay did the introductions. "Edgar, this is General Thompson Thorsen and Sergeant Thomas Manning from Washington. They came out here to make sure the wedding got me properly married." Clay turned his head toward the men. "Fellas, this is my uncle Edgar who's a federal court judge in Seattle. Aunt Sadie tells me he's very stern and tough." Everyone laughed. Edgar dismounted and came up the steps with his hand out.

Clay added, "General, you remember Lorenz from the last time you were here." Alorenzo nodded his head. "Lorenz, this is my friend Thomas." Again the old cowboy nodded.

Thompson leaned his hands on the railing. "Lorenz, you offered to teach me how to ride a horse."

"I recall, General. If you're ready, Edgar has this one quieted down."

"It better be, Lorenz, or you'll be picking me out of the dust."

Edgar touched the general's arm. "Don't be concerned, General. I have been riding this horse for three days, and she hasn't acted up even once." Edgar smiled. "It will be a relief for Lorenz when we city dudes go home and he can stop babysitting."

Alorenzo's face didn't change. "Clay, it would be a good idea for you to adjust those stirrups to fit the general."

Clay got Thompson correctly settled in the saddle and watched as Alorenzo led the way, heading toward the calving pasture. Alorenzo talked and pointed as they left the yard.

An hour later, Shoshone Mike and Peggy rode in from the line camp they were manning for the summer. Clay walked to the barn to talk to them and invite them to come to the house for the evening. Edgar and Thomas followed along and watched as they unsaddled, turned their horses into the corral, and left the barn, each carrying a Winchester.

Jennie organized the kitchen. She filled the oversized coffeepot and put it on the large commercial range to heat. When Sadie and Maxine volunteered to help, Jennie handed each an apron. Sadie scrambled eggs, Maxine cooked hash browns, and Jennie fried sausages and bacon. Clay walked in, and Jennie smiled at him. "Don't just stand there. Start making toast." The warming oven began receiving bowls of food and platters of meat.

The house filled up as the hands arrived. Lars and Hilda arrived just as the food started going on the table. Stacks of plates, silverware, and coffee mugs waited beside the food, and Alorenzo opened a fresh bottle of Jack Daniels. Jennie called, "Come and fill plates for yourselves and find a place to sit—anywhere you choose." She elbowed Clay in the ribs. "You lead the way." Jennie had finished organizing her first meal for a large group of people. She told herself, *Wasn't so hard with this large kitchen to work in.*

Jennie supervised the table while the men filled their plates, with the ladies following. From the den, she could hear the men teasing Clay about giving up his bachelorhood and how Jennie would be making a new man out of him. When her turn came, Jennie helped herself to food and carried her plate to the den. She sat beside Clay on the fireplace ledge, leaning her back against the stone wall. With her head close to him, she whispered, "Don't listen to them. There's nothing about you to change."

Clay whispered back, "Don't be concerned; they're just having fun."

Peggy called, "Hey, you two, didn't your mothers tell you it's not polite to whisper in front of company? What are you telling him, Jennie?"

"I told him he has one more day before he starts taking orders." Clay grinned, and everyone laughed.

Maxine advised, "You have a large problem, Jennie. While working with him for several years, he turned out to be too independent to take orders. Clay always seemed to find a way to twist them around." Again everyone laughed and poked fun at Clay.

Jennie finished her food, and Hilda came to take the plate. "It's okay, Mother. I'll start the dishes in a few minutes."

"No you won't. You stay with Clay while I load the dishwasher." Peggy went to the kitchen and came back with the coffeepot to refill mugs and told Jennie, "After topping off everyone's coffee, I'll help Hilda." Jennie relaxed.

Conversations started up in different parts of the family room. Thompson walked over to Jennie and asked, "Will you go for a walk with me, Jennie?"

Obviously Jennie had received a surprise. She glanced at Clay, who winked at her. She looked up. "Of course, General Thorsen. Give me a moment to put on a sweater."

When they went to the mudroom to put on their boots, the silence stretched.

They strolled across the yard to the corrals. "He's a good man, Jennie."

"He's always been a good man, even when he was a boy."

"We recruited him into the army because of his computer skills, and we quickly found he is very skilled at a number of other things. He qualified as a sharpshooter and as a sniper. Out here on the ranch, it's easy to understand why. These people grow up using a rifle. There's almost nothing I can tell you about his time in the army, except that he provided a great service to his country. Everything in his record is classified. Under the secrecy act, he can't tell you the things he did. My suggestion to you is don't worry about it, just be proud."

Thompson leaned his arms on the corral bars and looked at the horses. "Today is the first time for me riding a horse. If I were a few years younger, it's something I could enjoy." Jennie waited; she was accustomed to Clay and his pauses. "Want to tell you about the two people who came with me. Mrs. Cherrett has been my assistant for many years, and she mothers everyone, including Clay. She always badgered him about finding a nice girl and getting married, and he would laugh at her. She wanted very much to meet you. By the way, she approves of his choice." Jennie smiled.

"You will have noticed Thomas carries a cane and limps. He served under Clay. When he was wounded, Clay carried him several miles to reach help. Clay saved Thomas's life, and he will never forget it. Now he'll know Clay is settled, with a good life ahead of him. There is one other thing you should know. Clay still works for me on a consulting basis, so if at times you see strange messages on the computer or phone calls you don't understand, please don't concern yourself. Occasionally Clay flies to Washington, and he has been told to bring you with him when he does. Hopefully we can entertain you, and you can do the tourist thing; there is a vast amount of history to pursue in DC."

"Thank you, General. All Clay has mentioned to me are bases where he trained, not a word about where he served or what he did. I must admit to wondering; it seemed obvious he was hiding something."

"Please call me Thompson. Clay isn't hiding anything from you; he's just following his orders. He did nothing he needs to hide." The silence lasted as they watched the horses eating hay. "We should get back to your guests."

Jennie turned and immediately saw dust from a car coming along the ranch road. She hurried Thompson so they arrived at the house ahead of the car, where they stood and waited. Jennie recognized the sheriff's car, and when it came to a stop, she saw he had Clay's best man with him. Jennie shook their hands and did the introductions. "Tom, Donald, this is General Thompson Thorsen, Clay's commanding officer from his army days. General, this is Sheriff Tom Odleson and his son Don."

They shook hands. "A great pleasure to meet you, General. Don and Clay are the same age and went through school together. Don drove up from Boise today for the wedding and wanted a chance to catch up with Clay. Hope we aren't interrupting anything, Jennie?"

"Not at all, Tom. Come into the house. Clay will be happy to see you."

Jennie led the way, and when Clay saw who she was bringing, he hurried to welcome them. He and Don hadn't gotten together often in recent years. Don clapped Clay on the shoulder. "You old devil, getting married. I expected you would be a bachelor your whole life."

"Being a bachelor was always an option," Clay grinned, "except I kept waiting for Jennie to grow up."

All the guests were well fed and settled in comfortably, talking and laughing. Clay joined right in the middle of it all and seemed to be enjoying his last evening as a single man. Jennie smiled to herself, knowing he would be no different after the wedding. She caught Hilda's eye and nodded toward the kitchen. Jennie washed the coffeepot and refilled it while saying, "It's time we went home. I want to ride with you and leave the Suburban so Clay can use it to bring people into town tomorrow."

Hilda reached for the coffeepot. "Let me finish getting the coffee ready. You go and tell Lars and say good-bye to everyone."

Lars stood up immediately and watched Jennie go to kneel on one knee beside Clay's chair. When Clay looked at her, she made her announcement. "We're going home now. Thank you all for coming. It's been a good time, and we will all be together tomorrow. Clay, I'm going to ride with Mom and Dad and leave the Suburban for you."

Jennie stood up, and Clay came to his feet. "Peggy, I just put a fresh pot of coffee on the stove. Please look after it?" Clay held her hand as they walked to the mudroom and said good-bye.

A small wedding, in a small church, was held at noon. With his military friends included, Clay had more family in attendance than Jennie. A photographer from Idaho Falls recorded the event. Ranch hands, neighbors, and friends of both families filled the pews.

In consideration of those with travel plans, the reception started at one thirty. Clay made sure he and Jennie greeted everyone in the crowded hall. There were very few people both hadn't known for years. Ladies from the church served a hot dinner with wine for those who wanted it, and Sheriff Tom Odleson emceed a short program. Clay talked for a few minutes, being well received. When he sat down, Tom announced, "There is one more item on my agenda. Our special guest, US Army General Thompson Thorsen, wishes to make a presentation." Clay's head came up, surprise showing on his face as he looked at the table where the general sat with Alorenzo and the Winehousers. Jennie put a hand on his arm and smiled at him.

Thompson stood up, wearing his full dress uniform, which Clay hadn't seen until earlier that morning. "Ladies and gentlemen, first I wish to extend my congratulations to Mr. and Mrs. Bamford on their marriage. To all of you who are part of this community, whether you live in town or out in the surrounding area; what fine people you are. You cooperate, help, and care for each other and are a shining example to the rest of the country of what neighbors should be. Mr. Gonzales, sitting here beside me, tried to teach me how to ride a horse, something I never had an opportunity to do before. To be honest, I wasn't very good." The crowd laughed politely. "Lorenz never raised his voice as I continually bumbled along, trying to follow his riding instructions. He must have felt like yelling, and all the time, he sat on his horse looking very much like he was born in the saddle.

"I am wearing this stuffy uniform because I have a special presentation to make today. Mrs. Cherrett, please bring me the case." Maxine walked across the room with a velvet case in her hand. Clay fidgeted again, not understanding what this could be about. Jennie patted his arm. Maxine opened the case, and Thompson removed a metal and held it up by the dark purple neck ribbon it was suspended on so everyone could see it before he continued.

"Major Bamford served most of his time in the army under my command. In fact, all of his time, except when he was in basic training. Because of his abilities, he was promoted rapidly and would have gone much further in the army except for his decision to return to your community. After visiting here and meeting Mrs. Bamford, it's easy for me to understand why. Although a disappointment to me and others, it was obviously the correct decision on his part.

"Major Bamford's performance in all areas of activity was superb, marred only by his strong streak of independence and his ability to interpret orders in a way to enable him to conduct operations in his own manner. The new Mrs. Bamford told me this is a longstanding, well-known Bamford trait, which all of you are most likely aware of.

"This special metal"—Thompson held it up again—"was approved by the Secretary of Defense, with special engraving on the back, which I will read for you in a moment. Sergeant Manning, will you please escort the recipient to this table." Clay started wondering. Thomas wasn't in the army, hadn't been for several years. What was going on? He started to get to his feet and decided not to. Glancing at Thompson, Clay caught a hint of a smile. Thomas, wearing his old dress uniform, left his cane behind as he walked slowly to the head table, coming past Hilda and Lars to stop in front of Jennie and Clay. Clay's chair started to slide back, and Thomas grinned. "Remain seated, Major. You aren't needed; this award is for Mrs. Bamford."

Clay eased himself back down and relaxed, now understanding. The Washington office gang had planned a trick to play on him. He turned toward Jennie, whose feelings were going from concern for her husband to shocked amazement. Her eyes grew overly large.

Clay whispered, "It's okay, honey. Go along with the general and enjoy whatever he's up to."

Thomas came around the table and pulled back the chair for Jennie, who stood and smoothed her long white dress. Thomas stood erect with his right hand on his hip. "If you please, ma'am, take my arm." Jennie linked her arm with Thomas's, who walked with her to where Thompson now stood beside Maxine. The camera kept flashing as it had done almost continuously.

"Mrs. Bamford, it is my honor to inform you that you have been awarded a special appointment to the officer ranks of the US Army. It is our wish that you enjoy a long and happy marriage. Since Major Bamford earned a reputation for disobedience, you have been appointed an honorary two-star general. If said major should ignore any orders you issue to him, please contact my office; we will arrange a court martial to be held here in this hall."

After a brief silence while the crowd digested the words, the hall erupted in laughter. Jennie smiled broadly and turned to look at Clay, who was standing beside their table, clapping his hands, grinning from ear to ear. The photographer began snapping pictures rapidly, trying to capture all the reactions. Edgar and Sadie stood to clap, and the crowd followed suit.

Thompson still held the metal. When the noise faded away, he continued. "Let me read the inscription to you. Engraved on the back are these words. *J. M. Bamford is officially appointed an Honorary Two-Star General, Army of the United States of America.*" Thompson grinned. "Today's date is on it."

Holding the ribbon with both hands, Thompson hung the metal around Jennie's neck. Maxine came to rearrange Jennie's long blonde hair. With the ribbon properly in place, Thompson held out his hand. Jennie shook the hand and leaned in to kiss Thompson's cheek. "Thank you, Thompson. I shall use my authority with great discretion."

Thompson stood up straight. "Sergeant, please escort the general to her seat." Clay held the chair for her when she arrived, and she smiled sweetly at him, with laughter in her eyes.

Tom stood up for the last time. "My goodness, such a surprise. What did you folks think about that?" The clapping was loud. "It is nice to know when I need support for my police work in the future, I can go to General Bamford and have the army come in to help me." Tom got his expected laugh. "That is the end of our program. A number of you are travelling, and we wish you a safe journey. For the rest of you, stay around and talk. Many of you will want to have a look at Jennie's metal. Once again, thank you for coming today."

The Winehousers left to drive to Boise and catch their flight to Seattle. At four o'clock, the helicopter landed, and Clay watched his friends go on board to leave for Mountain Home. After the helicopter took off, he drove to the Johansson home to find Jennie wearing jeans and relaxing with a house full of friends. Clay changed into jeans and joined the cocktail party.

A number of people asked Jennie where they were going for their honeymoon, and she replied each time that Clay wouldn't tell her. It was just a small white lie. The truth was they had no plans to go anywhere except back to the ranch and didn't want friends dropping in to bother them.

Jennie Mae Bamford knew exactly how and where she wanted to spend the first night of her marriage, something she had thought about since she was a young girl, her mind fueled by summer vacations at the ranch and stories she read over the years.

Clay insisted on purchasing the new GMC Suburban as a wedding present, and now it rolled smoothly along the county road, leaving a long, trailing dust cloud behind. Jennie listened to the rumble of tires on the gravel road and marveled at the smoothness of the ride. She understood Clay's effort was to give her independence—enabling her to leave the ranch, to pursue her writing interests, or visit her mother and friends, whenever she wished.

Jennie glanced at the car clock and calculated she had now been married for almost eight hours. The wedding and following reception went much as planned, and Clay gave a well-worded, if somewhat short, speech, which surprised the attendees with its elegance, because he was known for his reticence.

As they arrived in the ranch yard, Clay pressed the button on the door opener and drove into the new double garage attached to the house. It had its own door for access to the kitchen. With Jennie's input, Clay made changes to the ranch house in preparation for their marriage. A contractor remodeled the large master bedroom, and Clay filled it with new furniture, just for her. The attached bathroom expanded to include a walk-in shower big enough for two people and a large Jacuzzi tub. Jennie now had her own office, the walls lined with bookshelves, where she could work without being interrupted. Clay did all these things because he wanted to make it her house.

Jennie opened the Suburban's door and got out to stand on the freshly painted concrete floor. The garage door went down, and Clay came around the vehicle. Jennie held out her arms, and he walked right into them to hold her closer than ever before, squeezing her tightly in his strong arms. Clay had been very circumspect since their relationship took off the previous fall, and several months had passed before he kissed her with passion. Afterward, Jennie stopped wondering, expecting he would become more aggressive. The closest he came to intimacy was to pat her on the shoulder or the hip on occasion. Clay treated her with utmost respect, the way she knew he believed a lady should be treated.

Now he was holding her so close she could barely breathe, and she could feel his desire for her. She didn't plan to keep him waiting very long. When his arms loosened, Jennie found her heart pounding in her chest, and she was gasping for breath. Jennie reached for his hand. "Come on, Clay, let's go into the house. Do you want me to make coffee for you?"

Clay held the kitchen door open for her. "No thanks, Jen. I'm good until breakfast."

They didn't turn the kitchen lights on. Jennie led the way into the large living room and bent to switch on a reading lamp. When she straightened, Clay was right there and put his arms around her, kissing her hard. Several minutes went by before they broke apart. While her breathing slowed, Jennie looked at him, her eyes large and a slight flush on her cheeks. Her knees felt weak. Smiling prettily, Jennie put her hands on Clay's chest and pushed him so he fell into his favorite armchair. "You sit there while I take a quick shower. I'll be right back." She turned to go and stopped, her wifely instincts kicking in. "I'll get you a sip of Jack before I go."

Jennie hurried to the kitchen and came back with a glass containing two fingers of Jack Daniels, which she set on the table beside Clay. She leaned down and kissed him. "You enjoy your Jack; be back in a minute."

Jennie came back wearing Clay's white terry-cloth robe, a robe far too large for her, and stopped in front of his chair. Clay thought once again how beautiful she is, how lucky he was. He noticed she seemed a bit intimidated or maybe shy. He set his glass on the table and held out his arms. Jennie slid onto his lap, put an arm around his neck, and kissed him.

Clay could smell the shampoo in her damp hair and the soap she used to shower. His whiskey forgotten, he held her close and kissed her passionately. Soon Jennie squirmed around to get closer to him, feeling a hand touch her bare hip and slowly slide upward to cup one breast. Her body moved slightly as she became aware, and she quickly decided she liked the feeling. Soon her breath started catching in her throat.

"Are you ready to go to bed?"

Jennie's eyes flew open, and she smiled. "Oh yes, Clay. Please pick me up and carry me to your bedroom."

Surprised, Clay asked, "Why my bedroom? There's only a single bed, which isn't very roomy for two people to sleep in."

Jennie giggled softly, inclining her head to better see his face. "Didn't think you were planning to sleep for the next few hours."

She got a gentle smile. "I wasn't, but you tell me why you want to go there instead of to our new bedroom?"

"That's where you always slept."

"What in the world are you talking about, Jen?" Now he sounded slightly exasperated.

Jennie sat up, making no attempt to keep her robe closed. "Do you remember the summer Mrs. Compton was here?"

Clay frowned, suddenly afraid of what might be coming. "I guess so. That was years ago, and you were just a child."

"Ten years ago from this coming summer, the year of my twelfth birthday. You snuck out every night to be with her, and my thoughts were to scratch her eyes out. You would open your bedroom window and tiptoe across the porch. I watched you go and waited for you to come back, night after night. Even kept track of how long you were gone and recorded the time in one of my notebooks. The average was close to three hours."

Clay pondered how he could get out of this. "Sorry, Jen. If I knew you were aware of what was going on, I'd never have done that."

Jennie laughed gaily. "Oh yes you would have, Mr. Bamford. You may have been more discrete, that's all, and don't be sorry. I'm expecting you to teach me everything you learned and how I should do the things that please you."

Shaking his head in wonderment, Clay asked her, "How did you know what was happening with Mrs. Compton?"

Jennie kissed him before answering. "At the time, there was only the vaguest idea in my head of what you were doing. In the years afterward, I figured it out from descriptions in my books. Probably still don't really, truly understand. Having no experience to judge by makes it difficult. It's your responsibility to educate me. Now, are you going to take me to bed?"

She received a hard look from Clay. "You still haven't told me why you want that bed."

Jennie smiled sweetly. "Because, for all these years, I have dreamed of starting our marriage in that bed. When you're ready to sleep, we'll go to our room."

"Okay, honey." Clay stood up with her in his arms, the robe trailing below on the floor. "You have to understand, Jen, at that time I was young and eager, and she was willing."

"Of course, Mr. Bamford. Now things have changed. Now the new Mrs. Bamford is young and willing and hoping you're still eager."

CPSIA information can be obtained at www.ICGtesting.com
Printed in the USA
LVOW11s2029170315

430945LV00002B/71/P